MASQUERADE

Calum McSwiggan is an author, journalist and LGBT+ advocate. He's worked for *Attitude* magazine, written for *Metro*, *Gay Times* and the *Independent*, and was recently placed in the *Guardian's* list of the fifty most influential LGBT+ figures in the UK. Putting LGBT+ stories at the heart of everything he does, he's produced award-winning films, presented radio, and racked up millions of views on his online videos.

Follow Calum across all social media channels
@CalumMcSwiggan

MASQUERADE

Calum McSwiggan

PENGUIN BOOKS

PENGUIN BOOKS

UK | USA | Canada | Ireland | Australia
India | New Zealand | South Africa

Penguin Books is part of the Penguin Random House group of companies
whose addresses can be found at global.penguinrandomhouse.com

www.penguin.co.uk   www.puffin.co.uk   www.ladybird.co.uk

First published 2025
001

Text copyright © Calum McSwiggan, 2025

The moral right of the author has been asserted

Excerpts on p216 and p258 are from 'Stayin' Alive' by The Bee Gees,
written by Barry Gibb/Robin Gibb/Maurice Gibb/Robin Hugh,
© 1977, Universal Music Publishing Group

Penguin Random House values and supports copyright.
Copyright fuels creativity, encourages diverse voices, promotes freedom
of expression and supports a vibrant culture. Thank you for purchasing
an authorized edition of this book and for respecting intellectual property
laws by not reproducing, scanning or distributing any part of it by any
means without permission. You are supporting authors and enabling
Penguin Random House to continue to publish books for everyone.
No part of this book may be used or reproduced in any manner for the
purpose of training artificial intelligence technologies or systems. In accordance
with Article 4(3) of the DSM Directive 2019/790, Penguin Random House
expressly reserves this work from the text and data mining exception.

Set in 10.5/15.5pt Sabon LT Std
Typeset by Jouve (UK), Milton Keynes
Printed and bound in Great Britain by Clays Ltd, Elcograf S.p.A.

The authorized representative in the EEA is Penguin Random House Ireland,
Morrison Chambers, 32 Nassau Street, Dublin D02 YH68

A CIP catalogue record for this book is available from the British Library

ISBN: 978-0-241-55441-8

All correspondence to:
Penguin Books
Penguin Random House Children's
One Embassy Gardens, 8 Viaduct Gardens, London SW11 7BW

MIX
Paper | Supporting
responsible forestry
FSC® C018179

Penguin Random House is committed to a
sustainable future for our business, our readers
and our planet. This book is made from Forest
Stewardship Council® certified paper.

1

'Prom night, baby!'

Chase startles me awake by hitting me squarely in the face with a pillow. I squint up at him through tired eyes and can see him grinning from ear to ear. 'Come on, day's a-wasting!' he says cheerily, grabbing my arms and tugging on them. He's been my own personal alarm clock ever since we started sharing a room.

'Seriously, Zach, how can you lie in on a day like today? You slept right through breakfast!'

'Why, what time is it?' I groan, pulling my hands free and rubbing my eyes. I feel especially groggy today, like I've barely even slept.

'Eleven fifty-nine,' Chase says, as the details of our dorm room slowly come into focus. He's wearing a backwards blue baseball cap, tufts of his soft black hair poking through it, and an extra-large Miami Dolphins shirt that completely swamps him.

'You can't sleep all day, Zach. Come on. You're missing it! The rugby team are outside doing naked laps!'

'They're doing *what*?' I say, suddenly more awake.

'Naked laps!' he repeats as I jump up and rush to the window.

'They are *not*,' I say, spotting them throwing a ball around, very much fully clothed.

'Well, it got you out of bed, didn't it? Honestly, Zach, I don't think I've ever seen you move so fast. You say you're not athletic? We could get you running in the Olympics if we just stacked the finish line with guys in their underwear.'

I laugh at that. I'd like to say I'm not so shallow, and yet here I am, leaping out of bed at just the suggestion of a hint of nudity. It's been a long year, OK? And all quiet on the romance front. I feel betrayed by all the movies that convinced me private school would be inherently debaucherous. I was led to believe I'd be fighting off boys with a stick. In reality? Sometimes we stay up late reading queer manga. That's about as debaucherous as it gets.

I push open the creaky old window, and the smell of summer fills the room. We're up on the sixth floor, in the east wing of the building, sitting atop a hill with nothing but woodland surrounding us. With just one road in and out, it's easy to forget that the outside world exists. For two years now, there's been this and only this. Oakbrook Academy. It really does feel surprisingly like home.

'I can't believe we're about to leave it all behind,' I say. 'This time tomorrow we'll be saying our final goodbyes.'

'Yeah,' Chase says, a little softer now. I can tell he's been thinking about it too. 'What will you miss the most? Besides me, of course. Obviously you're gonna be inconsolable when we say *our* goodbyes. I've got tissues ready and everything.'

'I'll be weeping for weeks,' I tease, though secretly I know that will, in fact, probably be the case. Growing up as an only child, sharing a room here took a lot of getting used to, but now I can't imagine waking up without Chase. 'I'll definitely miss our movie nights,' I finally settle on. 'I'll have to find someone new to educate on quality cinema.'

'*Quality cinema?*' He raises an eyebrow. 'If I recall correctly, I'm pretty sure you said that *Ratatouille* is the best film ever made.'

'That's because it *is* the best film ever made,' I say. 'It's got romance, drama, an incredible score! And don't even get me started on the subtext!'

'I can't get you to *stop* on the subtext, Zach. You've spoken at *length* about the subtext. The subtext surrounding a talking mouse –'

'He's a *rat*! We've been through this! It's literally called *RATatouille*!'

'Mouse, rat, whatever.' Chase laughs. 'It's still a three out of ten at absolute best.'

'You're a three out of ten at absolute best,' I say. 'You know, I seriously can't wait to get to film school and be surrounded by people that *actually* understand me.'

'Or ridicule you for describing *A Bug's Life* as an "emotional masterpiece"?'

'It *is* an emotional masterpiece!'

'If you say so,' he replies, further mussing up my bed-head. 'But what else will you miss? Come on, besides movie nights?'

'Well . . .' My gaze drifts back towards the rugby team. One member of the team in particular. 'I suppose I *am* gonna miss seeing Cameron in his kit . . .'

'Or without his kit . . .' Chase adds as one of the boys slowly peels his shirt off, his body glistening in the morning sun.

'That's not even Cameron.' I laugh. 'That's *Ethan*. You *still* can't tell them apart?'

'I really can't.' He looks back and forth between the twins.

In fairness, they do play up to the identical-twin thing. They style themselves with the same soft boy-band look. All dimples and cheekbones and sleek black hair that falls down in nineties curtains. But Cameron has this aura about him. It's unfathomable to me that people can't spot him a mile off. It's like he actually glows.

'It's so easy to tell them apart!' I say. 'Ethan is *such* a straight boy!'

'It's not like Cameron has a rainbow flag printed on his forehead.'

'Yeah, but he has this, like . . . *gay energy* about him!'

'*Gay energy?*' Chase squints at me. 'You know, I saw this TikTok that said if one twin is queer there's, like, a seventy per cent chance the other will be as well?'

'So you're saying Ethan's a secret closet case? Don't let Tiffany hear you. She hates you enough without you implying her boyfriend's a secret homo.'

'I'm not implying anything,' he says with a smile of pure innocence. 'I'm just pointing out the statistical probability. We Asians are *really* good with numbers, remember?'

I laugh. 'I still can't believe she said that.'

'Or that she thought it was a compliment.'

'You should have reported her for racism,' I say. 'Zero tolerance, remember?'

Chase shrugs his shoulders. 'Since when do any of the rules apply to *her*?'

Tiffany and Chase have a long-standing rivalry. They played a lot of sport together before he transitioned, and he beat her at absolutely everything. She always disliked him for that, but then he came out and started playing with the boys, and was no longer competition. You'd have thought that would have been the end of it, but somehow it only seemed to exacerbate her hatred. At first I thought it was a classic case of deep-rooted transphobia, but now I think it's something else. Like she always thought she'd eventually beat him, and now she's furious she'll never get the chance.

'Anyway,' I say, watching as Cameron finally peels his own shirt off and throws it into the pile with the others, 'Cameron is *clearly* the better-looking one.'

'The clue's in the name, Zach – *identical* twins.'

'Oh, for God's sake.' I laugh as I go to grab my phone from the bedside table.

I see there's a message from Bec, our mutual best friend. She's written **HAPPY PROM!** into the group chat with a long string of suggestive emojis. She's clearly got only one thing on her mind for this evening. I'd be lying if I said I wasn't thinking about that too.

'Take a look,' I say. 'Cameron's *way* hotter.'

I zoom in on their '*twinstagram*' – a joint account that's racked up well over sixty thousand followers. Admittedly I probably spend far too much time looking at these pictures.

'Do you see? He has softer features, styles his hair better, and he has that adorable little love-heart-shaped birthmark.'

'What birthmark?' Chase snatches the phone and squints at it. 'That tiny thing underneath his eye? It looks more like a pimple.'

I snatch the phone back. 'It's a love heart,' I say firmly.

'All right, it's a love heart . . .' He holds his hands up defensively.

'Besides,' I say, 'it's his personality that makes the real difference.'

'Yeah,' Chase drawls. 'I'm sure it's his *personality* you're thinking about under the covers at three a.m. . . .'

I'm sure I don't know *what* he's talking about.

'I'm serious!' I say, looking at a picture of the two of them in their burgundy school blazers. They're standing outside the main entrance, the castle-like structure towering behind them. Ethan is clenching his jaw, smouldering, while Cameron is cheesing with this big dorky grin. 'Cameron isn't afraid of what others think of him. But Ethan? He's just so . . .'

'Arrogant? Pretentious? Deeply unlikeable?'

'I was about to say "insecure".' I laugh. 'But whatever. He just doesn't have that . . . *something*. That special spark that Cameron does.'

'Oddly romantic,' Chase says. 'You really should make a move, you know. You've mooned over him from afar for *two years*. Now here we are on the last day of school. With a masquerade-themed prom ahead of us! It's *begging* for a little romance, Zach.'

'I know.' I let out a long-drawn-out sigh as I hear Cameron laughing with one of his teammates. How is it possible that one boy can be so perfect? 'I want to make a move. Like I *really* want to. But look at him. He could have literally anyone he wants.'

'Yeah, I hear he's got both Kit Connor and Joe Locke sliding into his DMs.'

'I wouldn't be surprised!' I'm already conjuring up images of *that* episode of *Heartstopper*. But it would never happen. Putting so many cute boys in one place is against the laws of physics. I'm pretty sure the universe would fold in on itself.

'I know you think he's on this whole other level, Zach, but he's single and not dating anyone. Sure, he's hot, but you know that under the flawless skin he's no different to the rest of us, right? I'm sure he wants his prom-night kiss just like everyone else.'

'Everyone else?' I say. 'But what about you? You don't want that. What happened to "*no boys till university*"?'

Chase flaps me away. 'That's because I'm not ready yet. It's different. You know, I often wish I had some trans friends to talk about this stuff with? I love you, Zach, but sometimes it's like you really don't get it.'

'No,' I say, 'I get it. I understand why you're not ready.

I just think maybe Cameron has his own reasons too? Maybe he's not ready yet either?'

'Or maybe you're making up excuses.'

'Maybe,' I say, going back to look at Cameron from the window.

I know Chase is right, but he's making it sound way easier than it actually is. It's not like I can just walk up to Cameron and tell him I like him!

Chase sighs. 'Think about every single one of those *awful* high-school movies you made me sit through. Tonight is going to be a checklist of those classic prom-night moments. Someone will spike the punchbowl, someone's gonna give an unexpected speech and, most importantly, the underdog is finally going to wind up kissing their crush. It'll be wall-to-wall joy, sex and underage drinking –'

'Except I'm the *only* one who hasn't yet turned eighteen.'

'Then you'll have to do enough underage drinking for the rest of us, won't you?'

I groan at the thought. Every time I drink anything alcoholic, I just end up saying something stupid. Last time we smuggled in a few beers, I got a telling-off from Bec. **Being a gay man doesn't excuse misogyny,** she texted me the next day. I apologized profusely, but the worst part is that I don't even remember what I said.

'Go long!' Ethan yells, tossing the ball. Cameron sprints after it. He's so focused on catching it that he doesn't spot how close they are to the car belonging to Mr Harrington, our miserable headmaster.

'Fuck!'

The car alarm cuts through the air, and the boys all scatter.

'See?' Chase says. 'You put him on a pedestal, but he's just as clumsy and flawed as the rest of us. Honestly, I'm surprised that team even made it to regionals. They have the coordination of a bunch of drunken toddlers. No wonder they didn't bring back the trophy.'

'And that's *exactly* why you should've joined the team. They need some brains to go with all that brawn.'

'Are you saying I'm not brawny?' Chase flexes his arms and pretends to be offended. 'Besides, as I've told you a thousand times, I have literally *no interest* in rugby.'

'And yet you're wearing a rugby shirt . . .'

'This is *American football*. It's completely and totally different.'

'It's basically the same sport but with armour.'

'It. Is. Not,' Chase growls. 'You know, every time I start to think I'm gonna miss you, you reassert your status as an absolute dickhead.'

'And that's exactly why you love me,' I grin just as his phone starts blowing up with a million notifications. 'Someone's popular . . .'

'It's the results!' he says excitedly, his eyes scanning the screen. '*Most likely to be famous. Best dressed. Class clown.*'

It's the categories from the unofficial leavers' poll.

'*Hottest boy.*' He nudges me. 'Want to see how you scored?'

'I already know how I scored. Zachary Evans – zero votes. Honestly, who thought this was a good idea anyway? As if we're not already dripping in insecurity . . .'

'Speak for yourself,' he says. 'It's just a bit of fun, Zach.'

'Fine,' I say. 'Hand it over then.'

Chase passes me his phone, and I scan the results. It's essentially a long list of everything that's wrong with this school. A hierarchy based on money and popularity and little else.

'*Hottest boy – Rhys Kingsland*.' My eyes roll so far back they almost come full circle. 'Why am I not surprised?'

'He *is* hot, Zach! You can keep saying you don't see it, but the boy is practically a supermodel. Those biceps . . . those dimples.'

'You mean the ones his parents paid for?'

'Unsubstantiated gossip,' Chase snaps. 'I thought you were better than that. Besides, who cares? You know I'll be paying for a *lot* more than cheekbones, right? If a person has the means to make themselves happier in their body, why shouldn't they?'

'I guess so,' I say, continuing to scroll. 'Well, this is *clearly* rigged. Tiffany has won *everything. Most popular. Hottest girl. Most likely to become prime minister . . .*'

Chase snorts at that, taking the phone back with a look of pure disbelief. 'These votes don't even add up. Bec got forty-nine votes for hottest girl. Tiffany got fifty-one. That's a hundred votes, Zach. There's not even that many students in our year! She probably made a bunch of fake accounts just to vote for herself.'

'Well, I can't say I'm surprised. Cheating is sort of her MO. I'm just shocked she went to all this effort for an unofficial student poll! It's not like any of this actually matters.'

'I'm half tempted to hack in and fix it.'

'Could you actually do that?' My ears prick up.

'Course,' Chase says. 'The coding behind this thing is *basic*.'

'Then why don't you?' I say, devil horns practically sprouting from my head.

'You know I don't like cheating, Zach.'

'It's not cheating if the whole thing is already rigged. You're just . . . putting the universe back how it should be. Besides, it's the last day. What are they gonna do?'

Chase looks at me for a moment as he thinks about it. 'Fine,' he finally says with a grin, opening his laptop. He clicks around for a minute or two, his face deep in concentration. He says it's '*basic*', but watching him do stuff like this will never cease to amaze me. He says writing code is no different to writing a story, but all I see is numbers and gibberish.

'OK,' he says after no time at all. 'We're in.'

'Just like that? You're a criminal mastermind!'

'It's not like I'm hacking into the Pentagon,' he says. 'So what are we changing?'

'Hmm.' I scroll through the results on my phone. '*Most likely to win gold at the Olympics*. That should quite obviously have gone to you!'

'Nah,' he says. 'My future is right here at the keyboard. Let's give it to Bec. She's the one who's actually got a shot at a career in this.' His tongue sticks out as he concentrates. 'Bec for hottest girl too, right?'

'Obviously.' I refresh the page to see the results changing in real time.

It's incredible to watch. He could probably have hacked into the school system and given us all perfect grades if he wasn't so honest. Humanity would do well not to piss him off and create the next supervillain. The world should be grateful he insists on using his powers for good.

'I'll let Tiffany keep *Most popular*,' he finally says as he finishes knocking her out of every other category. 'Just so she doesn't have a meltdown.'

'Generous,' I say. 'Though she's gonna have a meltdown regardless. God forbid she doesn't win absolutely *everything*.'

Chase gives me a satisfied smile and goes to close his laptop.

'Wait,' I say. 'Do you think you could change one last thing?'

'You want Cameron for hottest boy, don't you?'

'He deserves it! Rhys already gets everything.'

'But I think Rhys won this one fair and square. We're not snatching that away from him just because you disagree with the result.'

I groan. 'I just hate how everyone is so *obsessed* with him. If I hear about his dancing pecs one more time! I get it – we *love* masculinity. It's the holy grail of attractiveness. But can we just have a *little* bit more love for the feminine boys?'

'And by "feminine boys" you mean Cameron?' Chase raises an eyebrow. 'Need I remind you that he and his brother have over sixty thousand followers? That sounds like plenty of love to me.'

'Rhys would probably have double that if he wasn't so

bad at social media.' I snort. 'The other day he posted a picture of the toilet, Chase. The *toilet*.'

Chase laughs at that. 'Do you know what I think, Zach?'

'I have a feeling I'm not gonna like it . . .'

'I think maybe – just maybe – you're a teeny-tiny bit jealous.'

'Oh, whatever!'

'The only reason you dislike Rhys is because you *quite clearly* fancy his boyfriend.'

'Kellen?' I splutter. I don't know why Chase *always* says this. Him and Bec are *obsessed* with the idea of me and Kellen. 'I do not fancy Kellen.'

'Mmm-hmm,' he says. 'Sure you don't. And you don't secretly think Rhys is hot either. The three of you would make a cute throuple, actually. Maybe after prom you can all head down to the boathouse and engage in a little *ménage à trois*?'

'OK, now you're being ridiculous,' I say. 'I understand why you *might* think I fancy Kellen . . . but Rhys?! When have I *ever* expressed interest in basic jocks like him?'

Chase cracks up. 'It's *really* easy to wind you up, you know that?'

'Anyway, Kellen's dead to me since he ditched us,' I say. 'He's one floor up – it would take thirty seconds for him to come down and say hey.'

Kellen has a single room, making him one of the only Oakbrook students without a room-mate. Chase and I were very much his surrogates – he used to spend all his time in here – and now it's like we never see him.

'He could at least sit with us at lunch. Why does *everything* now have to be about Rhys?'

'He's just excited,' Chase says. 'He's still in the honeymoon period.'

'It's been a year!'

'He always wanted a boyfriend, Zach, and then he lands the hottest guy in school. I miss him too, but we've gotta let him have this. It might not be what you want, but at least try to be happy for him. That's what friends do.'

'I am trying,' I grumble. 'But Rhys is such a colossal meathead . . . and apparently nobody else sees it.' I glance back down at my phone. 'He got fifty-six votes, Chase. *Fifty-six!*'

'Well, I'm not changing it. But if it's any consolation, I didn't vote for him.'

'Who *did* you vote for?' I ask, studying the results a little more closely.

'Who do you think?'

'Oh,' I say. 'Zachary Evans – one vote. Well, I appreciate the sympathy –'

'No, you idiot,' he says, laughing. 'I voted for myself.'

'You did?' I check my tally to make sure I haven't misread it. But no, it's really there. Someone actually voted for me. 'Maybe it was Bec?'

'Nope, she also voted for me.' He grins. 'See: Chase Kwan – two votes.'

'That can't be right,' I say, double-checking.

Did someone really vote for me? Over every other boy in school? That's like voting for your favourite ice cream and deciding to go with vanilla. And not even the good kind. We're talking about that bargain block at the back of the freezer that you forgot about until you were *really* hungry at 3 a.m.

'Looks like *someone* has a secret admirer.' Chase beams. 'Who do you think it was? Josh perhaps? Maybe he wants to reignite the old flame . . .' He nudges me as he says it.

'There was no flame. I told you, we were just experimenting.'

'With your pants round your ankles?'

'Oh my God,' I say. 'We're *not* having this conversation again.'

I lost my virginity to Josh last summer. I wouldn't exactly describe it as romantic, but I don't mean that as a bad thing. I was so nervous about sex, but he took the pressure off and made me feel safe. It feels weird to describe it this way, but it was kind of like facing my fears and having my friend there to hold my hand. I'm genuinely so grateful to him for that, but we are just friends. That's all it is. We mutually decided it was a one-time thing. So why would he suddenly change his mind? It can't be Josh. Chase has definitely got that wrong.

'So if not Josh, then . . . Cameron?' Chase wiggles his eyebrows as he says the name.

'Honestly, someone probably just chose me by mistake.'

'Oh, whatever!' he says. 'Someone likes you, Zach! And I bet you tonight's the night you're gonna find out who it is. Before the clock strikes midnight!'

'So I'm Cinderella now, am I?'

'If the glass slipper fits! I'll be your fairy godfather.' Chase snatches a pencil and waves it like a wand. 'You will go to the ball, young Zachary! Your pumpkin carriage awaits!'

I can't suppress a grin. I really am going to miss him. 'Maybe you're right.'

'And if it goes wrong, at least you'll be able to say you gave it a shot!'

'I suppose I do wanna leave this place with at least one crazy story.'

I think about all those movies where the hero goes off the rails for one chaotically joyous day. Why can't I be the Ferris Bueller? I've always wanted to be that person. Even if it's not who I *really* am.

'We're talking about kissing a boy, Zach, not stealing a car. But yeah ... I mean ... that's what the last day is all about, right? *Everyone* wants a crazy story. Everyone wants it to be memorable. That's why people are more likely to take chances. Besides, I reckon we'll look back on our time here very differently anyway. Do you really think we're gonna remember Mr Draper's maths lessons? Or do you think we'll remember ... *this?*'

I glance around our dusty old dorm room. '*This?*'

'*This!*' Chase says. 'Peering out of the window on a hot summer's day. Gossiping about our classmates. Watching cute boys get all sweaty! Everyone is so worried about missing the "high-school experience" they forget they're already living it.'

'Maybe you're right.' I look back out of the window.

The car alarm is still blaring, and Mr Harrington has finally appeared to switch it off. We duck down as he looks around for the culprit. The last thing we want is for him to think we're somehow responsible. He's never liked me and Chase, but then he doesn't really seem to like anyone. Unless your parents are *exceptionally* rich, of course, and then suddenly you're his favourite.

'Anyway –' Chase looks at his watch – 'you better get ready. Madzikanda will be calling for team captains soon. We need to be there. Bec's gonna put herself forward . . .'

I groan. He's talking about the big game of Capture the Flag that always takes place on the last day of school. It's really just to distract us while an events company decorates the hall for prom, but at Oakbrook tradition is tradition, and everyone takes it *way* too seriously.

'Maybe I could skip it? It's not like I'll be any help anyway.'

'No, you can't *skip it*.' He throws me some side-eye. 'We're making memories, remember? Besides, imagine how turned on Cameron will be, seeing you getting all *sporty*.'

'You think so?' I say, trying not to sound too excited.

'I know so,' Chase says with a little wink. 'One way or another, you're gonna score today, Zach. I just have a feeling.'

There's a buzz of excitement in the air as Chase and I step out of the east wing and stroll round to the front of the school. There's a bunch of students lazing on the perfectly manicured lawn, soaking up the sunshine before they head inside for lunch. Excited conversation fills the air and everyone is talking about the *big game*. Everyone wants to prove that their house is the best.

In the east wing, we represent Sycamore, while over on the west side they represent Hawthorn. The only prize is seeing the hall decorated in your house colours for prom. Blue and white for Sycamore, red and gold for Hawthorn. A game of Capture the Flag might not seem like much, but it's a big deal for a lot of the legacy kids who so desperately want to do their families proud by following in their parents' footsteps.

I see Josh sitting on the grass, and Chase gives me a little nudge, reminding me that he could be my secret admirer. I still don't believe that, but I take an extra moment to look at him today. He's wearing a sleeveless white basketball jersey with *Young, Gifted and Black* written in cursive lettering across the front. He's tall and skinny, showcasing the unthreatening boy-next-door vibe that attracted me to him in the first place. I'm not convinced he's my secret admirer, though. There's never really been any romantic chemistry between us. He's cute. Exceptionally so, in fact. But we're friends. I don't think we were ever meant to be anything more than that, and I don't think he does either.

He spots us and gives a little wave. If there's one thing I love about being queer at Oakbrook, it's this unspoken alliance between us. We're all here for each other, even if it's just in these small gestures. All of us except for Rhys, that is. He's too preoccupied with fitting in with the elite.

Owen waves too. He's Josh's straight best friend, and the two of them are inseparable. They're about the same height, but Owen is built bigger. He's a little clumsy, but keeps an infectiously positive attitude about everything. His gentle demeanour is the perfect complement to his soft Irish accent. He's a nice guy, and he makes me feel comfortable in that I know I can talk about anything in his presence. I don't need to mask or dilute my conversations around him just because he's straight. It's easy to see why he and Josh are close. I don't remember when they first became friends. It feels like they've always been besties – and it wouldn't surprise me if they stay that way forever. One friendship that's destined to last well beyond their school days.

We head through the huge wooden doors at the front of the building, the ornate frame intricately carved with the school's motto: *Repetitio Est Mater Studiorum*. It's Latin for *Repetition is the Mother of Learning*. I always thought that was stupid. You learn by doing new things, not the same thing over and over.

We must have walked this corridor a thousand times, but today it feels different, knowing it's one of the last times we'll do it. We emerge into the grand hall at the heart of the school. It sits below ground level, with overlooking balconies tucked into the alcoves, making it feel twice as big as it looks from the outside. The summer sun blazes in through the huge skylight in the ceiling as we descend the ornate stone staircase to join our classmates below. It's a little quieter than usual because all the Year Twelves went home last week, but there's still enough of a buzz of gossip to make the room feel full.

Usually we sit wherever we want, but today the hall is divided, the two houses sitting at long tables on opposite sides of the room. Huge plates of food are laid out family style. They've gone all out on the catering today, and yet nobody's really eating.

'You OK, Bec?' Chase says as we find our friend staring into the glass cabinet that runs the perimeter of the room. It's full of hundreds of medals, trophies and ribbons, proudly celebrating a hundred years of academic and sporting achievement.

'Sorry,' she says, snapping out of her trance. She's wearing blue and white shorts – the colours of Sycamore – with a matching crop top, her black hair tied back in a pony. 'I just can't believe this was two years ago.'

She points at a photo of her and Chase in their football kit, holding up a trophy. They're grinning from ear to ear because they'd just won regionals. It was back when they were still room-mates, before Chase came out and moved over to the boys' dorm. The two of them bonded over their athletic ability and being two of the few students of colour in an overwhelmingly white school. Bec was born in the UK with a mixed South Asian heritage, while Chase moved from Singapore when he was just a kid. They were room-mates by chance, but best friends by choice.

'I swear this literally happened yesterday,' Chase says, studying the photo.

'Remember the look on Tiffany's face when we walked back in with the trophy?'

'Seething.' Chase laughs, glancing across the room at her. 'Absolutely seething.'

Tiffany is sitting at the head of the Hawthorn table in her designer trainers, blonde hair scraped back into a ponytail so tight it negates the need for her monthly Botox. 'Hottest boy' Rhys sits on her left, every inch the 'gay best friend' she patronizingly describes on Instagram. He's 6 foot 3 and all muscle, with short brown hair, and dimples that his parents *definitely* paid for. Ethan sits on Tiffany's right, the dutiful boyfriend, and she incessantly plays with his hair, as if marking her territory.

The three of them are surrounded by a small group who make up the school's wealthiest elite. Either it was a remarkable coincidence that they all ended up in Hawthorn or, more likely, cleverly engineered by the quiet exchange of their parents' money. These kids are simultaneously the most popular and most hated. Nobody likes them, and yet everyone wants to be liked *by* them.

Cameron is the only member of the elite in Sycamore. Apparently something to do with his politician father's insistence on 'healthy sibling rivalry'. That, and it's rumoured that Ethan has *always* been the favourite. His father allegedly called the day Cameron came out 'a PR nightmare' and, while there's always been a lot of false rumours flying around this place, to me that one has the ring of truth.

'I can't believe it's all over,' Bec says with a heavy sigh, placing a hand on the glass. 'I knew this day was coming, but now it's actually here . . .'

'There'll be time to get weepy when we actually leave tomorrow,' Chase replies.

'Yeah, but today's the last *official* day. There's no more celebration after this.'

'We'll see each other over the summer. What about Zach's birthday?'

'Oh, that doesn't count.'

'OK, wow.' I snort. 'Why don't you tell me how you really feel?'

'You know I didn't mean it like that,' she says. 'How long till your birthday anyway?'

'Five days,' I reply. I've been counting down for a while now. 'It feels like I've been seventeen forever. It's weird to think I'll officially be an adult.'

'An adult who still can't grow facial hair?' teases Bec.

'I *can* grow facial hair.' I scratch at my chin. 'I just choose not to.'

Chase smiles. 'Sure you do. I can lend you some of my hormones if you like?'

'Can you imagine if the papers heard you say that?' Bec laughs.

'*Drug-pushing Transgender Immigrant!*' Chase frames the headline in front of us. 'Making the front pages twice before leaving school *would* be quite the accomplishment . . .'

'Don't even joke!' I groan, remembering the hell he was put through last year. Chase made national front-page news when he moved over to the boys' dorm and somebody *allegedly* complained that him being in the bathroom 'made them uncomfortable'.

It was an entirely made-up story, of course. Chase has always preferred his privacy, so uses the accessible bathroom. He even had permission from the school. Nobody was bothered or inconvenienced, as there aren't any students with disabilities on our floor, but that part was conveniently left out.

'I still can't believe Tiffany got away with planting that story,' Bec says.

'Well, we can't prove it was her, so . . .'

'Her father literally owns the paper, but sure . . .'

'Even if we had proof,' Chase says, 'then what? The school's hardly gonna do anything about it. Imagine what Daddy would print then!'

'Yeah, but at least we could expose all her bullshit hypocrite advocacy,' Bec says. 'That post on Trans Day of Visibility? "*In solidarity with my trans brothers and sisters!*" Give me an actual break. She will do literally *anything* to gain followers. Imagine how they'd react if they knew what she was really like . . .'

'That sounds like a war I do not want to get into,' Chase says. 'I'm just glad it's over. We'll never have to see her again after tonight. She can fade into obscurity for all I care.'

'*Fade into obscurity?*' Bec scoffs. 'With her connections? She'll be making headlines until the day she dies. And then one of her devil spawn will take over. You know her and Ethan are already talking kids?'

'Well, that's ridiculous,' says Chase. 'They're barely even eighteen!'

'It's not just them,' she says. 'I heard Kellen talking about marriage the other day.'

'Marriage?' I choke. 'That's ridiculous.'

I scan the room for him and see him heading down the stairs. He looks like a younger Keiynan Lonsdale, all flawless skin and perfect cheekbones. He's got 24/7 resting bitch face, but when he smiles? I can totally see why Rhys is into him. He has a spring in his step today, and I don't know why, but it irritates me. He's Sycamore, so he should be on our side of the room, but he heads into enemy territory, wrapping his arms round Rhys's giant shoulders and laughing loudly at one of Tiffany's jokes. In return, she gives him a smile that comes nowhere near her eyes.

'Astonishing. You could almost believe she likes him,' Chase says.

'Forced to fraternize with us lower classes,' Bec replies. 'I bet she's furious with Rhys for slumming it. *Very* unbecoming.'

They're right. You can practically see her clench from all the way over here. Kellen is a scholarship student, like Bec, and if it wasn't for him being coupled up with Rhys, there's no way the rest of the elite would tolerate him.

'And yet she has to accept the relationship or she'll seem homophobic,' Chase says. 'That girl is made to be a politician. She knows the game and how to play it.'

'She'll slip up eventually,' I say. 'Every politician has their downfall. It's inevitable.'

'We can but hope.' Bec shrugs. 'Anyway. Enough about *them*. This day's supposed to be about *us*. Any idea what you guys are gonna write yet?'

She nods to the tattered old yearbook behind the glass before us. It's an Oakbrook tradition dating back more than a century. Each year, for one night only, the headmaster (and it's always been a 'master' – go, patriarchy!) takes it out of its cabinet so that the leaving class can write a message, and read those of the many that came before.

'I wanna see what's in there first,' Chase says. 'Like, is it meaningful words or just vulgar messages and gushing declarations of love?'

'It's probably the latter,' I say. 'I bet the kids in 1925 weren't really all that different to us. I'm sure it's just pages and pages of "*Melanie loves Thomas*" and cartoon drawings of questionably large dicks.' Humanity seems to have an obsession with those. I've visited the British Museum. I've *seen* the ancient crockery.

'Well, I'm leaving a quote,' Bec says. 'Some song lyrics or something.'

'You are *not* going to quote Taylor Swift in a one-hundred-year-old book,' Chase says, scandalized.

'Watch me! It's supposed to be like a time capsule. There's probably lyrics in there from Elvis and Springsteen, and quotes from old black-and-white movies. The point is to capture how it feels to be right here, right now. So I think Taylor lyrics are entirely appropriate, *actually*. I quite like the idea of kids looking back at this in another hundred years and trying to imagine what it was like to be a Swiftie.'

'I'm sure that's *exactly* what they'll be thinking,' Chase says.

'You really think Oakbrook will still be here in a hundred years?'

Bec nods. 'If we've not been killed by climate change.'

'Or enslaved by malicious AI!' Chase adds cheerily.

'What a comforting thought,' I say, imagining killer robots tearing through the dining hall, the class of 2056 fleeing for their lives. Maybe I *do* watch too many movies.

I see Josh and Owen entering the hall then, heading down the stairs and parting ways to join their houses. Josh is with us in Sycamore, and Owen is over in Hawthorn. They're the only two students who truly don't seem to care about the house rivalry. Like a modern-day Romeo and Juliet, except with less romance and significantly fewer stabbings.

Owen doesn't *really* belong with Hawthorn anyway. Like Bec and Kellen, he's on a scholarship, and, with no Rhys Pass, most of them treat him like dirt. They openly make fun of his size and his general clumsiness, but the irony is that if he wasn't such a gentle giant he could easily flatten any one of them. That's the thing about Oakbrook – here, it doesn't really matter how big and tough you are. Money is power within these walls, and those without it are made sure they don't forget it.

'It's gotta be one of them,' Chase says as I watch Josh sit down with Cameron.

'Huh?' Bec says. 'Who's gotta be one of what?'

'Someone voted Zach for hottest boy.'

'Oh my God, I saw!'

'Did you also see you won hottest girl?' I grin.

'I saw that *Tiffany* won hottest girl,' she says. 'And then the results magically changed about an hour ago.' She looks at Chase. 'Your handiwork, I assume?'

He smirks. 'I don't know what you're talking about.'

Bec smiles back at him. 'So this secret admirer, Zach? It has to be Josh, right?'

'We were kinda hoping for lover boy over there,' Chase says, nodding in Cameron's direction.

I can't take my eyes off him. He and Josh are whispering now, and I swear they just glanced over in our direction. Surely they're not actually talking about me?

'Can we just not?' I finally say. I'm getting carried away. I don't want Chase and Bec putting ideas in my head. 'Let's forget it. I feel like someone's just trying to fuck with me. Get my hopes up just to smash them right back down again.'

'That's ridiculous,' Bec says. 'Keep those hopes sky-high, Zachary. Someone's into you! And it's gotta be one of the boys. Right, Chase? The girls wouldn't waste their vote on a gay guy. They'd vote for someone they actually thought they had a shot with.'

'Exactly,' says Chase. 'It's either Josh or Cameron. It has to be. Unless it's one of the "straight" boys. You know what they say . . . everyone's a little gay at private school.'

We all laugh at that, but I don't actually think there's any truth in it. I doubt anyone's actually closeted at Oakbrook. This place has a long list of problems but, surprisingly, homophobia isn't one of them. Tiffany's transphobia aside, people are generally free to be themselves without worrying about the consequences. I've not heard anyone yell '*backs against the wall*' since I got here. It's a much-needed change from my last school. Things were *very* different there. So when Mum's business took off, and I was handed a fancy brochure offering me a 'new life' and a 'better education', it was the lifeline that I needed.

I joined after the start of the school year, so everyone already had a room-mate, and I ended up in a double room by myself. I found it hard to make friends at first, but then Chase came out and moved over to the boys' dorm, and we've been best friends ever since. Me, Bec, Chase and Kellen. That's how it used to be anyway, but four became three when Rhys entered the picture. Things haven't really been the same since.

'Think fast!' Ethan yells, snapping me out of my thoughts. He stands up from the table and hurls a rugby ball across the hall at Owen. It lands directly in the plate of food in front of him, spattering his T-shirt to the sound of sniggering laughter.

'So much for last-day camaraderie,' Bec says. 'They're *supposed* to be a team.'

'Are we really that surprised at Ethan being an asshole?' I watch as he laughs along with his friends. I glance across at Cameron, who's now glaring at his brother.

'I feel bad for Owen,' Chase says. 'You just know he's going to be the target later.'

'Shit, I forgot about that,' I say. 'I hate to say it, but I think you're probably right.'

He's talking about the leaver's prank – a severely messed-up Hawthorn tradition. Every year at prom, they carry out some toxic prank on an unsuspecting victim. Generally cruel and intended to humiliate. Usually a scholarship kid. Always someone who can't fight back.

'We should probably warn him,' Chase says. 'I don't wanna be the bearer of bad news or anything – nobody wants to hear that they're a walking target – but . . .'

'I heard they're going to strip someone naked and throw them in the lake,' Bec says.

'Wow, so imaginative.' Chase rolls his eyes. 'Nothing says last day of school like sexual assault! Must have taken them hours of brainstorming to come up with that one. At least they've moved on from the stupid pig's blood thing they usually do.'

'*Vegan* pig's blood,' Bec corrects him. 'Beetroot and I don't wanna know what else . . . Apparently it *stinks*.'

'Literally the stupidest thing I've ever heard,' I say. 'So now bullying is fine so long as it's vegan? And did they not actually watch *Carrie*? A film about a kid who's bullied so badly she decides to *murder* her classmates. They thought *that's* an idea they should copy?'

'Apparently it originated here,' Bec says. 'That's where Stephen King got the idea.'

'He did *not*,' I say. 'The *master* of horror absolutely did not steal one of his most iconic ideas from a random British private school.'

'Well, when you put it like that . . .'

'Besides,' I say. 'In *Carrie*, it's a reference to menstruation! That's why it's so hateful. Here they're just dunking gloop over someone for no reason.' I look across at Kellen reapplying lip gloss while Tiffany insists that everyone admire her nails. 'Kellen must know what they're plotting. Why doesn't he say something?'

'I doubt he's in on it, Zach.' Bec shakes her head. 'And, even if he is, would *you* say something if you were in his position? That boy is like a tuna in a shark tank.'

'He *chose* the shark tank!' I say indignantly. 'It's not like anyone forced him in.'

'He's just lovestruck.' Bec shrugs. 'He's dating the hottest guy in school. Can you *really* blame him for getting caught up in that?'

'For the last time, Rhys is *not* the hottest guy in school,' I snap. 'How does an eighteen-year-old even get muscles like that anyway? I bet he's taking steroids.'

'He is *not* taking steroids, Zach.' Chase laughs. 'He's just down in the gym every morning, while you've still got your hand down your pants.'

'He's got you there!' Bec laughs. 'Though I bet you could beat him in an arm-wrestle. They do say it's all in the *wrist*.' She does the jerk-off gesture for good measure.

'Very funny.' I follow them to join the Sycamore table. We sit a few seats down from Cameron and Josh, and I can't help but steal a couple of glances. They're talking about their prom outfits and Josh is catastrophizing. Cameron is idly playing with his hair as he listens. I could actually pass out from how cute he is.

'You need to do something to get his attention,' Bec says, noticing me staring.

'Yeah?' I don't take my eyes off Cameron. 'He's ultra sporty . . . maybe if I put myself forward as team captain?'

'Absolutely not,' Chase says. 'Have you actually lost your mind?'

'Yeah, I don't mean to be rude,' Bec adds, 'but sport isn't exactly your forte.'

'Well, thanks for the vote of confidence!'

'I love this energy, Zach. I really and truly do.' Bec sighs. 'But maybe try something that doesn't screw the rest of us over? I still wanna win today.'

'Just because I'm not semi-professional like you two!'

'Remember when you fell over trying to kick a football? Twice, Zach.'

'It was slippery!' I say. 'And I wasn't wearing the right shoes.'

'Mmm-hmm.' Chase nods. 'I'm sure that's what it was.'

Bec laughs. 'There's other ways to get his attention, Zach.'

'Like, dare I suggest . . . talking to him?' Chase adds.

'And saying what?'

'Just have a normal human conversation maybe?'

'I'm not very good at those . . .'

Last time I tried to talk to Cameron, I gave him a lecture on the questionable ethics of fish farms. All he'd said was, 'How are you?'

'Oh God.' Bec is suddenly distracted by something behind me. I turn to see Tiffany heading right for us, her ponytail swishing with the precision of a scalpel.

'What does she want?' Chase says, gritting his teeth.

We all go silent as we brace ourselves for impact.

Three, two –

'So I think congratulations are in order,' Tiffany says brightly, smile fixed and unfaltering. Everyone around us falls silent. '*Hottest girl* . . . and *Most likely to win gold at the Olympics* . . .' She reads from her pastel-pink phone. 'You really did well, Bec.'

'Thanks,' she replies coldly, not giving Tiffany the satisfaction.

'Though it's funny –' she ploughs on, her voice climbing up an octave – 'Ethan said he could have sworn he saw my name against those results. Can you imagine? He said it was like they changed before his very eyes! Whatever could have caused such a thing?'

Chase sighs. 'Let's save ourselves the time, shall we? Yes, I changed the results. But you already know that, don't you? That's why you're over here doing this silly little routine.'

Tiffany's smile twists into something more sinister. 'So you admit it then?'

'I saw that you'd won practically every single category. So, yeah. I fixed it.'

'I wouldn't expect anything less from our resident hacker.' She says it like he's a criminal. 'You really care that much about some silly little poll? Kind of sad, isn't it?'

'Almost as sad as creating fake accounts to vote for yourself.'

Tiffany scoffs. 'It's always accusations with you, isn't it?'

'No smoke without fire.'

'And yet you never have any proof.' She shrugs. 'Doesn't matter anyway. I'm still gonna win Prom Queen. That's why we did *that* vote by paper ballot. So your meddling cyber fingers can't get at the results. Democracy in action!'

'You really think I care about who's crowned tonight?' Chase laughs. 'I mean, it would have been nice to see Kellen and Rhys make history. The first same-sex couple to take the crowns! A real friend would bow out of the competition. Be an ally. Let them have it. I mean, Rhys *is* your best friend, isn't he? Or is that just for the likes?'

'Of course he's my friend,' Tiffany snarls. 'And that's exactly why I'm giving them fair competition. That's the problem with people like you. You want everything handed to you. Well, not in my world. I'm not going to patronize them by letting them win.'

'No, far better to steal the crowns from under them,' Chase says. 'I'm sure you've already found a way to do that.' He's really on a roll today. I hate to give Tiffany credit, but she's hard to go toe to toe with. 'So what was it this time? Blackmailed Mr Harrington? Bribed half the student body?'

'How dare you –'

The sound of the double doors opening interrupts them and we all turn to see a tall Black woman striding into the room.

'For what reason is it this hot?' she demands of nobody in particular, and the hall falls silent. Tiffany glares at Chase before sweeping back to her table.

Miss Madzikanda has a way of commanding a room just with her presence. She's the 'head games mistress' (which is rich-people talk for 'PE teacher') and she's always been my favourite because she's the only teacher at Oakbrook that doesn't play favourites. It's rumoured she was on scholarship back when she was a student here, and I think that's why she doesn't bend to the rich kids. She's a hard-ass for sure, but she's a hard-ass to *everyone*.

She's wearing a stylish, slightly oversized mint-green tracksuit today, with her Afro loosely tied up in a matching headscarf. She has a whistle dangling around her neck, and she's carrying a cardboard box filled with red and blue bandanas. She drops the box on to the end of our table and wipes the sweat that's beading on her forehead.

'All right, you lot,' she says, clapping her hands together, 'I want volunteers for team captains.'

Tiffany's hand shoots in the air before she can even finish the sentence.

'Why am I not surprised?' Madzikanda says as Ethan gets an elbow to the ribs and his hand shoots up too. She takes out a couple of red bandanas and tosses them over.

'And Sycamore?' she asks, turning to our side of the room.

Bec puts her hand up, and so does Cameron, pitting the Clark twins against each other. Classic sibling rivalry. Exactly what we expected.

Madzikanda hands them both a blue bandana. 'Heads or tails?' She is looking straight at Bec as she takes out a large silver coin that looks more like pirate treasure than actual money.

'Heads?' she suggests, turning to her co-captain for approval.

Cameron nods. 'You know, a toss is statistically more

likely to come up heads? Something about the way the coins are weighted.'

'So you're telling me this isn't a fair process?' Madzikanda pretends to be shocked. She flips the coin and catches it. 'Tails,' she says. 'Hard luck.' She turns to Ethan and Tiffany. 'Top or bottom?'

'That's a bit personal, miss!' Josh jokes, demonstrating his class-clown credentials.

Madzikanda sighs. 'You know, when I tell my friends how many queer students we have here at Oakbrook, they always say, *Oh, how refreshing! They must be so well behaved!*' She looks around the hall, giving ample side-eye. 'If only that were true.'

'Ah, don't be like that, miss. You love us really,' Josh says, and she shoots him a knowing look, a glimmer of a smirk on her face.

'OK, well, allow me to rephrase,' she says. 'Which base do you want?'

'We'll take the hill,' says Tiffany.

Our half of the room lets out a collective groan because everyone knows that between the hill and the woods the hill is always the better option. Better for attack because you get a 360-degree view of the playing field, and easier to defend because the enemy has to run up the slope to steal your flag. We're already on the back foot and we haven't even started.

'Great!' Miss Madzikanda says. 'As for the rest of you –' she addresses those of us without bandanas – 'come on up and grab your team colours. Whistle is in thirty!'

*

35

Cameron bounces ahead of us, waving our blue flag proudly as he leads Sycamore through the woodland. He's enjoying this just a little bit too much, but he's so cute his enthusiasm is infectious. I never thought I'd say it, but Chase was right: we *are* making core memories today. There's just something in the air. I'm glad I didn't skip this.

'Nice of you to join us,' Bec says as Kellen comes running to catch up with us. I was honestly starting to think he wouldn't show. 'Did you forget which team you were on?'

'Course not,' he says, holding up his blue bandana. 'I'll always be Sycamore. I just got caught up chatting and didn't realize you were leaving.'

Bec smiles at that. 'Here,' she says, stopping to tie it for him. 'Blue suits you better than red. You know that, right?'

'Shame about the nails then.' He lifts his hand to show his ruby tips.

'You did *not* paint your nails in Hawthorn colours!'

'Of course not,' Kellen says, laughing. 'They're to match my masquerade outfit. I did them last night.'

'Well, they look great,' she says, admiring them a little closer. 'Can't wait to see what you're wearing. If it's anything like that look you pulled at Christmas . . .'

Everyone else had dressed up like elves and reindeer while Kellen went for this *'ice prince'* look. His cheekbones cut with silver highlight, his sparkling corset studded with fake diamonds. He'd glued them himself, and, although they were made of plastic, you'd have honestly never known. With £20 and a glue gun, he'd looked like the most expensive person in the room.

'For what it's worth,' Chase says, 'I know you're all buddy-buddy with Hawthorn now, but I'm really glad you're here. As long as you *swear* you're not on secret espionage?'

Kellen grins. 'Always did fancy myself a bit of a spy. Imagine me as a Bond girl. Shirley Bassey wailing as I do high kicks. Fur coat. Red lipstick. I'd be stealing secrets and stealing glances, with Chase on speed dial for when I need to hack the mainframe.'

'What mainframe?' Chase laughs.

'I don't know. It's what they say in the movies.'

'He's right,' I say. 'That *is* what they say in the movies. I'm glad you took something away from that Bond marathon.'

'Oh my God, don't remind me.' Chase groans. He stops in his tracks for a moment as if remembering the worst of all horrors. 'You made us stay up all night!'

'I didn't make you do anything!' I protest.

'You gave us espresso at two a.m., Zach.'

'Yeah, I didn't drink that,' Kellen says with a laugh. 'That's why I fell asleep. I tipped it out the window when you weren't looking.'

'You tipped hot coffee out the window?' I gasp. 'What if you'd hit someone?'

'Because there were just *so* many people taking a stroll at two a.m. ...'

'And where was my invite?' Bec pretends to be insulted. 'Maybe I wanted to stay up all night watching poorly written movies.'

'It was a boys' thing.' Chase shrugs.

'Oh, hello, misogyny,' she replies sourly. 'Because girls can't enjoy action movies?'

'You just said they were poorly written!' I say.

Chase is laughing now. 'I promise you didn't miss anything.'

'I did like the bit where they pointed the big laser gun at his genitals,' Kellen confesses. 'I like my men tied up and defenceless.'

'So that's what Rhys is into,' Chase teases. 'I thought you said you fell asleep?'

'I made sure to wake up for that bit.'

We all laugh at that, and, just for a moment, it feels like old times. It's bitter-sweet, though. I hate that it took a sporting event – *of all things!* – to get Kellen to hang out with us again. I'm still glad he's here, though. I would've been sad to leave without spending a bit more time with him. It seems silly to just be realizing that now. I guess it's only when you're at the end of something that you truly realize you're gonna miss it.

The match goes way better than I expected. They may have the superior base, but we counter that with a heavy defence, only sending Cameron, Chase and Josh after the enemy flag, while the rest of us stay back. I don't see much of Cameron, but Bec does a great job of leading, constantly yelling out encouragement and telling us how great we're doing. Even when Hawthorn get two flags away from us, she still maintains the positivity.

I'm not sure me and Kellen are contributing much, to be honest, but I suppose just adding to the mass of bodies does *something*. I even manage to tag one of the Hawthorn girls out at one point. In fairness, she tripped over her own feet, so it wasn't exactly like I *caught* her, but at least I was there to offer a 'helping hand' as she lay face down in the dirt.

Cameron leads our attack, successfully distracting the enemy team while Chase and Josh manage to score a flag each. They say queer people aren't good at sport, and Kellen and I may live up to that stereotype, but the three of them are proof to the contrary. I can tell they're getting tired, though, but luckily, after being tied two–all for what seems like forever, Madzikanda mercifully blows her whistle to signal a short break.

'I have an idea,' Cameron says as we regroup by our flag. His hair is messed up and he's got dirt scraped up one side of his face, but he somehow looks hotter than ever. 'We've played such good defence, so what if we mix it up a bit? Put everyone on attack? Hit them hard right off the bat? They'll never see it coming.'

'It's risky,' Bec says after a moment's thought. 'But I like it!'

'We just need someone to stay back,' Cameron says, glancing around all of us. 'We need the right person.' His gaze suddenly lands on me. 'How about it, Zach?'

'Me?' I say, completely flummoxed. 'Why me?'

'Why not?' He grips me by the shoulder, and I feel myself beginning to melt. 'You're as capable as anyone else here. I certainly believe in you.'

'You do?' I say, forgetting for a moment that he absolutely should *not* believe in me.

'Course,' he says with a smile that fully turns me into a puddle.

'O-OK,' I stammer. All thoughts have left my brain now. I'll do whatever he says.

'Are you sure about this, Zach?' Bec drags me back to reality. She doesn't look at all convinced. I'd be offended by her lack of faith in me if it wasn't absolutely justified.

'Yeah, Zach isn't exactly ... *excellent*.' Chase tries to put it gently.

'He's terrible,' Bec says, less gently.

'I'm sure he's not *that* bad.' Cameron defends my honour. *My hero!*

'No, he really is,' Bec says.

'OK, fine, maybe he's terrible!' Cameron laughs. Not exactly the words I was hoping would come out of my crush's mouth today. 'But it doesn't matter. Zach, we just need you to stand here. Pin yourself to that flagpole and don't move. If they know you're terrible, it might even work in our favour. They'll think it's a trap. There's no way they'd believe we'd leave our flag with only our worst player standing guard.'

'I don't think anyone's saying I'm the *worst* player –'

'I am *definitely* saying that,' Bec says.

'What about Kellen?' I say defensively.

'What about me?' Kellen raises an eyebrow. 'I'm not as bad as *you*, Zach.'

'You're so much worse than me!'

Bec laughs. 'OK, so why don't you both stay back? Work as a team? And then the rest of us can go on offence.'

'That works for me,' Cameron says. 'As long as you guys are happy?'

He looks directly at me as he says it. If I can pull this off, successfully defend our flag, maybe he'll see me differently. Maybe that's all I need to do to finally get him to notice me.

'We'll do it,' I say. 'Right, Kellen?'

'Fine.' Kellen shrugs. 'But I'm not taking any responsibility if this goes wrong . . .'

'It won't,' Cameron says confidently just as Madzikanda's whistle shrieks in the distance, signalling the start of the final round.

'We've got this!' Bec says. 'Everyone with me. Good luck, boys!'

And, before I can even really process what we've agreed to, they all disappear into the surrounding woodland, leaving me and Kellen alone.

'So you still have a thing for Cameron then?' Kellen says as the sound of footsteps and breaking branches grows quieter and quieter.

'Huh?' I say, feeling myself instantly turning red. 'What makes you say that?'

'Because you practically fainted when he spoke to you,' Kellen says with a laugh. 'It was quite entertaining to watch. All this time and you've still never made a move?'

'I'm working up to it,' I mutter. I don't want to have this conversation *again* today.

'Doesn't look like it.'

'Why are you interested all of a sudden?'

'I'm just saying ... You'll never know if you don't go for it. What could be more romantic than a prom-night dalliance?'

'And what could be more embarrassing than a prom-night crash and burn?' I reply. 'What if he rejects me? Then what?'

'Then nothing! If he rejects you, he rejects you. I don't understand why everyone has this debilitating fear of rejection! Worse things have happened, Zach.'

'I just feel like there's been so much building to this these past two years.' Admittedly I think I've enjoyed the fantasy as much as anything. 'I'm not sure I could take it if suddenly that was over. If it all came to nothing.'

'That's why you should have made a move two years ago!'

'Rome wasn't built in a day!'

'You're not establishing an ancient civilization, Zach. You're telling a guy that you like him. That can, in fact, be done in *less* than a day.'

'Well, I've been trying!'

'You *have not* been trying.' Kellen laughs. 'You've been being all *Zach* about it.'

'What's that supposed to mean?'

'I think you know what that's supposed to mean.' He raises an eyebrow.

'Yeah, well ...' I'm at a loss for words now. 'You're being very *Kellen* about this too.'

'Good, I love being Kellen.' He sounds awfully pleased with himself. 'You don't need to make this so complicated,

Zach. Just make the move. Shoot your shot! Better to leave having given it a go than be left wondering what could have been.'

'Easier said than done,' I say, shuffling my feet. 'I'm not good at this.'

'You think I am?' Kellen says. 'I still put on my big-boy pants and talked to Rhys. At least you don't need to go down into the trenches of Hawthorn! Cameron's on our side!'

'I know,' I say. 'I just need a bit more time.'

'Well, we're fresh out of that, I'm afraid. It's now or never, Zach.'

'Maybe I could just –'

The sound of snapping branches interrupts me.

'What was that?' Kellen springs up, on the alert.

'Stay here,' I say, stepping away from the flag, heading in the direction of the noise.

'Maybe it's just a deer . . .'

'There aren't any deer at Oakbrook.'

'A bear then? I don't know.'

'A *bear*?' I say, turning back round to face him. 'What do you mean "a bear"?'

'There are bears in the countryside.'

'Not in the UK there aren't. Where do you think we are? Svalbard?'

'Well, how do we know if we've never seen one?'

'We know *because* we've never seen one!'

'Seems like pretty flawed logic,' Kellen says. 'It's a false alarm anyway. Look.'

I turn back round and see that he's right. There's someone in a blue bandana running through the woodland towards us. At least it's one of ours.

'They're coming!' they yell, and I realize it's Cameron. His ears must have been burning. 'They're coming!' he pants, looking back over his shoulder. 'Their whole team.'

'What?' I say. 'Their whole team?!'

'Their whole team,' he repeats, bouncing on his heels, ready to defend. We're clearly done for. With just me and Kellen at his side, Cameron may as well be by himself.

We peer into the woodland, but I can't see anyone. I can't hear anyone either. There's nothing but the sound of my own heartbeat thundering in my ears.

'Are you sure?' I say, turning to look back at Cameron.

And that's when I see it. Or, rather, *don't* see it. His birthmark.

'That's Ethan!' I yell, but it's too late.

'Yoink!' he says, snatching the flag.

'Stop him!' I scramble forward, but we're far too slow. He sprints into the woodland, getting rid of the evidence by tossing his stolen blue bandana as he goes. We try to follow, but he's so quick and agile that we can barely keep up. He pulls his red bandana out of his shorts and reties it as he reaches the treeline, sprinting out into the open.

'Get him!' I yell to any of our teammates within earshot. Some of them immediately go after him, but he ducks and dives and manages to evade them. I see Chase running with the red flag in the opposite direction, but a Hawthorn lad steamrollers him, taking the flag back like it's nothing.

'Someone stop him!' I yell again, but it's hopeless. Out of breath, Ethan passes the flag to Tiffany, and she effortlessly runs up the hill, scoring their final point.

'Fuck this,' I say as their team erupts with celebration. 'He can't do that.'

'Where in the rules does it say that he can't?' Kellen says, out of breath.

'I don't need to read the rules to know that's cheating. I'm telling Madzikanda.'

'Don't,' he says. 'It's not worth it. Snitches get stitches, Zach.'

'I'm sorry, I didn't realize we were in a prison yard all of a sudden!'

'Just leave it,' he says. 'If we report them, they're just gonna hate us for it.'

'I'm sorry to break this to you,' I say, 'but they *already* hate us, Kellen. I know you want them to like you, but Tiffany and Ethan? They're never gonna *really* accept you.'

'I know,' he says, and it surprises me. 'But it's the last day. I just want everything to be chill. They're Rhys's friends. I'm going to have to spend prom night with them. I just don't want anything to ruin it.'

'That doesn't mean we have to let them get away with this.'

'Zach, please . . .' he says. He looks at me with a sense of desperation I've never seen from him before. 'I need tonight to go perfectly.'

I think on it for a moment. I don't really understand why, but this seems to mean a lot to him. Maybe Bec and

Chase are right. Maybe I do need to try harder to accept his relationship. 'OK, fine,' I finally say. 'But you owe me.'

'Thanks, Zach,' he says, opening his arms for a hug.

'Don't mention it,' I grumble, reluctantly accepting it. He squeezes me tightly for a moment, and it actually feels kinda nice. I let it linger for just a second before pushing him off. I don't want him getting the wrong idea about us. It'll take more than a game of Capture the Flag to mend our relationship. We're not suddenly best friends again.

'I'm gonna go say congrats,' he says, looking over at Rhys. I can tell he's already starting to itch from being away from him. This is exactly why we can't just go straight back to being besties. His friends will always be his second choice.

I take a deep breath and try not to let it bother me.

'OK, have fun.' I try to sound sincere. 'But see you later, yeah?'

I'm not sure he even hears me. His boyfriend consumes his whole world again as he rushes over to throw his arms round him. And, just like that, me, Chase and Bec are forgotten about all over again. I wonder if he'll even bother to talk to us at prom.

'Three–two to Hawthorn!' Miss Madzikanda booms through her loudspeaker. Hawthorn erupt all over again. 'Congratulations to this year's winners!'

I watch as Kellen fist-bumps Ethan and exchanges air kisses with Tiffany. I almost choke on the venom that sits in the back of my throat.

'I really thought we could beat them,' Chase says as he

and Bec come to join me. 'Just this once. Show them that they're not better than the rest of us.'

'They're not,' I say. 'They cheated. Ethan stole a blue bandana. He pretended to be Cameron to get close to our flag, then stole it from right underneath us.'

'What?' Bec says. 'Are you serious? Why didn't you say something?'

'Because what's the point?' I say. 'It'll be my word against his. It'll just make us look like sore losers. I'm not sure that's even against the rules anyway.'

'What about Kellen?' Chase says. 'He'll back you up, right?'

'What do you think?' I say, watching him fawning all over his Hawthorn boyfriend.

'Well, you know what? Let's just not give them the satisfaction,' Bec says. 'We go high. It's just a game. Who honestly cares, right?'

'Right,' I say.

But I do care. More than I'd like to admit.

Golden afternoon light pours through the windows of the old shower block as I peer inside. *Result!* There's nobody here yet. Getting the showers to yourself at Oakbrook is a rarity. And I know: communal shower, private school – that's a gay teenager's wet dream, right? But honestly? The whole thing just makes me uncomfortable. It's like forced exhibitionism. As if the students of Oakbrook aren't already judgemental enough in the classroom and the dorms. I don't want them sizing me up in the shower too.

The pipes groan as I turn the tap and step under the hot water, and just as the room starts to slowly fill with steam –

'Oh, there you are!'

It's Cameron. He only glances in my direction for a second, but even that's enough to make me want to cover up. 'I've been looking everywhere for you.'

'You have?' I squeak back. *And yet you had to find me here . . .*

'Yeah,' he says, peeling off his T-shirt and throwing it down on one of the benches. He keeps his eyes averted. Good locker-room etiquette, but he's still making me nervous. He's still got dirt on his face from the game, drops of sweat beading on the tips of his jet-black hair. 'So is it true?'

'Is what true?'

'What Bec said.'

My heart stops. If she's told Cameron I fancy him, I swear to God –

'That my brother cheated?'

Relief floods through me.

'Oh. Yeah. He pretended to be you. We shouldn't have fallen for it, but –'

Cameron swears. 'He's such an asshole. Why didn't you say something?'

'As if anyone would have believed me.'

'I'd have believed you,' he says, glancing over again as he kneels to untie his shoes. He holds eye contact for a moment, and I try not to get flustered. 'I don't blame you for not speaking up, though. They can be kinda intimidating, but you know you can talk to me, right? Just because he's my brother, it doesn't mean I'm gonna take his side.'

'I thought twins were supposed to have this unbreakable brotherly bond?'

He laughs, pulling off his shorts so he's just in his black designer briefs. I turn away so I don't feel like I'm staring. This is *exactly* why I hate communal showers – it's unreasonable to expect anyone to act *normal* under these circumstances. It's so much easier for straight people. They don't have to deal with any of this.

'I guess I was close with Ethan once,' Cameron begins. 'When we were younger. But we've both changed so much since then. These days I sometimes wish we weren't related.'

Shucking his underwear, he comes to join me in the showers, no concrete divider, no nothing. Just his naked body confronting me.

'I get that,' I say, feeling my mouth go dry. I try to keep my gaze fixed firmly on the wall. *He's trying to open up to you. Don't ruin the moment by making this weird.*

'Anyway,' he says with a shrug, 'it's whatever.'

I feel like Cameron wants to talk about it more, but I don't push it.

'You know,' he continues, rubbing shampoo into his hair, 'I never understood why you didn't join the rugby team. You'd be perfect, you know that?'

'I can't catch a ball to save my life,' I say, feeling myself blush.

'It just takes practice,' he says. 'And with your build? A

little bit of training, you'd be unstoppable. I'm jealous, to be honest. I've always struggled to put on muscle.'

'Muscle?' I say, glancing down at my shapeless body. 'There's no muscle on me.'

'Are you kidding?' He laughs. 'You've got good genes, Zach. Lift a few weights and you'd be bigger than me in no time.'

'But you're totally ripped,' I say, my eyes trailing down to his abs, and snapping back up to his eyes before they travel too far south. *Be careful, Zach.*

'That's just low body fat,' he says. 'I can't put on muscle to save my life. No matter how much I eat. No matter how much I lift. It's a curse, really. Look, flex for me.'

'What?'

'Flex,' he says, flexing his own arm to demonstrate.

I tentatively do as he says. I have never felt more self-conscious.

'You see? Your biceps are bigger than mine, Zach.'

'Huh,' I say. He's actually right. 'I guess I never noticed.'

'We're all our own biggest critics.'

'Well, I think you look great,' I say, holding eye contact for longer than is sensible. It's the closest I've ever come to making a move on him. I can feel my heart thundering.

'Thanks, Zach.' He smiles. 'We should hang out later. Me, you. Chase. Bec.'

'Yeah?'

'Yeah. It's funny – I feel like I should have made more of an effort to get to know you all these past two years. It just seemed like we had all the time in the world, you know? And now suddenly . . .'

'We don't.'

'Exactly,' he says. 'We've still got tonight, though.' He twists the tap until the water comes to a stop. 'See you in a bit, yeah?'

And, with that, he strides back over to the lockers and throws a towel round his shoulders instead of his waist. I open my mouth to reply, but I'm cut off by a bunch of the other boys noisily filing into the room. They go about tearing off their clothes and making a mess of the place in rowdy straight-boy fashion, completely unaware of the gay romance playing out right under their noses. At least that's what I'm calling it.

Even if it is just wishful thinking.

'Looking forward to seeing your outfit later!' Cameron calls over the noise, wrapping a second towel round his waist and heading for the door.

'Yours too!' I call back as he disappears and leaves me to the straights.

'Are you kidding me?' Chase says. 'Of course he was flirting!'

'It was just banter,' I say. 'Isn't that what guys do in the locker room?'

'What? Compliment each other's bodies? That's gay as hell, Zach.'

'It's a thing! I'm telling you. "Sick gains, bro." The straight guys do it all the time.'

Chase rolls his eyes hard. 'But Cameron's not straight, is he? Of course he was flirting. I don't know how he could make it any more obvious. The boy was literally naked!'

'Is he supposed to keep his clothes on to take a shower?'

Chase laughs at that, taking his usual spot on the window sill. 'Maybe I'm wrong,' he says. 'But you really need to wise up to the idea that you're a catch. First Josh, now Cameron. At this point, I'm surprised you didn't get more than one vote for hottest boy. Everyone seems to want a piece of you, Zach.'

'OK, well, that's just two people . . .' I say. 'Not *everyone*. Besides, I'm telling you, Josh isn't into me either. Whatever we had back then is over.'

'If you say so.' Chase shrugs, peering outside. 'What on earth is Bec doing now . . .'

'Huh?' I say, looking out to see her scaling the fire escape. 'What *is* she doing?'

She's wearing blue jeans and a white T-shirt, her hair's still wet from the shower, and she's precariously carrying a garment bag and a pair of high heels. She disappears from view, and then, a few moment later, there's a knock at the door. It's her, calm and collected; she hasn't even broken a sweat.

'What was that? You're like an Asian Lara Croft.' Chase laughs, pulling her in. 'You're not supposed to be up here. What if someone sees you?'

'That's why I took the fire escape,' she says. 'Anyway, what's the big deal? It's not like it's the first time I've been in the boys' dorm . . .'

'It isn't?' Chase says. I'm as surprised as he is.

'I've been in Jacob's room ... and Kyle's for that matter ...'

'Isn't that the same room?' Chase says.

'Yeah, but I was there for two very different reasons.'

'Oh my God,' I say, laughing. 'Why is this the first time we're hearing about this?'

'I told you I hooked up with them!' she says. 'Where did you think it happened?'

'I don't know,' Chase replies. 'I just assumed you did it in the boathouse or something. That's where *everyone* goes to hook up! Tell her, Zach!'

'What do you mean "tell her, Zach"?' As if I'm the authority on hook-ups!

'You and Josh!' he says. 'I don't know why you insist on playing innocent ...'

'Well, whatever!' says Bec. 'I'm not having sex in some crusty old boat! I don't understand why you boys all want to do it in there. You realize there's, like, two hundred beds in this place?'

'Where's the fun in that? Zero risk of splinters!' Chase says. 'Besides, do you really think these beds are any better?' He shakes the squeaky frame of his bed vigorously.

'The sound of passion,' she says. 'Music to my ears.'

Chase laughs. 'You're disgusting.'

She shrugs. 'Not like I'll be getting any tonight anyway.'

'Why would you say that?' I ask. 'Course you will! You're a catch!'

'Yeah, but apparently I'm *intimidating* ...'

'Who said that?' Chase looks annoyed.

'That's what all the boys say about me. They call me the *praying mantis*.'

'Like the weird bug thing?' I say.

'Exactly. The females eat the males after having sex. They use them and then mercilessly rip them apart.'

'Well, as far as nicknames go,' Chase says, 'that *is* kinda iconic.'

'I guess.' Bec sighs. 'But now none of them dares ask me to prom. Is it so much to want some guy to knock on the door with a big bouquet of flowers?'

She looks at the door as if she expects that to happen. It would be romantic for it to suddenly fly open, but alas, this isn't some romance novel. The door remains firmly shut.

'I didn't think you bought into all that anyway,' Chase says. 'You're a feminist!'

Bec gives him a flat stare. 'I can be a feminist and still want to be given flowers.'

'It's not like there's a florist on campus . . .'

'They don't need to *buy* me flowers, Chase! There's meadows out there full of them. I just wish one of these boys would step up. Why does it *always* have to be me who initiates?'

'Maybe there's a boy outside your room as we speak?' I say. 'There could be hordes of potential suitors lining up down the corridor. It's not like anyone knows you're up here.'

'Why *are* you up here?' Chase asks.

'Isn't it obvious?' Bec shakes her garment bag. 'I didn't

wanna get ready alone so I came to prep with my besties. My last room-mate abandoned me, remember?'

'I didn't abandon you!' Chase laughs. 'You're the best room-mate I ever had!'

'Hey! What about me?' I protest. I'm just as good as Bec!

'What about you? You snore and you wipe your juices on the bedsheets.' It's true, but he doesn't need to say it. 'I said what I said, Zach. Bec was a *way* better room-mate.'

'Damn straight,' she says, sticking her tongue out at me. 'So are we finally going to get to see this outfit you've been oh-so-secretive about?' She turns to the wardrobe.

'It's not in there,' Chase says. 'It's in the box.'

He gestures to the trunk in the corner of the room. It's sat there for so long, unopened, that I sort of forgot about it. I always assumed it was empty.

'Mysterious,' Bec says, crouching down to get a closer look. 'It's padlocked?'

'Here,' Chase says, reaching under the corner of his mattress to pull out a tiny silver key. Who knew this whole time he was holding on to a secret? He tosses it to Bec and she pops the lock, peering inside like she's unearthing hidden treasure.

'Remember my mum's old prom dress?' Chase continues as Bec delicately lifts up the elegant gold fabric. 'The one she gave me and always wanted me to wear tonight? I obviously wasn't gonna wear a dress, but –'

'It's incredible,' Bec says, marvelling at the craftsmanship.

It's been transformed into a type of formal masculine robe. The original gold fabric has been cut with white, transforming the western dress into something that connects both him and his mum with their heritage. I don't know the exact terminology, but there's this cute guy I follow on Instagram who posts these incredible martial arts videos while wearing something that looks just like it.

'So you made this?' Bec asks.

'Yes, I made it.' The sarcasm is thick in his voice. 'I'm actually not going to study computer science at all. I'm going to secretly run off and become a tailor.'

'Really?' Bec says, oblivious.

'No!' He laughs. 'Of course I didn't make it, Bec. You think I've been hiding a sewing machine under mine and Zach's bunkbed and working away in the middle of the night?'

'Well, I don't know! Everyone knows Zach's a heavy sleeper!'

It's true. Before Chase moved in, the fire alarm went off and we all had to evacuate. The headcount came up one person short because I was still upstairs dreaming about having a sleepover with all seven members of BTS. I wish I was joking, but that's actually what my dream was about. I was kinda miffed when I instead woke up to a frantic Mr Harrington.

Chase takes the garment from Bec and holds it up against his body. 'I sent it to a family friend who works in fashion. They weren't sure about cutting up Mum's dress without asking her, but I think it works, right? I just hope she's OK with it . . . She's either gonna be really touched or really, *really* angry . . .'

'Why would she be angry?' I say. 'You made something special, something even better. And this is like . . . super Chinese, right? She'll love it.'

56

'Yeah, it's *super Chinese*,' Chase says, mocking me. 'You sound like an idiot, Zach.'

Bec laughs at that. 'It's Hanfu, right?'

'Exactly,' he says, starting to get changed. 'I'm actually impressed you know that.'

'You showed us some outfits a while back,' Bec says. 'Right after you transitioned.'

I think I do sort of remember that.

'Always said you'd love to be able to wear them one day. But you were worried about somehow being disrespectful.'

Chase smiles. 'I'm glad you remembered,' he says, adjusting the outfit. It really does look incredible on him. 'Though I am still worried about it being perceived as disrespectful. I just hope Mum likes it. I'm kinda nervous about showing her.'

'Don't be,' Bec says. 'She's lucky to have a son like you. Anyone else would have sold the dress and bought themselves an outfit on ASOS. This is . . . *something else*.'

'Thanks,' Chase says with a smile.

'Uh-huh.' Bec is now busying herself with her own outfit. In a second, she strips down to her underwear – in front of us because apparently we're that close. I never realized before, but she's got a set of abs to rival Cameron's. 'Could you give me a hand?'

'Sure,' I say, helping her into her sparkling black dress and zipping her up.

'Thanks, Zach, you're a peach,' she says, stepping into her shoes. 'What do you think?' She puts on a matching feathered mask and spins round so we can get a good look at her. 'Obviously we need some make-up, and I need to sort out this hair . . .'

'Wow,' Chase says. 'I have literally never seen this side of you.'

'Me neither,' I add.

When not in uniform, Bec's always dressed in jeans or sportswear. In all the time we've been here, this is the first time I've seen her in anything even close to formal. I think of all those movies where the girl walks down the stairs in her prom dress and the guys' mouths fall open. That's what Chase and I must look like right now. And both of us prefer guys.

'Little black dress,' she says with a smirk. 'Every girl should have one.'

'Ten out of ten. Five stars. Absolutely no notes,' Chase says.

'He's right,' I say. 'Talk about a forty-five-second transformation. You always look good, but this? It's amazing! You're starting to make me feel underdressed.'

Fashion's never really been my thing, but as I look down at my plain white suit I wonder if I should have made more of an effort. It's been in my wardrobe for a while, and I must have had a late growth spurt or something because it's ever so slightly tight on the chest. It kinda looks deliberate, though, as if I've done it as a style choice. I feel the tightness in the sleeves and remember what Cameron said in the showers. Maybe he's actually right?

'What do you think of this?' I say, holding up the mask I panic-ordered last week. It's one of those intricate

Venetian masks, the colour of ivory with sparkling silver stones. It only covers one side of my face – phantom of the opera style.

'Well, it's a terrible disguise.' Chase laughs. 'I can see your entire face, Zach.'

'It's his moneymaker,' Bec says. 'If he covers that up, what's he got left?'

'Er, thanks?' I say. I think there was a compliment in there somewhere.

'Now *this* is a mask,' Chase says, reaching into the trunk and revealing the final part of his costume. It's shaped like the head of a dragon and far more elaborate than mine and Bec's. He puts it on, and it matches the rest of his incredible outfit perfectly. Now I *really* feel underdressed. 'The perfect disguise! Nobody's gonna know it's me!'

'Yeah, the Singaporean guy with the obviously Asian dragon mask.' Bec smirks. 'Nobody will see it coming! You'll have everyone totally stumped.'

'Shit,' he says. 'I actually hadn't thought of that.'

I laugh. Only Chase wouldn't see the parallel. 'It's gonna be obvious who everyone is anyway. A mask doesn't disguise a person's identity. The whole concept is ridiculous!'

'I think you might be surprised . . .' Bec says. 'All those Hawthorn boys look the same to me. And you just know they're all gonna be wearing identical black tuxedos. There's no way I'm telling them apart once they've got masks on.'

'So you don't think I'll stand out too much?' Chase asks, looking in the mirror.

'Of course you're going to stand out,' Bec says. 'But that's the point, isn't it? You look stunning. Like someone straight off the latest catwalk. Not to mention you look hot as fuck.'

'Thanks,' he says. 'But I know what people are gonna say. *I thought Chase was supposed to be a guy. Why's he wearing a dress?*'

'It's not a dress,' Bec reiterates, smoothing down the fabric. 'You're twice the man of any one of those boys. And this outfit just proves that!'

'Couldn't have said it better myself,' I say. 'Come here. I wanna take a selfie.'

'That's how you know you look good,' Bec says. 'You've even got Zach wanting to post on social media.'

'It's not for social media.' I roll my eyes. 'It's for Mum! I promised I'd send her one.'

'I need to fix my hair first,' Chase says, holding his hand up to stop me taking a picture. 'Though that reminds me. I better call my mum, actually. I want to show her the outfit before I spill something all over it. I overheard Harrington talking about brie and cranberry canapés. I don't want either of those things anywhere near this!'

'You'll be fine,' Bec says with a laugh. 'I promise to protect you from the canapés, but you absolutely cannot call your mum right now.'

'Huh?' Chase says. 'Why not?'

'Because she'd lose her mind if she saw us drinking *this*.' She reaches into the bottom of her garment bag to pull out some questionable-looking tequila. 'I haven't got shot glasses so it'll have to be straight from the bottle. Some

Dutch courage to start the evening!' She unscrews it and passes it over.

'Jeez,' I say, grimacing as I take a sip. 'Toxicquila,' I read from the bottle. There's a picture of a cartoon cactus with a culturally insensitive moustache and sombrero who's violently throwing up. 'Where the hell did you even get this?'

Bec shrugs. 'It'll put hairs on your chest.'

'I'll take all the help I can get.' Chase takes a big gulp, grimaces and then peers underneath his binder. 'Nothing yet.' He frowns. 'How long does this stuff take to kick in?'

'Give it a year,' Bec says, smiling. 'I'm sure it'll happen a lot sooner than you think.'

We manage to get through a third of the bottle of Toxicquila, and I completely forget about taking that picture for Mum. But it's fine – there'll be plenty of opportunities later. Even if it does mean that Hawthorn banners will be in the background. Not that she'd care about that in the slightest. I guess that's what separates us from the legacy families. They describe us as *new money* and make it very clear that we're not like them. Not yet anyway. We have to earn our place if we want to be a part of their silly little club.

I don't know if it's the tequila swishing around our bellies, or if we're just genuinely in a good mood, but the three of us head downstairs with a spring in our step. We're some of the last to join the big huddle of students gathered by the fountain on the front lawn and, surprisingly, Bec was right. As I glance around the crowd of designer suits and thousand-dollar dresses, I realize it's *really* difficult to tell anyone apart. There are a few outliers, of course: Sam's the only girl with bright pink hair, and no mask is gonna hide the fact that Brett is 6 foot 5.

'All right, put your dicks away,' Bec says as wolf whistles come from the throng of suited and booted salivating straight boys. 'Two years with these idiots and all it takes is a pretty dress to turn them into Neanderthals.'

Golden hour is upon us, and the sky is slowly coming to life with dashes of orange, pink and blue. The fountain features a statue of the founder of the school from, like, a hundred years ago. A stern expression is chiselled into the cold stone, and a carved bull mastiff sits obediently by his side. Nobody can ever remember the name of the man, but we all remember the name of his dog – Huckleberry. He's a bit of a school mascot around here. Petting him is supposed to bring good fortune and, although nobody *really* believes that, the top of his head is polished smooth from everyone taking it in turns to give him a good rub.

'And you're sure the outfit isn't too much?' Chase asks self-consciously. 'Not to sound narcissistic or anything, but it kinda feels like everyone is staring at me . . .'

'It's because you look incredible,' I say, putting my arm round his shoulder.

'You really think so?' He tugs on his sleeves a little.

'I'm telling you, you might just be the best-dressed person here. You're probably even gonna upstage Kellen.' I look around, but he doesn't seem to be here yet.

'Thanks, Zach,' he says, smiling. 'You look great too by the way. Never would have thought the whole suit thing would look good on you . . . but yeah. Masc.'

'Masc?' I actually cackle. 'Seriously?'

'One hundred per cent,' he says. 'I'm as shocked as you are.'

Bec smiles. 'Just wait till Cameron gets a look at you.'

'Where is he anyway?' I ask, scanning the crowd for him.

'Over there.' She nods towards the grassy bank where he and Ethan are posing for photos. They've gone for a yin and yang look, Cameron in white with sparkling black accents, and Ethan in the exact opposite. It's weird that I can tell them apart, even like this, but there's something about the way Cameron moves that just stands out to me. He has an easy-going energy about him, whereas Ethan seems more rigid.

They snap a few photos in their masks before taking them off, along with their suit jackets, and continue to take pictures. Cameron jumps on Ethan's back, and they seem to be actually having fun. I think of what he said in the shower block – '*I sometimes wish we weren't related*'. And yet right now that doesn't seem to be the case at all.

'We kinda match them,' Bec says, holding the slack of her black dress up against the white of my suit.

'I suppose we do,' I say. 'Maybe we should be a couple?'

Chase laughs. 'As if you'd know what to do with her, Zach.'

'I'll have you know I used to have a girlfriend,' I say. 'I was thirteen, but . . .'

Bec snorts at that. 'Well, if it's any consolation, none of these straight boys know what to do with me either. And I'm speaking from experience.'

I raise an eyebrow. 'Got your eye on anyone this evening?'

'There is one person,' she says. 'But I think he's got eyes for someone else.'

'Someone else? Have you seen yourself? You're the hottest girl here!'

'That's true,' she says, flicking her hair back. 'But that doesn't mean I'm everyone's type.' A ridiculous statement, honestly. You'd have to be blind.

'Why don't you two get a photo with them?' Chase says, nodding in Ethan and Cameron's direction. 'In your matching outfits. It'll give you a chance to talk to Cameron, Zach.'

'But then we'll also have to talk to Ethan,' I say with a groan.

'You know, sometimes I think he's just Tiffany's puppet,' Bec says. 'He's a dick, I'm not denying that, but ... maybe he'd be nicer if it wasn't for her pulling his strings?'

'He bullies Owen for no reason,' I say. 'Let's not forget that.'

'And I think one day he'll regret it,' she retorts. 'Tiffany on the other hand ...'

I glance across at her. She's wearing a red dress with a matching mask and shoes. I can hear her loudly dropping names like Marc Jacobs and Jimmy Choo. I don't really know who those people are, but I know they're synonymous with *expensive*. Her designer bag is shaped like a glittering heart – not a love heart, but an actual human heart. Ripped from someone's chest no doubt. Some of the other girls are fawning over her, admiring every detail as she holds the hideous thing up for them to get a closer look. Her outfit is probably worth more than Mum's house. The bag alone would probably require a mortgage.

Rhys is standing next to her, dressed in a plain black suit with a plain black mask. It's funny because Kellen used to complain about exactly this. He'd say it was misogynistic for girls to be expected to dress in extravagant colours while guys wore the same dull suits to every occasion. I look around for him again. He's still not here. I'm sure I'm not the only one who's excited to see what he's wearing – he must still be working on the finishing touches.

'Where is he?' I overhear Rhys complain. 'I don't understand what's taking so long.'

'Oh, let him take as long as he likes.' Tiffany waves him away. 'If he wants to miss his own prom, then that's up to him.' I'm sure she'd absolutely *love* that.

'It's just so annoying,' Rhys replies. 'He has to be late to *everything*. He looks the same with or without the stupid make-up. I don't understand why he always does this!'

As someone who never leaves her room without a full face, I sort of expect Tiffany to say something to that. But she doesn't. Though I'm not really sure she's even listening.

Rhys continues to complain, calling Kellen 'high maintenance' one moment and a 'ball and chain' the next. I hate that about him. Whenever Kellen's not around, he always has something bad to say. I can't remember the last time I heard him say something nice.

Luckily, everyone else has Kellen's back. A ripple of compliments surges through the crowd as he finally makes his entrance. Not a single head remains unturned as he strides out from the main building and goes over to join his boyfriend. I'm shocked to see he's wearing a black jacket too – though he's put a Kellen twist on it, and that's what's got people talking. The jacket has a hint of a sparkle to it and he's not wearing a shirt underneath, there's just his bare torso, and he's paired the outfit with glimmering black heels. I have to admit I'd expected him to wear something more colourful – he had painted his nails red, after all – but now I see he's stripped the colour from them too. He must have changed his outfit at the last minute to match his boyfriend's. He's holding his mask, and it's exactly the same as the one Rhys is wearing. He's gone to so much effort to match his boyfriend's distinct *lack* of effort, but I see Rhys glance at the heels and grimace. I could actually punch him, but Kellen doesn't seem to notice as he loudly tells him how handsome he looks in his *plain black* suit. I literally can't watch this.

'OK, who is *that*?' Chase says, pulling my attention away from the *happy* couple.

Someone's coming towards us. They're wearing an extravagant blue-and-gold-patterned jester's costume, the little bells on the tri-pointed hat jingling as they approach. Their hands are covered by silk gloves, and a grinning white mask obscures their identity.

'It's Josh,' Bec says confidently as he reaches us. 'Class clown, right?'

'Ta-da!' he says, pulling off the mask, the artificial grin replaced with the real one. 'Whaddya think? Outrageous, right?' He shakes his head to make the bells jingle.

That's what I love about Josh. Everyone else is so preoccupied with looking *hot* or *expensive*, but here he is making himself look ridiculous. Anything to get a few laughs.

'It's definitely something,' I say. 'You know it actually kinda suits you?'

'I know, right?' He adjusts himself *down there*. 'I think it's the spandex. It shows off my best features. And, by best features, I mean my ass.'

'Such a way with words.' Bec laughs. 'How are you not boiling alive in there?'

'Oh, I absolutely am.' Josh lolls his tongue out for emphasis. 'But we must suffer in the name of fashion.'

'And jester outfits are in this season, are they?'

'They will be after tonight.' He beams. '*Vogue* are gonna slide straight into my DMs.'

'Oh, absolutely,' Chase says. 'I hear Anna Wintour is *constantly* checking Instagram to see what random teenage boys are wearing to prom.'

'Who?' Josh says, oblivious, fiddling with his hat. 'Have you guys seen Owen yet? He's really trying to solidify his allyship status. He's actually wearing a Pride flag.'

'I am not,' Owen says, approaching. He's wearing a plain suit with a shimmering sparkle and a matching sequinned mask. Josh is kinda right: it does sort of look like he's dressed as a rainbow, almost as if he got lost on his way to a Pride parade.

'Allyship!' Josh says, making him do a twirl so we can get a better look.

'It's not a rainbow,' Owen says with a laugh. 'It's iridescent.'

'Sure it is,' Josh says, letting his hand fall limp for emphasis. Some straight guys would be annoyed by the implication, but Owen is just taking it with his usual dopey grin.

I hear raised voices then and look across to see Cameron and Ethan seemingly in some kind of argument. Their energy has changed drastically in the past thirty seconds.

'What's going on?' I ask.

'I've no idea,' Bec says, noticing it too.

I look around and see people checking their phones. They're whispering and pointing very unsubtly in the direction of the twins. Tiffany marches over to Ethan, their conversation growing heated before she pulls out her own phone and makes a call.

'Oh shit . . .' Josh mutters, looking down at his phone now too.

'What is it?' I ask. Chase and Bec appear equally confused.

'Pictures of Ethan,' Josh says. 'They must have been leaked . . .'

'Pictures? What kind of pictures?' Chase says, peering at the screen. I realize what Josh is talking about before Chase does. 'Oh. *Pictures*.'

'They're everywhere,' Josh says, showing us his phone now. 'Celebrity Buzz . . . Girl Gossip . . . Influencers Gone Wild . . .'

'I don't think we should be looking at this,' Bec says, pushing the phone away.

I see one of the images for just a split second. It's Ethan, posing in the mirror. He's completely naked, but sort of half covering himself with one hand. You can't see *that much*, it's more playful than pornographic, but even so – for a picture like this to leak without his consent . . .

'How did this happen?' Chase says.

'Someone must have gotten into his phone . . .'

'You mean you think it was someone at Oakbrook?'

'That or he's been sending them to other girls behind Tiffany's back.'

I find her in the crowd again. She's acting erratically now, waving her free arm about as she speaks to someone on the phone. She's understandably furious. I never thought I'd say it, but I actually feel bad for the two of them. Of all the times this could happen.

'Just make it go away!' she screeches, pacing up and down. 'I don't care, Daddy! I swear to God, if I see *anything* about this in the *Herald* . . .!'

So that's who she's talking to. Surely the *Herald* wouldn't publish pictures of a teenage boy? I mean this in the nicest possible way, but he's not even *that* famous.

She hangs up, looks around for a moment as if searching for someone. Does she actually know who did this? I follow her gaze as she searches for the culprit.

And then her eyes land on Chase.

'What's going on?' I say as she heads in our direction.

'I know it was you!' she says, on the warpath. 'Do you really think we're that stupid? That we wouldn't figure it out?'

'Figure what out?' Chase says, baffled.

'Drop the act!' She's practically foaming at the mouth. 'Don't even try to deny it!'

'Tiffany, I have literally no interest in pictures of your boyfriend.'

'So it's just a coincidence, is it? This morning you hacked into my laptop and –'

'Now wait a second!' he interrupts. 'I never *hacked into your laptop*. I changed a few results around in that stupid leavers' poll. I never touched your laptop!'

'What's the difference?' she says. 'You're still hacking things!'

'Oh my God,' he says. 'This is ridiculous.'

'Is it? You've had it in for us ever since you had your ten minutes of fame. Obsessing over me, telling everyone it was me who leaked that story.'

'That's because it *was* you,' I interject. I can't believe she can be so brazen.

'And do you have any proof of that, Zach? Or are you just making baseless allegations as always? You know that's defamation, right? I'd watch what you say if I were you. You do realize my father knows *everyone* in the media? Whoever you sent those pictures to, there's gonna be a paper trail. A couple of phone calls and I'll have all the evidence I need. Honestly, Chase, you're supposed to be the clever one. With all those big-boy brains, I'm quite surprised you could be so stupid.'

'Call him stupid again, I *dare* you . . .'

'It's fine, Zach,' Chase says, stepping in between me and Tiffany. 'It *obviously* didn't come from me. What could I possibly gain from doing something like that?'

'You *know* something like this could ruin us. That's why you did it, isn't it? Thought you could take us down a peg? Bring us down to your level?'

'What level? What are you even talking about?'

'You know what I'm talking about! And you're not gonna get away with it!'

Everyone's listening now, and people are starting to whisper. Surely they're not actually believing her? Chase would *never* do something like this.

'Do your worst,' he finally says. 'You can't prove *anything*.'

'We'll see,' she says. 'Oh and Chase?' She looks him up and down. 'Just *love* the outfit. I hope nothing tonight *ruins* it.'

'The prom prank,' Bec says. 'You wouldn't . . .'

'What prank?' Tiffany smiles innocently.

'You know *exactly* what prank . . .'

'I heard a *rumour* they're going to toss someone in the lake . . .' She shrugs. 'But that's nothing to do with me. It's not like I could lift Chase anyway – he's a big strong man now, remember?'

'Watch it,' I say.

She smirks at that. 'Have fun tonight, won't you?'

'I'm going to murder her,' Bec says as Tiffany turns on her heel and walks away. She's so angry she's shaking. I look down at my hands and realize I'm shaking a little too.

'It's fine,' Chase says. 'Tiffany is full of shit. They said they'll expel any students that try to pull off a prank this year. Zero tolerance, remember?'

'They say that *every year*. Expulsion on the last day of school is hardly a threat. Besides, do you really think they're going to try to expel Tiffany? She could push Harrington in the lake and still leave with a glowing letter of recommendation.'

'Just don't worry about it,' Chase says. 'If they throw me in the lake, they throw me in the lake. It's not a big deal.'

'But your outfit . . .'

'Will dry . . .' he says with finality. Then frowns. 'She doesn't really think I leaked those photos, though, right? Like, this is just an act? To get back at me?'

'I don't know,' I say. 'But we *know* it wasn't you. That's all that matters.'

'But she just seems so convinced. Even she's not that good an actress.'

'Let her believe what she wants,' Bec says. 'Nobody's gonna listen to Tiffany. I know this might surprise you, but people actually like you, Chase. They *love* you, in fact. Nobody says a bad word about you. Doing something like this? They know it's not in your nature.'

'I don't know,' he says, looking around with trepidation. You can hear the sound of gossip obscured behind masks. 'It feels like people might actually believe her.'

'She's just trying to get in your head,' I say. 'Don't let her. She can't prove it was you because it wasn't you. You've absolutely nothing to worry about.'

'I guess,' he says. 'I just have a bad feeling, that's all . . .'

I don't say it, but I have a bad feeling about this too.

'It'll be fine,' Bec says, wrapping her arm round him. 'And, for what it's worth, at least Ethan seems to be taking it pretty well.'

I look across and see him laughing with his friends. They're pointing at the screen as if revelling in the attention. I don't know how he's so unbothered by it. I'm not sure I would cope if the whole world was looking at pictures of me like that.

I haven't long to think about it, though, because prom night is about to get under way. The huge wooden doors open and the teachers step out. They line up, looking only marginally less bored than we do as Mr Harrington gives some grand speech about *preserving tradition*. He drones on and on about tonight being a night to connect with the many who've walked through these doors before us. It's not a sentiment I disagree with, but after he's said the same thing eighty-six times it definitely starts to wear on me.

'And on the subject of traditions,' he says, after speaking for a full ten minutes, 'some of them are best left in the past. I know the leaver's prank has been a long-standing institution here at Oakbrook. I know some of your parents might even have been involved when they were students. But such behaviour is tantamount to bullying, and what might have been winked at in the past is no longer acceptable today. So this is your reminder that there is to be no prank this year.'

'You all look wonderful in your prom outfits,' Miss Madzikanda says, cutting in. 'So let's keep it that way. I know you think the staff are entirely oblivious to what goes on in this school, but we've got eyes and ears in places you've never dreamed of. So let me assure you when I say that *nobody* is going into the lake this evening, and I mean *nobody*. Got it?'

'What about skinny-dipping, miss?' asks Josh.

'There's nothing I'd rather see less than your bare backside,' she says.

'You don't have to look!'

'Well, I'm sure your classmates don't want to see it either.'

'I'm not so sure about that.' He grins. 'Half of them have *already* seen it.'

Madzikanda squeezes the bridge of her nose. 'I'll pretend I didn't hear that.'

'I meant in the showers, miss. I'll have you know I'm still a *virgin*.' He shoots me a wink, as if him not being a virgin is our little secret.

Madzikanda groans. 'I truly do not need to know anything about your sex lives.' She claps her hands together to change the subject. 'And on that note I think that's enough speeches, don't you?'

There's a sigh of relief from all of us. Mr Harrington tries to indicate he's not finished, but she mercifully cuts him off by throwing open the giant doors.

'Welcome to the masquerade!'

'That's my line,' Harrington grumbles as she shoos him away, the crowd surging forward excitedly. Half a dozen smartly dressed waiters hold out trays of sparkling drinks as we enter. They're non-alcoholic, of course. The school can't sanction underage drinking, but the staff will turn a blind eye. They *know* every student fully intends to 'secretly' get drunk.

'Who lit all these?' Chase says as we walk through the corridor. The lights have been dimmed, and hundreds of tiny candles are nestled in gaps between the old bricks. 'Like, seriously, this must have taken forever. I feel like I'm in a movie or something!'

He's absolutely right. I've walked this corridor a thousand times, but tonight it feels like a different place. It's amazing how the right lighting and decoration transforms it completely. As we walk beneath an archway, it makes me feel like I'm going back in time.

'That's what *money* can do,' Bec says. 'Gotta keep the Hawthorn Elite happy or they'll be demanding a refund . . .'

The sound of a string quartet reverberates round the old walls, and silence falls upon us as we reach the top of the stone staircase that overlooks the hall.

'Wow,' Chase breathes.

Candelabras are lit in every corner, with banners hanging in crimson and gold, the colours of Hawthorn – their reward for winning Capture the Flag. That should annoy me, but right now it's hard to care. It's beautiful. I can't believe this is the same room we had lunch in just a few hours ago. A stage has been constructed on one side, where the string quartet are playing now, but they've already cleared away all the tables to make room for a dance floor, so presumably the music will get livelier later on.

Phones rapidly appear to snap photos, people lift their masks to get a better look, and, even though I probably only post on social media once a year, I find myself reaching for mine too. You expect a lot from a private school, but this is truly *beyond*.

'I don't think anyone's gonna be asking for that refund,' Chase says.

'I wouldn't speak so soon,' Bec says, nodding in Tiffany's direction. She's actually pouting as she looks at the decorations. 'Literally, what is her problem?'

'I don't think that girl will ever be happy,' he says.

'Oh well –' Bec shrugs – 'more for us to enjoy. Shall we?'

She holds out her arms. Chase and I take them and lead her down the stairs together, as if we're her double prom dates, and in that moment I feel so grateful to have them both as my friends.

'Yearbook?' Chase says as we reach the bottom, pointing to the candlelit table that now houses it. This is the first time I've seen it not behind glass. It's open to a random page, and there's dozens of scrawlings fighting for space, all in different handwriting. The top of the page reads Class of '26 in elaborate lettering.

'It's hard to believe anyone was really here back then,' I say, staring up at the interior of the building, trying to imagine how it looked all those years ago. 'Don't you feel weird, thinking about a time before any of us existed?'

'Because the whole universe revolves around you?' Chase teases me. 'A world without Zach Evans? The unimaginable horror!'

'Funny,' I say, leaning closer to the book.

I thought it would be full of uplifting messages of positivity and affirmation, but someone has written To the night I never thought would end. Jeez. Surely their prom can't have been *that* bad?

'No drinks near the book!' Mr Harrington interrupts us, rushing over. 'There's a hundred years of history right there!'

'Sorry,' I say, taking a big step backwards. They should put a sign up or something. How was I supposed to know?

'Pick a year,' Bec says, handing me her drink.

'Erm . . . sixty-nine?' I say.

'You're an actual child. I guess you really can't get Cameron off your mind.' She starts flicking through the pages. 'Here,' she says, 'class of sixty-nine. Wasn't this the summer they wrote songs about?' She reads some of the words on the page. 'Huh . . . I'm right.'

'What do you mean?' I say, still holding both our drinks, trying to see from a distance.

'See right here? These are Beatles lyrics!' She flicks forwards a few pages. 'And look, this is that song by The Police!'

'The song about watching every move a person makes? Truly the creepiest thing anyone has ever written,' Chase says, horrified. 'I'm not sure what point you're trying to make.' He pushes his drink into my hands so I'm now holding three glasses.

'Look,' he says, 'this is ridiculous. Someone has just written "*Long live the mullet!*"'

'Mullets *are* back in fashion . . .' Bec says.

'Don't remind me,' he says with a groan.

'Miss!' Bec calls, spotting Madzikanda. 'What year did you graduate? Seventy-six?'

'Ninety-eight!' she says, scandalized. 'How old do you think I am?'

'Sorry!' Bec laughs. 'Numbers were never my strong suit.'

'It's lucky you're good at sports then, isn't it?'

'I'll take that coming from you!' Bec beams, flicking through the pages again. 'Here it is. Class of ninety-eight.' She studies the page for a moment. 'Which one is yours, miss?'

'The only one without a signature,' Madzikanda replies, mysterious as ever.

'Why doesn't it have a signature?' Bec says, looking for it. And then her jaw actually falls open. '*Oh my God*,' she says. 'You didn't wanna incriminate yourself!'

'What?' I say. 'What on earth does it say?!'

'There's a reason we don't let you read that thing until the last night,' Madzikanda says with a twinkle. 'How are we supposed to discipline you if you know what we used to get up to?'

'Yeah, but this, miss . . . This is . . . I didn't know you had it in you.'

'It's not as bad as it sounds . . .' She chuckles. 'Trust me.'

'What did she write?' I say again, desperately trying to get a look at the book.

'Never you mind,' Madzikanda says, turning the page to the class of 2025.

'Write whatever *you* want.' She hands the pen to Bec. 'Don't let them influence you.'

'Thanks, miss,' she says, watching as Madzikanda goes to busy herself elsewhere. Bec thinks for a moment, staring at the empty page, and then she scribbles something down, looking incredibly proud of herself. Chase leans in to read what she's written.

'Taylor Swift.'

'I don't know why you thought I was joking . . .'

'I just thought maybe you'd write something more meaningful.'

'*Pfft!*' She scoffs. 'Come on then, Plato, your turn.'

'I need more time,' Chase says, pushing the pen away. 'It'll come to me.'

'I look forward to being wowed.'

'OK, I've had enough of being a cupholder,' I say, holding out their drinks.

'Sorry!' They laugh as they relieve me.

'Did you want to write something, Zach?' Bec asks.

'Not yet,' I say. 'I was kinda hoping to talk to Cameron.'

'I get it,' Bec says, her tone suddenly changing. 'I'm a bit worried about him.'

'Huh?' I say, following her gaze to where he's sitting on the stairs. He's staring down at his phone, not engaging with anyone, a worried look spread across his face.

'Do you think it's what happened with Ethan?' Chase says.

'Maybe,' Bec says. 'It wasn't his pictures that were leaked, but they're twins, so . . .'

'Fuck,' I say. 'I hadn't even thought of that.'

'Me neither,' Chase says. 'Maybe you *should* go and talk to him?'

79

'I dunno,' I say. 'Perhaps now's not the right time.'

'Of course it's the right time!' Chase says. 'Go and be a friendly face.'

'OK,' I say. I have no idea what to say to Cameron, so I just go over and sit down next to him.

'Hey,' he says, putting his phone down and letting out a long-drawn-out sigh. 'I guess you heard the news then?'

'Yeah,' I say. 'Kinda. I mean, I didn't look or anything, but . . .' I fumble over my words awkwardly for a moment. 'I just don't understand why anyone would do that.'

'I can think of a few reasons,' Cameron says. 'It's not like he's short of enemies. Not that he's bothered anyway. "*As long as it boosts our followers*" . . .' He looks at his phone again. 'You know we've gained almost five thousand since the news broke?'

'Seriously?' I say. 'Are people really that shallow?'

'Evidently so. It's all he ever talks about – gaining followers? He wants to make a career of it. Says we can make a killing if we start doing a few lip-syncs.'

'But you don't want that?' I ask. I always assumed that's why they were doing it.

'I don't know what I want,' Cameron says. 'It'd be nice to make my own money. Not have to rely on Dad going forwards. But that's not why we started the twinsta. It was just supposed to be a bit of fun. And then the followers started rolling in and –'

'Your brother started seeing dollar signs?'

'I don't know,' he says. 'Sometimes I think he doesn't

care about the money. But the fame? The way he lights up when he talks about it. That's the thing Ethan really wants.'

'I mean, doesn't everyone? That's the goal, right? To be rich and famous.'

'It depends what you're famous for,' Cameron says. 'Everyone thinks we're the same, just because we're twins. And maybe we used to be. But I don't even know who he is any more. I might have called him my best friend once. But this place has changed him.'

'Well,' I say, 'have you talked to him? Tried telling him all this?'

'I've tried,' he says with a shrug. 'I just don't want being a *hot twin* to define me. That's all anyone thinks when they see our account. *Oh my God, look how cute they are . . .*'

'People have said worse.'

'I know . . .' he says. 'I'm not trying to play the victim or anything. I just want people to follow us because they care about what we say, not what we look like.' He takes out his phone. 'See these girls? They're the same age as us and they have over a million followers!'

There's a lesbian couple onscreen doing some dance challenge and kissing for the camera.

'They're from Woodside. That's, like, three towns over from here.'

'Are you sure? It looks like they're in London.'

'They're visiting friends,' Cameron says. 'See.'

I spot a guy in football kit with **CHENG** written in bold letters along the back.

'Oh, he's cute,' I say, pulling the phone right up to my face to get a closer look.

Maybe I shouldn't be gushing over other boys in front of Cameron. But maybe it's good he sees this side of me. Maybe I should play a little hard to get? That's what you're *meant* to do, right?

'Yeah, he's really cute,' Cameron says, nodding. 'I prefer his boyfriend, though.' He points to an adorable floppy-haired boy in the background. He has painted nails, a crop top and a pair of shoes that can only be described as outrageous. 'That boy is the fantasy.'

'Really?' I say. Is he now playing hard to get too?

'He looks a bit like you, actually.'

'Huh?' I say. It catches me off guard. 'Me?'

'Yeah,' he says. 'You don't see it? It's something in the eyes, I think.'

I look closer at the video that's now playing on a loop. He's definitely attractive, it's a compliment for sure, but I really don't think I see the resemblance.

'Anyway,' Cameron says, bringing us back to the original point, 'these girls use their platform to talk about things that matter. See, here's a post on queer book bans.'

'Then why don't you do that? You can make whatever content you want.'

'Because Ethan doesn't wanna "*make things political*",' he says. 'He just wants to wear matching outfits and take cute pictures. And the thing that bothers me most is that it *works*. It doesn't matter that we don't have anything to say as long as we look cute, right? They call us "influencers", but what the fuck are we actually influencing?'

He taps into a web browser to show me the comments from one of the gossip blogs.

We need Cameron's nudes to leak next! Just how identical do you think they are . . . ?! says the first, followed by a string of suggestive emojis.

'I'm sorry,' I say. 'People are awful . . .'

'Yeah.' He sighs, and an awkward silence falls over us. I wonder then if my thoughts about Cameron have ever crossed into the inappropriate. Just this morning – watching him from our dorm-room window – wasn't I objectifying him then too? Am I any better than the people in the comments? I want to say something to set the record straight, to let him know that I like him for his personality and not just his looks. But the words refuse to come. Another moment of silence passes.

'Love the outfit,' he finally says. 'I knew you'd turn it out. Cute mask too.'

I get what he's doing. If you can't think of something to say, just compliment something they're wearing. My mum taught me to do that as well.

'Yours too,' I say. 'Definitely prefer the white . . .'

'Black for the *evil twin*,' he whispers, nodding in Ethan's direction. He's trying to wave Cameron over. 'Duty calls.' Cameron sighs and stands. 'Come save me later?'

'Sure,' I say, watching him plaster on a fake smile as he goes to join his brother. I don't know why he feels the need to keep up the charade. Surely he could just cut ties with him? Though I suppose that's easy for me to say, being an only child.

'Making any progress?' says a voice from behind me, making me jump. It's Kellen. I'm surprised. I wasn't sure he'd speak to me at all tonight. That's something at least.

'I don't know,' I say with a shrug. 'With everything that's happened tonight, it doesn't seem like the right time to be making a move on him. It feels like taking advantage.'

'I get that,' he says. 'But it's the last night, Zach. You're not some predator. You're just talking to a guy you like. You won't get a second chance.'

'I know,' I say, groaning. 'I just wish I had a bit more time! Just a few more days! Expecting me to conjure up a romance in one evening is unreasonable. This isn't some fairy tale.'

'You've had, like, two years . . .'

'I'm not very good with time management.'

Kellen laughs. 'You've got a few more hours. You can still get your kiss by midnight.'

Everyone is obsessed with a kiss before midnight. Cinderella has a *lot* to answer for.

I look across the room at Cameron. 'Do you really think so?'

'I know so,' he says, placing his hand on my shoulder. 'You've got this.'

'Thanks,' I say. 'How are things going in the shark tank?'

'Oh, they're going.' He chuckles. 'Tiffany won't stop going on about being Prom Queen. She's talking like it's a given that she'll win. I mean, she probably will, but even so.'

'Well, for what it's worth, I hope you beat her to the crown.'

'I don't need a crown to be a queen,' he says, flashing perfect white teeth. 'But thanks for the vote of confidence. See you later, yeah?'

Despite Kellen's encouragement, it's almost eleven and I still haven't managed to make my move with Cameron. Every time I think it's *the moment*, something happens to distract me. He asked me to come save him later, but he always seems wrapped up in something. Whenever I want to go over, it just feels like I'd be interrupting.

Looking around, it doesn't seem as if anyone else is having the same issue. Everyone is losing their inhibitions and getting much more flirtatious. Half the students have ditched their masks, and I see people coupling up left, right and centre. People I would *never* have imagined getting together. I guess people actually do wait for the very last moment to say how they really feel. That or the spiked punch is a lot stronger than I originally thought. I look down at the cup in my hand and take a big gulp.

'Still staring at Cameron?' Bec says, joining me.

'Oh, I actually wasn't.' I laugh. 'For once.'

She smiles at that. 'He totally wants to take you to the boathouse.'

'I don't know,' I say, watching him. He's laughing with Owen and Josh about something. 'I don't think he's like that, you know? He doesn't seem the type to have a meaningless one-night stand? I think he's more the *take it slow* kinda guy.'

'One-night stands don't have to be meaningless,' says Bec. 'Think about you and Josh. That wasn't meaningless, right?'

She makes a good point. It might not have been romantic, but it's certainly something I'll always remember. It was special, in its own way.

'Besides,' she continues, 'you can't keep delaying the inevitable. You do realize we're leaving tomorrow, right? I'm not sure you have the time to *take it slow*, Zach.'

'I think it would be nice to just . . . hang out, you know? Spend some time with him. We don't *need* to tear each other's clothes off.'

'Easy to say when you already saw him naked today . . .'

'I didn't look!'

'Course you didn't.'

'I didn't!'

She smiles at that. 'You're sweet, Zach. You know that? They don't make a lot of guys like you. Cameron would be lucky to have you. Even if it is just for one night.'

'It's hot as balls in there,' Owen says, wiping sweat from his brow and unbuttoning his shirt.

'You're *such* a straight boy!' Josh laughs as he comes to sit down on the grass next to me. 'You put in all that effort dressing up in a snazzy suit, grooming and manscaping to make yourself look like a real gentleman, and then you come out with "*hot as balls*". And you wonder why you're single.'

'Hey!' Owen fake frowns. 'I'll have you know my mum says I'm a catch.'

Bec and Chase laugh at that. We're out by the lake, moonlight rippling on the surface, fireflies hovering. It's getting *far* too hot in the hall. People's outfits are already starting to look a little dishevelled, and most of the students have revealed their not-so-secret identities by taking off their masks to escape the heat. I get the aesthetic of all the candelabras, but open flames on an evening as hot as this one? Ice sculptures would have been better. Imagine a frozen sculpture of Huckleberry! I wonder if they have a suggestion box . . .

'Who do you think's gonna be first in the boathouse?' Chase gestures to the old wooden building. Nobody has gone in yet, but it's early. It's more of a late-night institution.

'I'm ready for round two just as soon as you are, Zach.' Josh squeezes my leg. I try not to read too much into that – he's flirty by nature. It doesn't mean anything.

'Mind if I join you?' Cameron says from behind, dropping down next to me so I'm sandwiched between the two boys.

Considering the temperature, they're both sitting unusually close, and it feels deliberate. Maybe one of them really is my secret admirer. I swallow hard, and Bec gives me a knowing look, barely managing to conceal her smirk. Chase has noticed too and uses the opportunity to do some not-so-subtle stirring.

'So I'm curious,' he says, leaning back on his hands. 'Who did everyone vote for in the leavers' poll? I wanna know who you all picked for hottest boy.'

'It was a tough choice,' Owen jokes. 'I mean, there's just so many fit guys here . . .'

'Oh, come off it,' says Josh. 'I still placed a vote for hottest girl. Bec obviously.' He shoots her a wink. 'I hate it when straight guys pretend they can't see that a guy is attractive! Just because you're hetero, it doesn't mean you shouldn't vote!'

'He's right,' Bec says. 'I voted Sam for hottest girl. Easy choice, really. I think it's the pink hair. If I was a lesbian, I would slide into her DMs *so hard*.'

Owen laughs at that. 'I never said I didn't vote!'

'I fucking knew it!' Josh says. 'It was *you* that voted for me!'

'Pity vote, naturally.'

'Yeah, whatever. I know you're secretly in love with me.' He blows him a kiss and Owen catches it, pretending to push it deep into his chest. If these two were in a romcom, everyone would ship them. The class clown and the gentle giant. It practically writes itself.

'So was this a *reciprocal* vote?' Bec pushes the point. 'Who did you vote for, Josh?'

'I'm not telling,' he says. I feel his fingers grazing my leg. 'Maybe I voted for Owen. That's what a good friend would do. Or maybe I voted for someone else. Maybe they're sitting here right now.' I feel my heart rate quicken slightly. 'Or what if I just voted for Rhys like *everyone* else?

Maybe I'm gunning for Kellen's man. That boy really *does* have muscles.'

'Not you as well.' I groan. 'Please tell me you didn't.'

'Why, are you jealous?' He smiles mischievously. 'Who did you vote for anyway?'

'Oh ... erm ...' I can feel Cameron's leg pushed up against mine. 'I ... erm ...'

'He voted for me,' Chase says, coming to my rescue. 'Best friends stick together.'

'I'm just *that* good an ally,' I joke, shrugging my shoulders.

Chase actually groans at that. 'He knows I hate that word.'

'What, "ally"?' Josh says, intrigued, sitting upright.

'Yeah,' he says. 'I just hate how some people claim it as such a badge of honour. *I'm an ally!* Cool, congrats for not being phobic. And don't even get me started on people who think it belongs in the LGBT+ acronym.'

'I think it belongs!' says Josh. 'Laura Ann Carleton!'

'Who?' Owen looks baffled.

Josh throws him some side-eye. 'She was that incredible woman who was murdered in California. People kept tearing down her rainbow flags, but she kept putting up new ones. She ended up paying the ultimate price. She wasn't queer, but she will *always* be one of us. There's space for her in our acronym, and I *will* fight you on that.'

'That's fair.' Chase nods like he's deep in thought. 'I guess what I'm trying to say is that I don't want every straight person with a *LOVE IS LOVE* tote bag to start claiming they're part of the community. That's the "allyship" I have an issue with.'

'You mean the T in LGBT doesn't stand for "tote bag"?' Josh pretends to be shocked.

I laugh. 'OK, if we're being controversial,' I say, 'I hate *LOVE IS LOVE* as a slogan.'

'What?' Cameron says. 'Hate is a strong word for something so inoffensive.'

'I hate it *because* it's inoffensive!' I say. 'It's like diet allyship. Being supportive without actually being supportive. It doesn't *mean* anything!'

'Not to mention it's not trans inclusive . . .' Chase says.

'OK, I hear you,' Josh says. 'But I think it's about context, right? Sure, *LOVE IS LOVE* isn't the *most* inclusive statement, but imagine you've got a homophobic grandparent, and you spend *years* trying to convince them that your identity isn't criminal. And then one day they show up wearing a T-shirt with that written on it? It would mean the world to a queer kid. It's accessible because it's easy. Allyship doesn't *always* have to be radical. Sometimes it's the little gestures that mean the most . . .'

'Well, *fuck*,' Chase says. 'I guess you make a good point. Just a shame I can't take it seriously because you're dressed like an actual court jester.'

'Just here to entertain the royal court,' says Josh, jingling his bells. 'Speaking of which . . .' He looks at his watch and hops to his feet. 'We should probably head back inside. They're about to announce our prom kweens.'

'Kellen and Rhys are not going to win,' I say. 'It'll go to Tiffany.'

'Oh ye of little faith!' Josh says. 'I think you might be forgetting something . . .'

'And what's that?'

'That love —' he grins, offering me his hand – '*is love.*'

We gather in the hall, at the front of the stage, ready for the crowning ceremony. The music has already stopped, and the crowd murmurs, waiting for Harrington to approach the mic. The votes are counted by an independent adjudicator and sealed in a little golden envelope, meaning even he doesn't know who's going to win.

'Here,' Tiffany says, pushing her phone into Owen's hands. 'Live-stream this.'

It wasn't a request; I can't believe the audacity.

'You know you don't have to do what she says, right?'

Tiffany shoots me a death stare. 'I'm sorry, Zach, how does this concern you?'

'I'm just saying. You do realize he's not your servant?'

'It's fine, Zach,' Owen says. 'I don't mind, honestly.'

'See,' she says. 'He doesn't mind.'

'What makes you so certain you're going to win anyway?'

'Do I ever lose?'

'So you *have* rigged it then . . .'

'I'll let you in on a little secret, Zach.' She leans in close and lowers her voice. 'I don't need to rig anything. I know you *think* everyone wants the gay couple to win.

But nobody's gonna vote for them because everyone *knows* their relationship's done for. Being prom king and queen is part of mine and Ethan's story. It's something we'll tell our grandkids one day. But Kellen and Rhys? What's the point in them winning if they'll be broken up in a couple of months?'

'What?' I say. 'How can you say that?'

'I'm sure Rhys thinks it's *fun* to rough it with a scholarship kid. But they haven't got a future together. Not like me and Ethan. I doubt they'll even make it through the summer.'

She says it with a smirk that actually turns my stomach. Rhys is supposed to be her best friend, but she couldn't care less about his happiness. I don't exactly love him and Kellen as a couple either, but now? I want them to win just to spite her.

She turns to Owen. 'Start the stream as soon as Harrington starts talking.' She goes to disappear into the crowd. 'And may the best *woman* win.'

Just when I think I can't hate her any more. My eyes burn into the back of her head. I can't stand her arrogance; it's all I can think about as Mr Harrington approaches the microphone to launch into *another* long-winded speech about tradition. Owen starts the live Instagram stream and, over his shoulder, I can see people already starting to comment. It amazes me that people actually care about this. The viewing numbers go from double to triple. Countless strangers who don't even go here. Why on earth are they all so invested?

Mr Harrington drones on for so long that even the people in the live stream are getting impatient. I've got it open on my phone now, just so I can read the comments.

Get on it with it, old man!

Is he getting paid by the word or something?

Am I the only one who thinks he's kinda hot? OK, Daddy.

I'll pretend I didn't see that last one.

'And so, without further delay,' Mr Harrington *finally* says, after delaying for fifteen whole minutes, 'it's my honour to announce this year's Prom King and Queen.'

'Prom Royalty!' Josh yells from behind me. 'It's gender neutral.'

'Oh ... erm, yes,' Harrington says. 'This year's Prom Royalty ...'

The crowd groans as he fumbles with the envelope.

It's been eighty-four years ... some *Titanic* fan quotes in the live feed.

I look for Kellen and Rhys in the crowd. I know it isn't going to be them, but I *will* it to be anyway. Surely our classmates know how important this is? A school like ours finally crowning a same-sex couple? I have to believe people would vote for that at least. Even if it is going against the queen bee and her endless reign of tyranny.

The envelope opens.

'Tiffany White and Ethan Clark!'

I really shouldn't have got my hopes up.

Everybody claps as the two of them take the stage. They approach from different sides – it's all been perfectly choreographed. It wouldn't surprise me if they'd already rehearsed this. Mr Harrington crowns them, and gold confetti bursts from above, filling the room with tiny pieces of plastic landfill. I don't think Greta would approve.

'Thank you, Mr Harrington,' Tiffany says, taking the microphone. 'And thank you to everyone who voted for us. I know it's not really traditional to give a speech,' she says, 'but if it's all the same to all of you, there is something I'd like to say.'

'Oh God, here we go . . .' Bec whispers from behind me.

'Most of you are already aware that this afternoon somebody did something truly awful. Not to me, but to my dearest partner.' She squeezes Ethan's hand for sympathy points. Like a true politician. Of course she'd try to make this about her. 'So I just want to take this opportunity to say that revenge porn is *never* OK. There's no place for this kind of behaviour in civilized society.'

Her gaze drifts down to where Owen is standing, speaking directly to the live stream. 'And, although I could *easily* expose the culprit and tell you all his – or *her* – name right now, we've decided to rise above it. Refuse to give them the attention they so clearly crave. Karma will out eventually. I have every faith in that.'

She pauses for a moment, and the crowd actually goes wild with applause. She can't seriously still be trying to imply this was Chase? And people are actually eating this up? I look down at the live stream to get the general consensus.

I heard it was the trans guy.

She should expose him!

He belongs in prison!

I glance back at Chase. He's white as a sheet.

'So let's not get caught up in all this negativity,' she continues. 'We're here to celebrate, so that's exactly what we're going to do. So we invite all of you to join us in a toast.' She raises her glass in the air. 'To the class of twenty-five.'

'The class of twenty-five!' everyone choruses.

'She's full of shit,' Bec says from behind me. 'If she had any proof it was Chase, she would have shared it *everywhere*. What an absolute cop-out!'

'Right,' I say. 'People aren't going to believe that.'

I look down to see Chase reading that people are, in fact, believing that.

'They're saying it was me,' he says, his voice cracking. 'You guys know it wasn't, right? I never went anywhere near her laptop.'

'Of course we know it wasn't you!' Bec says, pulling him into a hug. 'I'm gonna fucking kill her. Actually murder her. I'll do the time.'

'I need some air,' Chase says, breaking away from the hug and heading for the double doors at the back of the room. Bec weaves through the crowd after him.

I try to follow, but a squeal of feedback stops me in my tracks. I look up to see Kellen has picked up the mic.

He's taken off his mask and is standing centre stage. For a moment, I think he's going to decry Tiffany's slander, but of course he'd *never* do that.

'Sorry to interrupt your evening . . . again,' he says. 'And congrats to Ethan and Tiffany.'

He's fidgety and stumbles over the words, like he's really, *really* nervous. I want to go after Bec and Chase, but I also want to know what he's about to say.

'Tonight is the last time we're all going to be together,' he continues. 'So, if you'll indulge me, I wanted to take this opportunity to say something to someone special . . .'

Oh God. Enough with the mushy-gushy. The whole crowd instinctively turns to find Rhys. From the expression on his face, he had no idea this was coming either.

'I know we're going off to study in different cities,' Kellen says, looking him in the eye now. 'We're gonna be on opposite sides of the country, and people keep saying that there's no way we can make it work long distance. So that's why I want to make this promise, right here, right now, in front of everyone. I promise to find a way.'

People clap at that. It's a little *much* for my liking, but I clap too. And I do it loudly. *I doubt they'll even make it through the summer.* Fuck you, Tiffany.

But then I realize that's not the end of it. He's reaching into his jacket pocket as he bends forward, as if he's taking a knee . . .

Oh my God, Kellen, what are you doing?

'Rhys Kingsland . . .'

Make it stop.

'Would you do me the honour . . .'

Please, for the love of God. Make. It. Stop.

'. . . of being my husband?'

The voice in my head is screaming with second-hand embarrassment.

It feels like everything goes in slow motion after that. The entire room is looking at Rhys – students, staff, even the waiters – but he just stands there like a deer in headlights.

I see Madzikanda take a large gulp of wine.

'Husband?' he croaks finally.

'Yeah,' Kellen says softly, his eyes filling up with hope.

Please say yes, I think. This whole thing is completely preposterous, but I can't bear to see Kellen humiliated so publicly. What on earth possessed him to do this?

'Um . . .' Rhys licks his lips anxiously, eyes darting from face to staring face. He drags the silence out for far longer than is comfortable. 'I guess?'

So romantic.

The crowd parts as Kellen rushes down from the stage and dives into his arms. Rhys catches him and the two of them fumble an awkward kiss. It's like watching a car crash, but people weirdly seem to be enjoying it. The clapping is thunderous, the whoops and cheers close to deafening. Has everyone lost their mind? Surely they know this is ridiculous?

'Love is love!' I hear Josh yell from somewhere in the crowd. Surely not him too? Josh has more sense than to think this is what love is. I take it as my cue to leave.

I go towards the door again, but this time someone grabs my hand.

I seriously can't catch a break. But then I realize I'm wrong.

Because it's Cameron.

'Can we talk?'

'Huh?' I say, turning to face him. He's still holding my hand. His skin is a lot softer than I imagined. I always thought his hands would be rough from playing rugby.

'That proposal,' he says. 'It kinda got me thinking . . .'

'It did?' I swallow hard. Maybe Kellen has done me a favour here . . .

'Yeah. *Carpe diem* and all that.' He glances over his shoulder. 'There's something I want to tell you, but I don't wanna do it here. Maybe we could go somewhere quieter?'

And I want to. I *really* want to. But I can't stop thinking about what just happened to Chase. As much as I wanna 'talk' with Cameron, I know my best friend needs me right now. I won't be like Kellen. I'm not going to abandon my friends for some boy.

'I want to,' I say, 'but I'm kinda in the middle of something.'

'Oh.' He sounds deflated.

'I *really* want to. Just maybe a bit later?'

'OK,' Cameron says, looking at his watch. 'How about midnight then?'

'Midnight's perfect,' I say. Maybe I really am Cinderella.

'By the lake?'

'Sure,' I say, giving him a smile before heading for the door.

I expect to hear yelling or crying – or both – but when I get outside I just find Chase and Bec sitting quietly at the edge of the lake. Bec has her arm round Chase, and they're not saying anything, just looking out over the water.

'Chase?' I say delicately.

He turns and smiles softly when he sees me.

'What's going on in there?'

I think about telling him about Kellen's proposal. About Cameron asking me to 'talk'. But right now none of that seems important.

'Nothing much,' I say, sitting beside him. 'I'm so sorry about Tiffany.'

'I should never have changed those results,' he says. 'I don't know what I was thinking. I should have just left her alone. Let her have her victory lap.'

'That's my fault. I encouraged you. If I'd known this was gonna happen . . .'

'How could you have, Zach? It's not your fault.'

'Yeah,' Bec says. 'The only person we should be blaming right now is whoever leaked those pictures . . . That's what started this.'

'It could have been anyone,' I say.

'We need to find out who,' Bec says. 'Tiffany said it herself: somebody's bound to have left a paper trail . . .'

'I know who it was,' a voice says from behind us.

We all spin round to see the last person I'd have expected.

'Ethan?' Bec says, standing up defensively. 'Don't you fucking start . . .'

'I wasn't going to.' He holds his hands up defensively. 'I come in peace.'

Bec narrows her eyes, chewing her lip. I don't trust him either.

'Let him speak,' Chase says, getting up now too.

'I know who leaked the pictures,' he repeats. 'I know it wasn't you, Chase. If you come with me, I'll show you.'

'Show us right here,' Bec retorts.

'I can't,' he says. 'And I can only show this to Chase. It's kinda . . . personal.'

'What do you mean by personal?' Bec snaps. 'There's no fucking way.'

'Fine, suit yourself.' He goes to walk off.

'Wait,' Chase says. 'Why can't you just tell us?'

'Because I can't,' he says, annoyed. I don't understand why he's getting so defensive about it. 'I'll *show* you,' he says again. 'You just have to trust me.'

'Trust you?' Bec refuses to stand down. 'Why the fuck should we trust you?'

'Bec,' Chase says. 'It's fine . . .'

'It's not fine!' she snarls.

'You know what? Fuck this,' Ethan says, actually walking away now.

'Ethan, wait,' Chase says, going after him. 'It's chill, Bec. What's he gonna do? I'm a big boy. I can handle this.'

Bec looks unconvinced.

'I'll be right back, OK?'

'Fine.' She clearly isn't happy. 'I don't like this, Zach.'

'Me neither,' I reply as we watch them walk away. 'But if Ethan knows who really did this, isn't that worth pursuing? That'll clear Chase's name. Squash the rumours before they get out of hand. You've seen what they're saying online. We need to show he's innocent.'

'Yeah, but why can't Ethan just tell all of us? What could he possibly have that he can *only* show to Chase? It doesn't make any sense. And why is he going behind Tiffany's back?'

'Maybe he's been sending pictures to other girls and doesn't want her to find out?'

'But Chase will just tell us anyway. He knows that.' She watches as the two boys disappear inside the building. 'I don't like him being on his own. They could do anything . . .'

'What are they gonna do? Seriously?'

Bec turns pale. 'Oh my God,' she says, breaking into a run. 'How could we be so stupid?'

'Huh?' I say, hurrying after her as she races into the hall. 'What's happening?'

'We have to stop them!'

'Stop them from doing what?' I say, already breathless.

Music pumps. Everyone is on the dance floor. Everyone except for Ethan and Chase. I scan the room and see that the punchbowl has been knocked over, its contents spilled across the floor. For a moment, I imagine Ethan dumping it over Chase in some cruel prank, but then I realize it's a false alarm. The two of them are just standing at the top of the stairs, and Ethan is showing him something on his phone.

'See, it's fine,' I say. 'They're just talking.'

But Bec has seen something I'm missing.

'Chase!' she yells, staring up towards the ceiling.

I follow her gaze, but can't see what she's looking at.

'Chase!' she yells louder now, and that's when I finally spot it.

A glint of silver hanging way up in the rafters above them. We're too late.

Ethan steps neatly aside, leaving Chase alone. He looks up for a moment, confused, just as a metal bucket swings down, drenching him from head to toe in thick red liquid. Pig's blood. His pristine outfit is ruined.

The room erupts with screams – shock and laughter mingling as the crowd of students realize the leaver's prank wasn't cancelled after all. Chase is frantically trying to wipe the mixture from his eyes. Bec looks like she's seeing red too.

'What the fuck are you laughing at?' she screams at a Hawthorn boy as she pushes past him, throwing her arms round Chase, ruining her outfit as well. Everyone is staring, watching my best friend's humiliation. Phones are appearing everywhere, catching it in 4K from every conceivable angle. So much for allyship. They'll turn on anyone for content.

The music drops out suddenly: even the DJ must be in shock. The room falls deathly silent and just one voice cuts through the quiet.

'Oh dear,' Tiffany says, stepping out of the shadows at the top of the stairs, Ethan at her side. 'I guess karma works fast.'

The rage is bubbling inside me now.

'Shame you got caught in the crossfire,' she says to Bec, looking up and down at her bloodstained outfit. 'Ah, well. Hope it doesn't stain the ASOS.'

And that's when I snap.

I grab the half-empty bucket from where it lies at the foot of the stairs, and run after Tiffany. I can smell the beetroot now – at least they kept it vegan again this year.

'How's this for karma, you bitch?' I yell, throwing the contents towards her.

But Tiffany is too quick and dodges at the very last second, leaving Josh and Owen in the firing line. They take most of what's left over to the face, but not all of it.

Something else is hit too.

The yearbook.

Still out on its table, the antique volume now sits in a huge puddle of red liquid, sodden and dripping. It's ruined.

'*Fuck, fuck, fuck,*' I say, realizing what I've done.

'What the hell is all this?' a voice booms from behind me.

I turn and see Mr Harrington rushing towards me. That's when I realize the bucket is still in my hand, everyone around me covered in the red sticky mixture. Chase looks devastated. Josh and Owen are dripping on the flagstones. And Tiffany's face is a mask of triumph.

'What's going on?' Miss Madzikanda says, following closely behind Harrington. She looks down at the bucket in my hand. 'Zach, what happened here?'

'*She* happened!' I say, pointing at Tiffany.

'Me?' she says, effortlessly turning on her wounded princess act.

'Don't try to pin this on Tiffany,' Mr Harrington says. 'I saw you with my own eyes! I caught you red-handed! *Literally* red-handed!' I look down to see that my hands are, in fact, stained red. 'And after I explicitly forbade this stupid prank. Consider yourself expelled!'

'Hang on a minute, Alan,' Madzikanda protests.

'Save it, Joyce,' he says, glaring at her.

'You know what?' I say. 'Fuck you. Fuck this school. Fuck everything.'

'Zach, wait,' Miss Madzikanda says as I turn away. 'Let's talk.'

'About what?'

'About . . . *Huckleberry*.'

I spin back to face her. 'My friend's been assaulted, I'm getting expelled and you want to talk about a *statue of a dog*?' I say. 'What exactly are you on?'

'Zach, I think I might know what's happening here . . .'

'I'll tell you what's happening!' I say. 'What's happening is that Hawthorn have ruined everything, like they always do. They're spoiled and privileged and get a free pass to do whatever the hell they want!'

I throw the bucket to the ground with a clatter, sending a final splash of fake pig's blood up Harrington's trousers.

'Get out,' he says through gritted teeth. 'Get out before I throw you out.'

'Gladly,' I say, striding off in the other direction.

I hear Madzikanda calling after me – still waffling on about something to do with Huckleberry – but I ignore her.

I know she's usually on the right side with these things, but I'm beyond saving. Even she can't help me now.

I storm out of the front doors, thinking about what kind of punishment they're going to concoct for me. Expulsion won't be enough – they'll refuse to let me graduate, blacklist me from every university, destroy any chance I might have of a future.

I imagine Ethan and Tiffany rising through the ranks, becoming CEOs on six-figure salaries while I end up destitute and unemployable. I think of Mum and how disappointed she's going to be, having worked to put me through this school just to see me expelled on the very last day. Will she even believe me when I tell her what happened?

'Zach!' Bec calls, following me out of the building.

Chase is behind her, still covered with pig's blood. He rushes over to the fountain, splashing water on himself, trying to wash some of it from his outfit. But it's hopeless. It's completely ruined. He never even had the chance to show it to his mum. It's our fault he didn't get any photos.

'Tiffany's not gonna get away with this,' I say. 'She can't get away with this!'

'It looks like she already is,' Bec says, staring down at her phone. 'She's already done an Instagram story. That fucking bitch.'

'Already?!' Chase says, scrambling for his phone. He pauses for a moment and then starts to read aloud. '*I condemn the actions of some of my classmates this evening.*

We may have our differences, but two wrongs never make a right. Retaliation is never the answer. Nobody's prom should be taken away from them. Solidarity always.'

'Solidarity always?' Bec says with disbelief. 'After this transphobic bullshit? I mean you said it yourself, Zach. The whole pig's blood thing? It's about menstruation.'

'Oh.' The realization dawns on me. 'You mean, you think she did this because . . .?'

'I think you're giving her way too much credit,' Chase cuts me off. 'Tiffany isn't smart enough to make that connection. Besides, I don't care about that. I care about this . . .' He tugs on his ruined outfit just as his phone starts ringing in my hand.

'It's your mum,' I say meekly, handing it back.

'I can't answer like this.' His voice begins to crack. 'She'll be furious if she sees what I've done to her dress.'

'*You* didn't do *anything* to her dress,' Bec says. 'It was them that did this. Not you.'

'She told me to stay out of trouble . . .'

'As if any of this is your fault!' Bec says, but Chase tosses his phone into the fountain, his hands shaking.

I can feel my fury rising again. How dare they do this to him? He's literally never done anything to hurt anyone. Why is it that he somehow always ends up as the target?

'They can't keep getting away with this,' I snarl, turning back towards the building, feeling like every moment at this school has been leading up to this.

'Zach, don't,' Bec says. 'You'll only make things worse.'

'How?!' I say. 'What are they gonna do? Expel me a second time?'

'Just leave it. We can celebrate right here. Just us. That's all that matters, right?'

'Of course that's all that matters, but *she* took it away from us!'

A firework goes screeching up into the night sky, exploding in deep crimson red. The colour of Hawthorn. The colour of pig's blood. The colour of Tiffany's extortionate Jimmy Choos. At the centre of the fountain, Huckleberry's expression seems different now, the glare of the fireworks accentuating his bared fangs. He's calling for revenge.

'Zach, wait!' Bec calls as I march back towards the hall. I know I should stop, but I don't. I don't even know what I'm going to do, but I have to do *something*.

Repetitio Est Mater Studiorum. I read the school motto as I head through the doors. The candles have all gone out now, but I can see the lights of the masquerade flickering from the end of the corridor. The sound of music and laughter twists my stomach. How can anyone be enjoying themselves after what Tiffany and Ethan just did?

I step out on to the grand staircase and see happy faces turned to the skylight, watching the fireworks burst in time to the music. I see happy couples holding hands and sharing this moment, and think of Cameron waiting out by the lake. I look down at my watch: 11.59. I was supposed to be meeting him right now. Tiffany's fucked that up too. All this talk of a Cinderella story. I think I was actually starting to believe it. The idea that me and Cameron could have had our happily-ever-after, that I could have had the perfect last night with my friends. With Bec and Chase. Josh and Owen. Maybe even Kellen too.

It's then that I feel my rage give way to sadness. It's our last night here. Our last chance to be together. We've had all that snatched away from us. And for what?

'Zach?'

The voice is so faint I barely hear it beneath the sound of the music. I might even have imagined it, but then I turn and see someone's silhouette among the shadows. They walk towards me, and I can make out the sparkles in their outfit. A guy, wearing a glittering gold jacket and trousers. A matching mask and bow tie dazzling as they catch the light.

'Who is that?' I say, not recognizing the outfit. But they don't say anything. They just stand there, looking awkwardly down at their own feet. I'm not in the mood for guessing games right now, and I'm half tempted to walk away, but something about their energy holds me there. It's almost as if something tells me they feel just as lost as I do.

'I need to find Tiffany,' I say.

'Wait,' they reply, their voice cracking as they catch my hand and stop me, squeezing as if begging me not to go.

Our eyes meet, and I know I recognize them, and yet right now I can't seem to place them. He tugs my hand, inviting me closer, and there's a tenderness there that makes me want to give in. Maybe it's just the emotional weight of everything that's happened, but right now it doesn't seem to matter that I don't know who it is. I take a step forward, and then another, until he grips my waist and pulls me into him.

'Cameron?' I say hopefully, my body pressed against his. But he doesn't answer.

He doesn't say anything.

He just lifts his mask and kisses me.

It all happens too fast for me to process, but, as I feel his soft lips against mine, I can't help but allow myself to kiss him back. It's heavy and clumsy at first, but, as I close my eyes and fall deeper, I feel this tingling sensation coursing through my body. It's so intense it lifts me on to the tips of my toes, like it could carry me up into the air and sweep me entirely off my feet. I've kissed boys before, but I've never felt anything like this. Reels of old movies play through my mind, in black and white and then colour. Every kiss I've ever seen on the big screen. Vintage. Contemporary. From *Casablanca* right through to *Ratatouille*.

I hear the fireworks overhead, but it's like they're getting further away now. Fading into the background until there's nothing but the two of us.

Just me and this perfect stranger.

And then everything suddenly goes black.

2

'Prom night, baby!'

A pillow hits me in the face. 'Come on, day's a-wasting!'

Someone grabs my arms and tugs. I open my eyes to find Chase hovering over me, his trademark grin plastered across his face. What's going on?

'Seriously, Zach, how can you lie in on a day like today? You slept right through breakfast!'

'Huh?' I say, pulling my arms free. 'What happened?'

I'm in my bed, but how the hell did I get here? I reach my hand up to touch my lips – they're still tingling from that kiss. It feels like no more than a few seconds have gone by. Did I pass out? Hit my head or something? Was the kiss really *that* good?

'You overslept is what happened,' Chase says, and I realize it's morning. The daylight is pouring through the window. He must be freshly showered because he's free of fake blood, and wearing the same blue baseball cap and Miami Dolphins shirt as yesterday.

'You can't sleep all day, Zach. Come on. You're missing it! The rugby team are outside doing naked laps!'

'They're doing – wait, *what*?' I say, the déjà vu really hitting now.

'Naked laps!' Chase says.

This all feels *way* too familiar. I don't say anything, but eye Chase suspiciously as I slowly get up and go over to the window. Sure enough, there's the rugby team, fully clothed, throwing the ball around. It's almost like I can predict their movements.

'OK, what's going on?' I say. 'You're pretending it's yesterday?'

'I'm pretending it's . . . yesterday?'

'Yes, yesterday.'

'When all my troubles seemed so far away?'

'Stop it,' I say, unamused. 'Seriously, what's going on? You managed to get all the blood off? I thought that was gonna be stuck in your hair for weeks.'

'Blood? Zach, what in God's name are you talking about?'

'Last night,' I say. 'Prom.'

Chase frowns. 'Prom is tonight.'

'What?' I reach over to my bedside table and grab my phone.

The calendar says July 16.

This doesn't make any sense. I didn't dream all that, surely? It was far too real. Besides, I never remember dreams in their entirety. But this? I can remember every detail.

I see an unread message from Bec. I remember this from yesterday. I know exactly what it's gonna say: *HAPPY PROM!*

I open it and there it is. The capital letters seem to mock me. The string of emojis in perfect order. Like they've been copy-pasted from my memory.

Is this some kind of elaborate prank? Change the date in Zach's phone and then all pretend we're living the same day twice? Surely not? My friends may be quirky, and they may enjoy messing with me, but that would be the behaviour of the criminally *insane*.

'Are you sure you're feeling OK?' Chase says, staring at me as if I've absolutely lost it.

And honestly? I think I very well may have. Maybe I'm just dreaming. That's all this is. I mean, that's the logical conclusion, right? I try to remember going to bed, but all I can recall is that kiss.

I look around the room, searching for a '*flaw in the Matrix*', something that will give this away as a trick created by my subconscious. There has to be a piece out of place, but as I look around it seems everything's exactly where it should be.

'Zach?' Chase says again. 'Is something the matter?'

'I'm fine,' I finally say after a long pause, even though I'm absolutely *not*.

Act normal, Zachary. At least until you can figure out what's going on here.

'Go long!' Ethan yells from outside, tossing the ball.

'Car alarm!' I say, watching as Cameron sprints after it and tumbles straight into Mr Harrington's car. Sure enough, the alarm starts blaring, and the boys all scatter.

'They have the coordination of a bunch of drunken

toddlers,' Chase says, watching them. 'No wonder they didn't bring back the trophy.'

'That's exactly what you said yesterday,' I squeal. 'This can't be a coincidence!'

'What can't be a coincidence? You're not making any sense, Zach.'

'This has all happened already,' I explain, my mind spinning as I try to process it. I look around the room, searching for something – anything – that might explain it.

'OK, slow down,' Chase says, gripping me by the shoulders. 'Zach, can you chill out for a second, or do I need to call someone?'

'OK,' I say, trying to take deep breaths. 'I'm calm. I'm chill.'

Notifications start pinging through on Chase's phone.

'It's the results!' I say, entirely losing my chill.

'Huh?' Chase says, looking at his phone. 'Oh . . .'

'Tiffany wins *everything*,' I say, pointing at his phone wildly. '*Hottest girl. Most likely to be prime minister.*'

Chase snorts at that.

'Just check it!'

'All right, all right,' he says, scrolling through the results. 'Huh, you're right! Well, whaddya know?'

'That's all you have to say? "*Well, whaddya know?*"'

Chase gives me a confused little laugh. 'I don't know what you expect. It's not exactly rocket science, Zach. *Obviously* she was going to win everything. It's Tiffany. She probably made a bunch of fake accounts just to vote for herself. Look, these results don't even add up. Bec got forty-nine votes for hottest girl. Tiffany got fifty-one.'

'There's not even that many students in our year,' I say before he can. 'I know.'

'I'm half tempted to hack in and fix it.'

'Don't,' I say firmly. That's where everything started to go wrong yesterday.

'I'm not going to,' he says with a laugh. 'Can you imagine Tiffany's reaction?'

'I don't need to imagine,' I say, the image of him drenched in blood still prominent in my mind. 'I need you to listen to me. Something weird is going on. It's like everything is happening all over again. Like ... *twice*. Like we're in some kind of time loop or something!'

Chase looks at me weirdly. 'OK,' he says, putting one of his hands behind his back. 'So how many fingers am I holding up?'

'I don't know,' I say. 'You didn't do that last time.'

'So everything's not repeating then?'

'Most things are.'

'Convenient.' Chase chuckles. 'Zach, is this a joke or something? You're secretly filming me for TikTok? Is it revenge for that prank I pulled back in the spring?'

'I'm not filming anything. You know I hate TikTok!'

'Mmm-hmm,' he says. 'Where's the camera?'

'There's no camera! Chase, I'm telling you, something *weird* is happening.'

I look around the room helplessly, pinching the back of my hand, hoping that will wake me up. But nothing happens. I'm still here, in our dorm room, on the morning of prom. Harrington must have got to his car because the alarm stops.

'You don't believe me, do you?'

'I don't know what there is to believe, Zach.'

'OK, but have I ever lied to you?'

'Dozens of times.'

'When?!'

'That time last week I came in and heard you watching porn, and you said it was a workout video.'

He'd pretended to believe me at the time. I thought I'd got away with it. I should have known that would come back to haunt me.

'OK, but –'

'And when you repeatedly denied hooking up with Josh in the boathouse.'

'That's not the same!' I protest. 'Just listen, will you? I promise I'm not lying. Yesterday is repeating itself. I'm certain of it. I just need to find a way to prove it.'

'This is a really weird prank, Zach.'

'It's not a prank!' I say indignantly.

'Well, whatever it is,' he says, 'you better get ready. Madzikanda will be calling for team captains soon. We need to be there. Bec's gonna put herself forward . . .'

'I know,' I say. 'I already know all of this . . .'

'You OK, Bec?'

We find her in the hall, peering into the trophy cabinet exactly like she was yesterday. Same shorts. Same crop top. Same everything down to the last detail.

'Sorry,' she says. 'I just can't believe this was two years ago.'

'I swear this literally happened yesterday,' Chase replies as expected.

'This *did* happen yesterday,' I mutter. I'm already sick of hearing everything for the second time. It makes me realize how unoriginal our conversations are.

Chase sighs. 'So Zach has decided to make this the day he loses his mind.'

'What?' Bec says, looking back and forth between us.

'He says we're stuck in a time machine.'

'I never said we're stuck in a time machine!'

As if I don't sound crazy enough without him putting words in my mouth.

'Clearly been watching too many episodes of *Doctor Who*.'

'I've literally never watched an episode of *Doctor Who* in my life!'

Surely he knows I hate sci-fi by now? It's just about the only genre I don't have time for. He's just doing this to annoy me.

'OK, well, you both sound equally ridiculous,' Bec says. 'A time machine? This is bonkers even for you two. What's going on, Zach?'

I sigh with exasperation. 'What's the point? You're not going to believe me anyway.'

'Well, I think I might draw the line at time machines,' she says, leaning against the cabinet. 'But you never know. I'm listening. Try me.'

I take a deep breath. 'I think we're stuck in some sort of ... *loop*,' I say. 'Like in *Groundhog Day*. Where Bill Murray keeps living the same day over and over?'

'Never saw it,' Bec says with a shrug.

'You never saw *Groundhog Day*? It's literally a classic!'

'And I *literally* don't care . . .'

'I never saw it either,' says Chase.

Just my luck. Neither of them have seen the one movie that would explain my situation.

'But I think it's a bit like *Russian Doll*,' he continues. 'The one where Natasha Lyonne keeps falling down the stairs.'

'*Ohhhhh*,' Bec says. 'I loved that show! It's like *Happy Death Day* or *Palm Springs*!'

How have they seen *every* rip-off but not the original?

'I love those movies!' Chase says. 'Where they keep dying over and over! That's what you're saying is happening to you, Zach?'

'What? No! I never said anything about *dying*!'

'You said it was like *Groundhog Day*.'

'Nobody dies in *Groundhog Day*!'

'Well, that sounds very boring. You should watch *Russian Doll*, Zach.'

'Oh my God!' I say. 'Will you just listen?'

'I *am* listening,' Bec says. 'You're stuck in a time machine. Continue.'

'There's no time machine!' I blurt, so loud that people actually look in our direction. I see Kellen give me a really weird look before continuing to fuss over Rhys. At this rate, everyone is gonna think I'm a lunatic. I'll be spending prom night in a padded cell.

Chase is laughing now. 'See, I told you he'd lost it.'

'I'm stuck in a time *loop*!' I say. 'Prom was yesterday. Everything that is happening right now has already happened. I know everything – I'm impotent!'

Bec splutters. 'You're *impotent*?'

'It means "all-knowing".'

'That's not what it means, Zach.'

'Huh?' I swear that's what it means.

'OK,' Bec says patronizingly. 'So, if you know everything . . . what number am I thinking of?'

'It doesn't work like that.'

'What animal then? No, what vegetable!'

'I dunno – a carrot?'

Bec blinks in mock surprise. 'Oh my God, he's right!'

I pinch the bridge of my nose. 'I don't possess magical powers.'

'No. You just came from the future in a time machine . . .'

'That is *not* what I said!' Why are they both being so annoying?

'What's it like in the future?' asks Bec, trying not to smirk. 'Have we made it to Mars yet?'

'I'm not from the future,' I say through gritted teeth. 'And I'm not psychic either!'

'Well, I'm glad we all agree on that,' Chase says. 'So if we're finished with this nonsense . . .'

'Wait . . .'

I look around the room for a way to prove it. I think back to everything that happened yesterday. Hawthorn cheating to win Capture the Flag. Ethan's nudes being leaked. Chase being humiliated in front of the entire school.

'That's it!' I exclaim. 'I know how I can prove this! Your outfit for tonight. You've kept it secret, right? Locked away? But I know what it is. It's your mum's prom dress!'

Chase falls silent. His eyes narrow. 'How did you know that?'

'You keep the key under your mattress. I'm telling you. I know *everything*!'

'So you looked then?'

'What? No! You're not listening –'

Chase shakes his head. 'I can't believe you, Zach.'

'I didn't look! You showed me yesterday. Or today. Or however the hell this works.'

'That seriously wasn't cool, Zach,' Chase snaps. 'That outfit actually means something to me! Do you know how excited I've been to show you guys?'

'I didn't look!' I repeat. 'I'm telling you, it's the time loop.'

But I can hear the ridiculousness of that as it comes out of my mouth. The disappointed look on Chase's face tells me everything I need to know. They don't believe me, and I can't blame them. I don't know if I would believe me either. It is totally batshit.

'It's your mum's dress?' Bec says, sounding confused.

'Yeah,' he says. 'I repurposed it. I wanted it to be a surprise.'

'It's Hanfu, right?' I say, trying to make amends. 'I know it was always something you said you wanted to wear. You showed us right after you came out.'

'Yeah,' Chase says. 'At least you paid attention to that part.'

I can tell that he softens a little at hearing this, but he's still looking at me as if waiting for an apology. But how can I apologize for something I didn't do? There *has* to be a way to get them to believe me. I look around the room again, waiting for inspiration. But it's hopeless.

'I'm sorry,' I finally say dejectedly. It feels weird to confess to something I didn't do, but how else am I supposed to navigate this impossible situation? 'I shouldn't have peeked.'

'It's fine,' he says with a shrug. 'It's done. No point being angry.'

'Well,' Bec says, 'the cat may be out of the bag, but I still haven't seen it. I can't wait to see you wearing it, Chase! That's gonna be the real moment.'

'She's right,' I say. 'It's just a bit of fabric until you put it on.'

'Well, maybe lower your expectations *slightly*,' he says. 'It's not *that* special.'

'Think fast!' Ethan yells, standing up from the table. I'd forgotten this was going to happen. I watch the rugby ball fly across the room in what feels like slow motion, once again landing in Owen's food, spattering him with bolognese.

The Hawthorn crew burst into guffaws again, but, when I glance across, Kellen isn't laughing like the rest of them. I didn't notice it yesterday, but he shuffles uncomfortably. Maybe he feels partly responsible. He catches me staring, and we both quickly look away.

'I feel bad for Owen,' Chase says. 'You just know he's gonna be the target later.'

I think back to last night's prank, to Chase drenched in fake pig's blood.

'We should probably warn him,' he continues. It's like watching a play after sitting through all the rehearsals. 'I don't wanna be the bearer of bad news or anything – nobody wants to hear that they're a walking target – but . . .'

'I heard they're going to strip someone naked and throw them in the lake,' Bec says, right on cue. Someone in Hawthorn must have started that rumour as a red herring.

'Wow, so imaginative,' Chase chips in. 'Nothing says last day of school like sexual assault! Must have taken them hours of brainstorming to come up with that one. At least they've moved on from the stupid pig's blood thing they usually do.'

And that's when everything suddenly clicks into place. Maybe *that's* why this is happening? It all went so disastrously wrong yesterday. Perhaps this is my opportunity to set things right. Some greater power out there in the universe giving me a second chance?

'About that . . .' I say.

The two of them must pick up on the seriousness of my tone because they both turn towards me, concerned looks flashing across their faces.

'I overheard Tiffany talking about the prank,' I lie. 'They're sticking with the pig's blood again this year. And Owen isn't the target, Chase. It's you.'

'What?' Bec says. 'She wouldn't.'

'I assure you she would.'

Bec jumps up. 'I'll kill her!' she growls through gritted teeth.

'Wait,' I say, not wanting things to escalate. I see Kellen watching us suspiciously. A few other people are looking in our direction too. 'We're better off with them thinking we're none the wiser.' I coax Bec into sitting back down.

'I'm listening,' she says. I can tell it's taking all her restraint not to go over there.

I point to the top of the grand staircase. 'They're planning on hiding a bucket up there. Chase, they're gonna try to lure you to the top of the stairs and then . . .'

'So I just won't take the bait,' he says. 'They can waste their whole prom night trying to get me up there. Meanwhile, I'll be having fun.'

'Exactly,' I say. 'So . . . you're not upset? That they want to humiliate you like that?'

'Tiffany has been trying to humiliate me from day one,' he says. 'Being hated by her is the biggest compliment a person can get. If someone like her hates me, that means I must be doing something right.'

'You're right about that,' Bec says.

'Anyway,' Chase continues, 'enough about *her*. There's something more pressing we've yet to discuss!' He opens his phone to the results of the leaver's poll, and, just like that, it's as if he drops back into his original script. 'Zach has a secret admirer!'

'Oh my God, I saw!' Bec says excitedly. 'Who do you think it is, Zach?'

I think of the masked stranger from last night. The feeling of his lips against mine.

'I think it's Josh,' Chase says. 'It's gotta be, right? Ever since you two –'

He's cut off by the sound of the huge double doors opening as Miss Madzikanda strides into the room. I watch her taking each predetermined step, like she has no free will.

'For what reason is it this hot?' she demands. I look for any clues that things might be different today, but everything's the same. Not a single hair out of place.

'All right, you lot,' she says, clapping her hands together and commanding everyone's attention. 'I want volunteers for team captains.'

Tiffany's hand shoots in the air before she can even finish the sentence. She elbows Ethan and his hand shoots up too.

'Why am I not surprised?' Madzikanda says, taking out a couple of red bandanas and tossing them over.

I think back to yesterday. How Ethan cheated to win the game for Hawthorn. I can't bear the thought of them winning again.

Maybe this is something I can change as well? If I can prevent Chase from being drenched with fake blood, maybe I can stop Hawthorn from stealing the game too? I already know the outcome of the coin toss. Chase and Bec will think I've lost it if I volunteer for team captain, but if I put myself forward I can get us the hill . . .

'And Sycamore?' Madzikanda says, turning to our side

of the room. Bec puts her hand up, like before. I just have to get in before Cameron does.

I go to raise my hand and –

'I volunteer!' Kellen yells with the intensity of Katniss Everdeen.

The whole room turns to look at him. What the hell is going on?

'I volunteer,' he says again, going completely off script.

This doesn't make any sense. Did I do something to knock him off course, or does he actually know what's going on here? He can't know, surely? He would have said something.

I watch him closely as he takes his blue bandana from Madzikanda and ties it, and just when I'm convinced he's not in on it he looks directly at me and smirks.

Oh my God. He *knows*.

'Kellen, what the hell?'

It's taken me half an hour to get him alone. He called heads at the coin toss, meaning we lost and Hawthorn took the hill again. Now we're walking back through the woodland, the rest of our team up ahead of us, oblivious to the insanity that's going on around them. Cameron is leading the charge, bouncing along as he waves our flag. If only he knew that we've already lost this game once, and we're about to do the same all over again.

'Surprised?' Kellen says. 'Thought you were the only one?'

'Well, yeah, kinda . . .'

Kellen huffs. 'Of course, the world always revolves around you, Zach.'

'What's that supposed to mean?' Why is he immediately on the attack?

'I'm just saying, you find yourself caught in . . . whatever the hell this is, and you assume it can *only* be happening to you.'

He does make a good point. I realize now how self-centred that seems. But what was I supposed to think given the circumstances?

'So you really think there's more of us?'

'Why wouldn't there be?' Kellen shrugs. 'What makes us so special?'

'I don't know,' I say. 'But was anyone else acting any different?'

'Well, not as obviously as you, that's for sure. Yelling about a time machine?'

'It was them that brought up the time machine!'

'Well, whatever, you sounded completely insane.'

'That's because this *is* insane.'

'And what's the first rule of a crisis?' Kellen asks.

I look at him blankly. I'm not sure if that was rhetorical.

'Don't panic. Stay calm.'

'That's easier said than done!'

'Is it?' he says. 'Because I was kinda thinking that this whole thing might be a great big blessing in disguise. What if we're just being given a second chance?'

'Well, actually,' I say, 'I was sort of thinking that too. Yesterday was such a disaster . . .'

He groans. 'You can say that again.'

I think about his proposal. At least Rhys said yes.

'So now we can set everything right,' I say.

'Exactly. Starting with winning this stupid game.'

'So then why did you mess up the coin toss?'

'I didn't. You underestimate me, Zach.'

'You knew it would be heads. If you'd called it, we could have had the hill.'

'Too many variables,' Kellen says with a shrug. 'It would have changed the whole game. This way, we know exactly what's going to happen. The only reason we lost was because of Ethan's trick. He's not gonna fool us twice, Zach.'

I think on that for a moment. 'That's actually not a bad idea,' I admit. 'We just play it exactly like we did yesterday. Stop Ethan. Score the final point.'

'Exactly,' he says with a smile. 'Simple.'

'Why do I feel like it's not going to be that easy?'

'Because you struggle with chronic pessimism,' Kellen fires back. 'You have to be more positive! What else went wrong yesterday? What else can we fix for you, Zach?'

'Where do I even start?' I say. 'Chase getting pranked. The yearbook getting soaked. Me getting expelled.'

'What?' he says. 'I wasn't there for any of that.'

'You weren't?' I say, taking a few moments to fill him in. I give him the summarized version, but even that has him stunned as I explain exactly how much went wrong.

'OK, you win,' he says as I round out the story. 'I step away for two minutes . . .'

'Where were you anyway?' I ask. I can't believe he missed all of that.

'I was . . . *busy*,' he says, and I know exactly what that means. Him and Rhys consummating their engagement no doubt. Which reminds me . . .

'There was one more thing,' I say, realizing I left out the most important part.

'Oh yeah?'

'There was . . . *a kiss*.'

'Say what now?' His ears prick up. 'You kissed someone?'

'Well, more like someone kissed me.'

'Now that *is* extraordinary,' he teases. 'Have you told Tiffany? She could stop the presses! Get her dad to run a story about it in the *Herald*.'

'Hilarious,' I say, throwing him side-eye.

'So who was it then? Josh again?' I can see his mind going back to our conversation of yesterday. 'Or Cameron . . . ?'

'I don't know,' I say. 'Maybe. That's what I'm trying to figure out. I'm kinda hoping it was Cameron, but it was dark and I was . . . distracted.'

'So you have no idea who kissed you? You can't be serious, Zach! You're just randomly snogging strangers now? You heard "masquerade ball" and thought, *Wahey, this is my time for anonymous hook-ups!*? If you were that desperate, why didn't you just use the glory hole in the third-floor bathroom?'

'There is *not* a glory hole in the third-floor bathroom.'

'Course there is,' he says. 'Between the last two stalls. Ask Rhys.'

127

'You two are actually disgusting.'

'What? It's not like we drilled it ourselves.'

'Well, who did then?'

'You really think I know? Zach, you don't even know the identity of the guys you're kissing!'

'First of all, it's one guy, singular. Second of all, it wasn't like that. It just happened so quickly. And it wasn't just some ordinary kiss. It felt . . . different.'

'Different?' Kellen raises an eyebrow. 'Different how?'

'Just different,' I say. 'I felt something weird. Like a tingle.'

'It's called a boner, Zach. Grow up.'

'Oh my God, can you just stop and listen to me for one second?'

'I *am* listening,' he says. 'Someone kissed you. You don't know who it was. You felt a "*tingle*".' He does air quotes as he says it. 'Anything else?'

'Well . . . no. That just about covers it.'

'Interesting,' he says, glancing around at the other students. He looks like he wants to say something more, then stops himself. 'Well, what were they wearing?'

'This gold suit,' I say. 'Matching mask. All sparkly.'

'I don't remember seeing anyone in a gold suit,' Kellen says slowly.

'Exactly. Me neither. That's why it's weird. Surely one of us would have seen him? There's not even *that* many students in our year.'

'What if it wasn't a student then?'

'You think it was a teacher?!'

'No, you idiot!' He looks at me with absolute horror. 'I meant it could be someone from outside! Someone our age! From another school!'

'Oh,' I say.

'Oh, indeed.' The disturbed look is still frozen on his face.

I wonder if it could be someone from another school. It's not a bad theory. But why would they be here? Kissing random boys in the dark. That doesn't make any sense.

'No,' I finally say. 'They had to be a student here. They knew my name!'

'And you're sure you didn't imagine it?'

'I'm not hallucinating, Kellen!'

'I'm not saying you are,' he says, but he totally looks like he thinks I am. 'Did you get anything else at least? Was he Black? White? Hair colour? Weight?'

'Yes, he was a size eleven shoe,' I say sarcastically. 'I checked just before he kissed me, and then after I got his blood type.'

'Well, I don't know,' he says. 'That's how the prince found Cinderella!'

'By checking her blood type?'

'You're not funny,' Kellen says dryly.

'He was taller than me,' I add. 'At least I think he was.'

'But everyone's taller than you, Zach. You're our little pint-sized prince.'

'I'm five foot ten,' I protest.

'Exactly.' Kellen smirks. 'You can borrow a pair of my heels if you like. Save you going on your tiptoes to make out with strangers?'

'You're insufferable, you know that?'

'Oh, I'm fully aware.' He beams. 'Come on, let's win this stupid game.'

The game goes exactly as it did yesterday. We end up tied two–all, and Cameron once again suggests putting me and Kellen on defence. I thought about challenging that idea this time, keeping more people back, but Kellen's probably right about not changing too much. If we start pulling on every little thread, then the whole day will unravel.

Madzikanda's whistle blows, and our team scatters back into the woodland. Kellen and I stay behind to guard the flag. With much more determination than yesterday. Everything is now riding on what happens next. All we have to do is lull Ethan into a false sense of security and stop him taking our flag. If we can do that, we just might win this.

'So let's say we do beat them,' I say, leaning against the flagpole. 'Then what?'

'Then we enjoy prom,' Kellen says. 'In Sycamore colours for once.'

'Yeah, but what else are you gonna do differently?'

'I can't tell you *everything*, Zach! Where's the mystery in that!'

I look at him blankly. The last thing we need is more *mystery*.

'Isn't it obvious?' He sighs. 'That proposal. I'm dying just thinking about it.'

I try not to wince. 'I mean. It was . . . sweet.'

'It's fine, Zach. You don't need to tell lies.'

'OK,' I say. 'It was a bit cringe ... I mean, who gets engaged at prom? You're barely eighteen, Kellen. This isn't the Middle Ages.'

'I know,' he says. 'But I've heard what everyone's been saying about me and Rhys. How we'll never survive long distance. How we'll never make it through the summer.'

Words straight out of Tiffany's mouth. Is that who he's talking about?

'I just thought if I could make it official ... then we'd *have* to make it work.'

'Trapping him by putting a ring on his finger isn't going to make the difference,' I say. 'If you wanna try long distance, then go for it. You don't need a forced engagement.'

'So you don't think I should propose again then? Tonight, I mean?'

'Honestly?' I say. 'Please, for the love of God, don't do that.' I feel the second-hand embarrassment all over again. 'How did you even afford a ring anyway?'

'It was my grandfather's.'

'Oh, Kellen ...'

'I thought it would be romantic!'

'It *is* romantic,' I say. 'But this early in a relationship? When you're both still so young? It's just maybe a bit ... full on? It doesn't mean you can't do *something*, though. A gesture maybe? To tell him how much he means to you?'

'Like, maybe I could get onstage and –'

'No getting onstage!'

I hear a branch snap in the distance.

'They're coming!' Ethan yells. He's wearing the blue bandana, once again pretending to be his brother. 'They're coming!' he repeats, looking back in the direction he appeared from. 'Their whole team.'

I don't react. We can't let him know we're on to him.

This needs to be handled with surgical precision.

'Get him!' Kellen screams, completely not sticking to the plan at all.

'Huh?' Ethan looks surprised, darting out of the way. 'Wow,' he says, bouncing from side to side, easily evading us. 'I honestly thought you'd fall for that.'

'You really think we can't tell you and your brother apart?' I say.

'Most people can't,' he says with a grin, dashing to the right. Kellen almost grabs him, but Ethan slips through his fingers, ripping off his stolen bandana and beelining for the flag.

I try to catch him, but I trip over my own feet, and fall forward as he snatches our flag and sprints away from us. I get up and try to go after him, but it's hopeless: he's ten metres ahead of us by the time we break the treeline. We call for help, and our teammates do their best to stop him, but – just like yesterday – he passes the flag to Tiffany and she carries it all the way back to home base. They make it look effortless.

'Jeez,' I say, out of breath. 'How did we manage to screw this up twice?'

Kellen sighs. 'Because we're *terrible* at sport, Zach! We could repeat this day a hundred times and probably still mess it up. Maybe Hawthorn are meant to win this . . .'

'Oh, fuck that,' I say, frustrated. 'Don't give me any of that *everything happens for a reason* nonsense. They still cheated, Kellen. I'm going to Madzikanda.'

'What?' he says. 'Zach, don't. We talked about that yesterday.'

'Yeah, and I shouldn't have let you talk me out of it.'

'Zach, please . . .' he pleads. I really don't understand why this is so important to him.

'I'm sorry,' I say, walking towards Madzikanda. She's about to raise the loudspeaker to her lips when I interrupt her. 'Miss, wait.'

'Zach?' she says, lowering it again.

'They cheated,' I say. 'Ethan stole a blue bandana and pretended to be his brother.'

'What?' Ethan says, overhearing this. He clearly wasn't expecting to be called out. 'You little liar!'

'I'm not lying, and you know it.'

'He's making it up,' he says, turning out his pockets. 'See, no bandana.'

'That's because he tossed it!'

'All right, settle down,' Miss Madzikanda says. 'Did anyone else see this, Zach?'

'Of course they didn't,' Tiffany interrupts. Why does she have to insert herself into everything? 'He's just making it up. Attention-seeking as always.'

'Fuck you,' I bite back.

'Language!' Madzikanda snaps. 'Was anyone else there, Zach?'

'Kellen was.'

I don't even look at him as I say it. I know he really doesn't want to get caught up in this, but I need him to back me up. Hawthorn can't get away with this twice.

'Kellen?' Madzikanda asks. He's skulking off to the side, pretending he's not listening. Ethan and Tiffany glare at him. Rhys gives him a look that screams, *Don't you dare.*

'I didn't see anything, miss,' he lies. 'Zach must be ... *mistaken.*'

'Kellen, what the fuck ...' I say. I honestly don't know what I was expecting, but seriously? This shows where his true allegiance lies.

Madzikanda sighs, almost like she believes me, but can't do anything about it. 'I'm sorry, Zach, but if you two can't get your story straight, the result will have to stand.'

A huge smirk rolls across Ethan's face. Tiffany pouts as if to say *poor you.*

'Come on, miss,' I say. 'You know I'm telling the truth.'

'Sorry, Zach.' She raises the loudspeaker to her lips. 'Three–two to Hawthorn!' she booms, her voice carrying over the treetops. 'Congratulations to this year's winners!'

'Thanks a lot,' I mutter to Kellen.

'What did you expect me to do?'

'Tell the truth, maybe?'

'I told you,' he says. 'Tonight has to go perfectly. I'm not about to mess that up.'

134

'Why does it matter?' I say. 'We're leaving this place tomorrow! If you hate Hawthorn so much, why do you keep buddying up to them?'

'Because I want to be with *Rhys*!' he says. 'He's not like the rest of them.'

I snort.

'Don't be like that.'

'Sorry,' I say. 'But if he wasn't, then he wouldn't put up with their shit either.'

'He's just being loyal to his friends.'

'But not to his *boyfriend*.'

'Zach.'

'What do you want me to say?'

'I just want you to be supportive,' he snaps back. 'You dropped me the second me and Rhys started dating. You pushed me out of my own friendship group!'

'No, I didn't!' I say, outraged. How dare he suggest such a thing? 'You were the one who stopped spending time with us!'

'Because you made me feel like I wasn't welcome.'

'What are you talking about?'

'All the snide jokes. Constantly belittling our relationship.'

'That's because you don't belong with him! You don't belong with Hawthorn.'

'You can't be serious,' Kellen says, shaking his head. 'It's all made-up nonsense, Zach! Sycamore. Hawthorn. Who the fuck cares!'

He takes off his bandana and storms away from me. I watch as he goes to congratulate Rhys, kissing him on the cheek as he's lifted into the air. Ethan gives him a fist bump and he exchanges air kisses with Tiffany.

And, just like that, everything snaps back into place.

Today is once again no different to yesterday.

I thought Kellen and I could be a team, present a unified front, work together to find out what's really going on here. But we obviously want completely different things. His priorities are not the same as mine, so from here on I'm only looking out for myself. If I'm going to put this day right, I can't do it with him messing everything up.

The masked stranger comes back to the forefront of my mind, and I can't help but glance across at Cameron. He and Bec are chatting at the edge of the playing field. They're both laughing. They seem happy. Maybe the game really wasn't that important after all.

I think about heading to the showers, but decide to hang back a little. As much as I want my chance with Cameron, if I learned anything from yesterday, it's that there's truly nothing worse than fumbling your way through a naked conversation with your crush.

'Hey, good-lookin'!'

You have to be fucking kidding me.

I gave the boys a good half an hour before venturing into the showers. I thought that would be plenty of time, but here's Josh, just as I'm getting all soapy.

'What are you doing here?' I say, wanting to cover up.

'Um, taking a shower?' He laughs. 'What do you think?

This isn't your own private bathroom, you know. Or did you think you were back at the mansion?'

'The mansion? What mansion? I grew up in a two-bedroom house.'

'You did? Huh. I always imagined you with butlers and silver service.'

'I don't know what gave you that idea,' I say. Surely that's not the vibe I give off? 'How come you're so late anyway?' I ask. 'I thought you'd be getting ready by now.'

'I'm running a bit behind,' he says. 'Owen had a bottle of champagne, and . . .'

'You've been drinking? It's, like, four p.m!'

'It's the last day of school!' Josh starts peeling his shirt off. Drops of sweat bead on his skin, and the afternoon light accentuates his slender figure. 'Time doesn't exist here.'

'You can say that again,' I reply. If only he knew how right he was.

He looks directly at me then. 'You know it's nothing I haven't seen before, right?'

'That was a whole year ago,' I say. Why am I *blushing* now?!

'Yeah, I noticed things have grown a little since then.'

'Oh my God,' I say. 'You're not supposed to look.'

'I was talking about your biceps!' He ditches his shorts.

'Even so!' I say. 'Avert your eyes! Locker-room etiquette, Josh!'

'Never heard of her,' he says with a shrug, taking his underwear off and twirling it on his finger. 'It's just nice to see you so excited.'

'Huh?' I croak, looking down.

'For prom. Biggest night of our lives, right?'

'Oh, er . . . right,' I say, feeling increasingly flustered.

'I'm just fucking with you.' He comes over to take the shower right next to me. What is it with these boys and their complete disregard for personal space? 'But you can relax, Zach. That's the joy of being friends who've bumped uglies! Though I kinda hate that phrase. Mine definitely isn't ugly.'

I can't help but glance down.

'Made you look,' he says with the most infuriating grin. 'What were we even thinking back then?'

'What do you mean?' I say. I can't help but be offended by the statement.

'Well, I'm me and you're . . . well . . . *Zach*. It's such a mismatch.'

'Why do you say *Zach* like it's an insult?'

'It's a compliment!' he says, laughing. 'You're *Zach*. You're different to the other guys.'

'Different how?'

'I dunno. It's like you've got this whole unthreatening *boy-next-door* thing going on.'

'Me?' I exclaim. 'That's exactly what I say about you!'

'So you talk about me then?'

'I used to.'

'Cute.' He smiles. 'Maybe we weren't as mismatched as I thought. Good times, eh?'

'*Good times?* You make it sound like you're reminiscing over a camping trip.'

'Oh, I've had *good times* on camping trips too,' he says, grinning.

'You're terrible.'

'I *am* terrible,' he agrees, turning the taps off.

'You showered for, like, thirty seconds.'

'Were you hoping for a little longer? Hoping I'd drop the soap?' He throws a towel round his waist. 'I'm in a rush. I still haven't decided what I'm gonna wear tonight.'

'You haven't? I thought you'd have figured that out weeks ago.'

'Too many options! I've got, like, five outfits to choose from. Though I was thinking I might do a quick costume change later. Serve two different looks.'

Two different looks? I think of the masked stranger. I already know Josh has his jester outfit. Could that sparkly outfit be hanging in his wardrobe too?

'You don't have anything gold, do you?'

'Why do you ask?'

'I just thought it would suit you, is all.'

'Black and gold.' He gestures to his skin. 'I suppose they do say they go together.'

'That's really not what I meant . . .'

'Course you didn't,' he teases. 'Well, I'm not giving you any spoilers. You'll just have to wait and see.' He winks and heads for the door. 'Don't spend all day in there now!'

'Wait!' I call, but he's already gone.

Could that gold outfit really belong to him? I've spent all year telling Chase and Bec that Josh and me was a one-time thing. But maybe there is some chemistry there? Maybe they were right? Maybe they could see what I couldn't?

I think of the vote for hottest boy.

The kiss last night at prom.

Could it *actually* be Josh?

'Wow,' I say, walking back into my room to find that Bec and Chase are already dressed. Somehow they look even more incredible than yesterday. I don't even need to fake my reaction. Everything felt like such a whirlwind the first time round that it's kinda nice to get to live this moment twice, to pay attention to the details and savour these feelings. It's like going back to your favourite movie and noticing something different every time you watch it. I hadn't realized before how Bec's earrings matched her dress so perfectly, nor how Chase's belt buckle is shaped like a swirling dragon. 'You guys look amazing.'

'You should have seen Bec scaling the fire escape!' Chase says.

'That's how you got up here?' I feign surprise. 'You're like an Asian Lara Croft.'

'That's what I said!' Chase gasps. 'We really do spend too much time together.'

'Yeah, that must be it,' I say, and I have to admit that was kinda fun. Maybe I can do more with this repeating-day thing than I realized.

'You're just in time for a selfie,' Bec says, whipping out her phone.

'Well, maybe wait till I've got dressed?' I laugh, pushing her phone away. 'Why don't you get some pictures of Chase? He needs to send some to his mum.'

'Oh my God, please,' he says. 'Before I spill something all over myself. I overheard Harrington talking about brie and cranberry canapés. I don't want either of those things anywhere near this!'

The memory of the pig's blood plays over in my mind. It's not the canapés he has to worry about. At least today he hasn't made himself a target by hacking Tiffany's rigged poll, but I'm still worried. Even though he knows what the Hawthorn Elite are planning, it still feels like the night could very easily go sideways.

'Actually,' I say, interrupting them mid-photo, 'why don't you call her?'

'Oh, you absolutely cannot call your mum right now,' Bec says with a wicked smirk.

'Huh?' Chase says. 'Why not?'

'Because she'd lose her mind if she saw us drinking *this*.' She reaches into her garment bag to pull out the bottle of Toxicquila.

'The tequila can wait,' I say, plucking the bottle from her fingers and giving her a look to say *this is important*.

Bec hesitates for a second and then smiles. 'You're right,' she says. 'Call your mum! I need to know what she thinks of my dress anyway.'

'She's gonna say it's too short!' Chase laughs, pulling out his phone. 'Zach, can you hurry up and put some clothes on? My mum doesn't need to see your nipples.'

'All right, all right.' I pull on my shirt and button it. 'Better?'

'Much,' he says, hitting dial on FaceTime. His mum answers almost immediately.

'I thought you'd never call!' she shrieks from the other end of the phone, holding it way too close to her face. 'Let me see! What are you wearing?'

'Hi, Myra,' Bec says, waving into the camera. 'Here,' she says, taking the phone from Chase and stepping backwards so his mum can get a full view of his outfit.

'Oh my God,' she says, her smile faltering. 'Is that ... my dress?'

The smiles disappear from Chase and Bec too. I swear my heart temporarily stops beating. I knew today could go sideways, but I didn't think this would be the cause of it. There's an uncomfortably long silence and then ...

'*It looks incredible!*' Myra says, joy rushing through every muscle in her face. 'Let me see closer!'

Thank God for that. Their smiles return as Bec works all the angles.

'You're not mad?' Chase says after a few moments.

'How could I be mad?' his mum says. 'I have my alarm set for 11:11 every day. To wish for my son to be happy. And look at you. It looks like all those wishes came true.'

I see a wash of relief run through him. All his worries now replaced with a smile.

142

He switches to Mandarin, and they exchange a few more words. I don't understand the specifics of what they're saying, but I know they're having a *moment*. A moment they never had yesterday.

'Now let me see Bec,' she finally says, and Bec dutifully does a twirl for her.

'Not bad, not bad,' she says. 'Though that dress is a little . . . *short*.'

'Told you,' Chase says with a laugh. 'Zach, put your jacket on.'

'Oh,' I say, quickly pulling it on so Myra can take a look at my outfit too.

'Handsome,' is her final verdict. She looks like she might have some further critiques that she graciously keeps to herself. 'OK, have fun,' she says. 'Call me in the morning.'

'Will do,' Chase says. 'Love you, Ma.'

'Love you – don't kiss too many boys,' she replies, and hangs up.

'She's so sweet,' Bec says.

'She's just on her best behaviour because you're here.' Chase laughs.

'He's right,' I add. I've got to know Myra quite well over the past couple of years, and *sweet* isn't the first word I'd use to describe her. I've always been so surprised at how open her relationship is with Chase. There's *nothing* they don't talk about. She even knows what happened between me and Josh. I'd never talk to my own mum about that. She probably thinks I'm still a virgin.

'So are we ready?' Bec finally says. She retrieves the tequila from where I'd stashed it, the loop snapping back into place. 'I haven't got shot glasses so it'll have to be straight from the bottle. Some Dutch courage to start the evening!'

'You look great,' Josh says, scanning me up and down. I'm giving Huckleberry a good rub. Something I didn't do yesterday. I don't really believe in superstitions, but then I didn't believe in time loops either. So who knows what else I'm wrong about?

'You look good too,' I say, looking at him. I was hoping he might have switched to the gold outfit, but he's still wearing the jester costume from yesterday.

'Well, aren't we just the complimentary couple!' he jokes. 'Though I do think you looked better earlier. Without the clothes, that is.'

'Wait,' Bec says. 'Have you two been at it again?'

'No, we haven't been *at it*,' I say, squeezing the bridge of my nose.

'Zach tried it on with me in the shower,' Josh says. 'But I had to rebuff him.'

'That is *not* what happened.'

'Then why are you blushing?'

'He's right, you are blushing.' Chase laughs. He's giving Huckleberry a rub now too.

'Why didn't you mention this earlier?' Bec demands. 'Why so secretive!'

'Because there was nothing to mention!'

Josh gives them a big dorky grin, enjoying this *way* too much. 'It's all right, Zach. Plenty more fish in the sea!' He gestures to the crowd around us. 'I reckon one of these fishies is a secret closet case. I'll be damned if I'll let this evening end before I find them.'

'Well, the clock's ticking,' Bec says. 'You better get to it.'

'Patience,' he says. 'Here's one of my suspects now.'

'Huh?' Owen says, looking bewildered as he approaches. 'Suspects for what?'

'We were just saying that you're probably secretly gay. Hanging around with me all the time? Kinda seems like you might have a crush. It's starting to raise suspicions.'

'Oh,' Owen says. 'Shit, you caught me. Been fantasizing about you this whole time. And now you're dressed as *the Joker*? I've always had a secret Batman kink.'

'I knew it!' Josh teases. 'Boathouse in ten minutes?'

'See you there.' Owen's deadpan delivery is impeccable.

'Honestly, Owen.' Chase grins. 'You better *not* come out as gay. You're our token straight guy. We need you for diversity points!'

'It's true,' Josh says. 'I explicitly forbid you from kissing any boys!'

'I'll try my hardest,' Owen says.

I catch a glimpse of Ethan out of the corner of my eye. I'd almost forgotten what's about to happen to him, but now, knowing that moment is coming, it's hard to focus on anything else. In just a few minutes, he's going to find out that his private pictures are all over the internet. It feels wrong to just stand here, knowing it's coming, and do nothing.

Maybe I *should* do something. My gaze drifts across to Kellen.

Maybe *we* should do something.

I know I said I was gonna stay out of his way and do my own thing, but this feels important. This definitely warrants calling a temporary truce. I excuse myself from the others and head over. Rhys is loudly talking about tax breaks, and Tiffany and Ethan are hanging on every word like he's their actual messiah. I hadn't noticed before, but Kellen has toned down his look from last night. He's swapped the bare chest for a plain white shirt, and he's swapped the heels for flats. His suit still has a little sparkle in it, but that feels like just about the only part of his personality still showing. He's clutching Rhys's arm maybe just a bit too tightly. And Rhys's body language seems off. As if he wants Kellen to let go.

'Can we talk?' I ask. Tiffany scowls as if disgusted by my presence.

'I'm kinda busy,' Kellen says dismissively.

'It's important,' I say. 'It's about . . . *you know*.'

'OK, fine,' he says, breaking away from the others. 'I'll be right back.'

Tiffany looks at him as if to say *don't hurry*.

'OK, what is it?' he says as soon as we're out of earshot.

'I think we should talk about what's about to happen.'

Kellen sighs. 'I already know what's going to happen, Zach. I messed up yesterday. Now I'm gonna fix it. That's it. I don't know why you're caught up in this too, but I need to focus on myself. I want this night to go perfectly, and right now you're messing with it.'

'By talking to you?'

'By interrupting me,' he says. 'I was in the middle of a conversation.'

'About tax breaks,' I reply. 'Do you even know what those are?'

'I'm not an idiot, Zach.'

'I'm not saying you are. I'm just saying you're not a part of that world.'

'Because I'm on a scholarship? You sound just like them.'

'I'm just saying you don't belong with them. You're better than they are.'

Kellen scoffs. 'This is nothing to do with Ethan or Tiffany or the rest of Hawthorn. What you're really saying is that I don't belong with Rhys.'

'No, I'm not.'

I definitely am.

'If you're gonna say it, say it with your whole chest.'

'OK, fine,' I say. 'I don't think you belong with Rhys. There. Happy now?'

'Thrilled.'

'You're infuriating.'

'*I'm* infuriating?' He laughs. 'You're the one who's dragged me over here for this meaningless conversation.'

'It's not meaningless!' I say. 'Someone is about to leak Ethan's photos. Shouldn't we be doing something to stop that? He's meant to be your friend, right?'

'What are we supposed to do?' Kellen says. 'It takes time for something to go viral. Those photos were probably leaked hours ago. It's too late to do anything about it now.'

He's right, I realize, but that doesn't stop me. 'We could still figure out who it was . . . Expose them, get some justice.'

'Justice? You hate Ethan, Zach. Why do you suddenly care so much?'

'Why *don't* you care?' I say. 'I mean . . . it wasn't you, right?'

'Of course it wasn't me! How fucking dare you?'

'Well, it was *someone*.'

'And that someone wasn't me,' he growls. 'So why don't you run along and play Sherlock Holmes on your own. And while you do that I'm gonna go enjoy prom. With my boyfriend. If that's OK with you?'

'Whatever,' I say, stomping away. I can't believe I've actually missed hanging around with him. He's as insufferable as ever.

'Just make it go away!' Tiffany screeches into her phone, right on schedule. I guess I'm too late. 'I don't care, Daddy! I swear to God, if I see *anything* about this in the *Herald* . . . !'

She hangs up and glares around. Her eyes land on Chase for a moment, and you can see her scrutinizing him. I think she's about to charge over and accuse him like yesterday, but then she glances away and continues scanning for suspects. It looks like taking the heat off Chase by making sure that he didn't hack the results might actually have worked.

At least I did *something* right.

'Who do you think did it?' Bec says as I join them again. 'I know they have a lot of enemies, but . . . this? Could someone really be so heartless?'

'It could be anyone,' I say, looking around the crowd.

There's nobody at this school that Ethan and Tiffany haven't snubbed, bullied or demeaned at least once. Even Ethan and Rhys have locked horns a couple of times. Literally *everyone* is a suspect. Including Kellen. Despite what he said, I can't rule him out. With the way they treat him, he definitely has a motive. Maybe he just wanted to bring them down a peg on prom night.

Maybe that's why he doesn't want me sniffing around . . .

'At least Ethan seems to be taking it pretty well?' Bec says.

I look over and see him laughing with his friends, just like yesterday. He really *doesn't* seem all that bothered. It feels wrong to think – he is still a victim after all – but it seems like he might actually be *enjoying* it. Cameron said all his brother cared about was how many followers he had. Maybe Ethan really is seeing all this as a *good thing*. Maybe he doesn't need justice. No, I think. It's not just about him. This is about *all* victims of revenge porn.

People shouldn't be able to get away with this!

After all, this affects Cameron too. I look across to see him staring at his phone with yesterday's worried look spread across his face. I should probably go and talk to him, but then the front doors open and the teachers step out, ready for Harrington's eighteen-hour speech.

Great, I think. *As if listening to this once wasn't enough . . .*

After it's over, we file into the hall through the candlelit corridor, and I peer up into the rafters to see if I can spot

149

the bucket. If you look really carefully, you can just about see it hanging up there in the darkness. I point it out to my friends as we walk in. Chase is safe for now. Even Tiffany wouldn't be so stupid as to pig's-blood *everyone*.

'Are you OK?' I say when I finally get a moment with Cameron.

'It's just these comments . . .' he says, scrolling through Instagram to show me.

'I know it's easier said than done,' I say, 'but you really should try to ignore them.'

'I know,' he says. 'I just hate that everyone thinks they have the right to compare us. I don't know why I ever agreed to do the whole yin and yang thing.' He pulls on his jacket as if it makes him itch. 'I honestly wish I could go upstairs and change.'

'You mean you have a spare outfit?' I ask.

'Course,' he says. 'But Ethan didn't wanna do silver and gold. He said the colours weren't right for Instagram. Said we needed something more muted . . .'

'Silver and *gold*?' I say, my heart beating faster. 'Which one was yours?'

'I don't know. Ethan ordered them. Does it matter?'

'I suppose not,' I say, even though it *really* does. Maybe it *was* Cameron who kissed me after all? Maybe he got sick of matching with Ethan and did go upstairs to change?

'Sorry,' he finally says. 'I feel like I'm being a bit of a downer.'

'You're not,' I say, meeting his eyes for a moment.

'It's just annoying,' he says. 'I had other plans for this

150

evening. A little prom-night romance, maybe. I was kinda hoping I could talk to you about that actually . . .'

'You were?'

'Yeah.' He swallows hard and looks away. 'Though maybe I need a little bit of liquid encouragement first.' He glances over at the punchbowl. 'A few drinks and I'll be back.'

I want to stop him and tell him that he can talk to me right now, but we've got the whole night ahead of us. There really is no rush. I'm sure he just needs a little bit longer to open up. To change out of what he's wearing and put on that gold suit . . .

Maybe things are going to work out today after all. Sure, I could do without the Hawthorn banners, but generally? Things actually seem to be going pretty well. Bec still writes her Taylor Swift lyrics in the yearbook, and this time I write something too.

To second chances, I inscribe in my best handwriting. *Zach Evans. Class of '25.*

Having lived this day already takes some of the pressure off, and it's actually incredibly satisfying to know that Tiffany and her cronies have gone to all this effort to try to humiliate Chase, and knowing they won't succeed. It's sad, really, that they can't just enjoy their prom night without ruining it for someone else. They'd argue that they're just honouring Oakbrook tradition, but really it's nothing more than petty school bullying.

Eventually, we gather beneath the skylight and wait for Mr Harrington to crown Ethan and Tiffany. I'm tempted to skip this since I already know whose names are inside that envelope. The votes were cast yesterday, so it's not like I ever had any power to change it.

'And so, without further delay,' Mr Harrington says, after his incredibly long-winded speech – God, that's *four* I've had to listen to now – 'it's my honour to announce this year's Prom King and Queen.'

'Prom Royalty!' Josh yells, right on cue. 'It's gender neutral.'

'Oh ... erm, yes,' Harrington says. 'This year's Prom Royalty ...'

There's that same moment of tension as he fumbles with the envelope.

'Kellen Thomas and Rhys Kingsland!'

'Huh?' I say, watching as everyone claps excitedly, the two boys walking through the crowd to the stage.

What did you do, Kellen? Rigging the result isn't what I meant by a romantic gesture ...

'Could have seen that coming,' Bec says.

'It was obviously going to be them,' Chase agrees.

Except it wasn't obvious because this isn't how it was supposed to go at all. I glance across at Tiffany. She looks as surprised as I do. But, while she glares at Kellen furiously, Ethan seems completely unbothered.

The applause grows louder as Rhys and Kellen take the stage and Mr Harrington crowns them. 'Our first-ever same-sex royalty!' he says as the confetti canons fire and glitter rains down on us. Except it isn't gold this time, it's rainbow.

'Love is love!' Josh shouts from somewhere behind me. I turn and catch his eye, and he gives me this big smile. He's ridiculous, but he's cute. I can't help but smile too.

How on earth did Kellen do all this?

I turn back to the stage and see him kissing Rhys. Everyone has taken their phone out to capture the moment, but I'm not sure I want to remember *this* part of the evening. I don't know what it is, but something about this just doesn't feel right. My stomach twists as they hold the kiss for longer than feels comfortable. Kellen raises Rhys's hand in the air to thunderous applause before they descend back into the crowd to meet a sea of well-wishers and congratulations.

'Two guys winning?' I overhear Tiffany saying to Miss Madzikanda. 'It's misogynistic. How is it progressive to muscle girls out of their right to win Prom Queen?'

'Because one year it might be two girls,' she replies. 'When I was a student here, we wouldn't have even dreamed of seeing two boys taking the crowns. I think you're maybe forgetting the significance of that.'

'It's just a pair of plastic crowns,' Tiffany replies bitterly.

'And yet you're this bothered by not getting one,' Madzikanda replies. 'I know you're disappointed, but try to be happy for them. Rhys is your friend, right? Besides, you got to be here to see them make Oakbrook history. Put that on your Instagram.'

Yes, Madzikanda! Drag her!

Tiffany looks increasingly irritated. 'Where's Mr Harrington?' she finally huffs, realizing she's wasting her time with Madzikanda. 'I'm going to demand a recount. That's my right! That's how democracy works!'

'You do that.' Madzikanda shrugs, watching her walk away.

'Rainbow confetti?' I say as soon as Tiffany is out of earshot. A few stray pieces still float in the air around us. 'Something tells me that was your doing.'

She chuckles. 'I wasn't actually looking to take the credit, but . . .'

'Well, it was hardly gonna be Harrington's idea.'

'I'm sure I don't know what you mean,' she says, twinkling. 'I'm just glad we finally got to use it. I ordered it *years* ago. There was a young lesbian couple who were in the running. They didn't win, but I've been loading it into the backup confetti canons every year since. Just in case. I can't believe it's taken this long. It's about time it finally happened.'

'You made history, miss.'

'No,' she says. 'They did. Look how happy Kellen is. Makes it all worthwhile.'

I look over. Kellen has a huge smile on his face as he shows off his crown. Rhys seems a little awkward, but then that's his default setting if he's not on a rugby pitch. I still don't understand how Kellen managed this, though.

'I guess I should go and give them my congratulations.'

'You do that,' Madzikanda says with a smile.

I wait until there's a break in the crowd of people and pull Kellen aside. 'All right,' I say, 'enough games. How did you do it?'

He beams with a big mischievous grin. 'I just switched out the ballots.'

'What? When?'

'Earlier!' he says. 'Right after Capture the Flag. Can you believe Harrington's office wasn't even locked? You know we actually got more votes than I expected? It was *way* closer than I thought. I only had to switch a few.'

'But that's cheating!'

'They cheated in Capture the Flag!'

'Two wrongs don't make a right.'

'OK, Grandma,' he says, rolling his eyes. 'You saw what Tiffany did yesterday. Did you *really* want her to get onstage and start running her mouth again? I did us all a favour! Sure, I get a sparkly crown, but I was also looking out for Chase!'

'You were looking out for yourself,' I say. 'Don't act like you were doing some good deed. You did this because you wanted to win.'

'And what if I did?' Kellen pouts. 'It's not like I stole it from someone deserving, Zach! You know full well how many arms she twisted to get the votes for her and Ethan. It's not like it was ever a fair competition.'

'It's still cheating!'

'Maybe you're just jealous,' he finally says with a shrug.

That stings and I don't really know why. I'm not jealous. Am I?

'I'm going back to my boyfriend. At least try to enjoy the rest of your prom.'

'Whatever,' I say, striding away from him. I don't know

why I keep letting him distract me. I have my own objectives tonight, and they've got nothing to do with him and his stupid action-man boyfriend. I think of that kiss again, that magical spark when the stranger pushed his lips against mine.

Cameron or Josh. It has to be one of them.

I go through the motions for the rest of the evening. I try not to totally zone out of conversations, but it's hard because I've already heard everything people have to say.

My focus is constantly on Cameron and Josh. Waiting for one of them to excuse themselves to go and change. But it doesn't seem to be happening. They're both in their original outfits, Cameron still paired with his brother, and Josh still dressed as class clown. I'm half tempted to spill my punch over them just to hurry things along a little. I have to know who that gold outfit belongs to.

'What happened to the outfit change?' I finally ask Josh when I get him alone.

'Oh, I can't be bothered,' he says. 'More time dressing means less time drinking.'

'Well, hypothetically, if you *were* to change ... what would you change into?'

'Something slutty,' he says with a wink. 'Now, if you'll excuse me, I have some very important business to attend to.' He nods to the punchbowl where Owen is pouring two more drinks.

I'm not getting anywhere. Midnight is drawing closer and closer and I *still* don't know who kissed me.

'Zach!' Cameron says, approaching. 'I was looking for

you!' He's slightly flushed. Not hammered, but definitely several drinks in.

'You were?'

'Yeah,' he says. 'I think I'm ready for that talk. Before I get too merry.' He looks around to see if anyone's listening. 'Maybe we could go somewhere a little quieter?'

'Cameron, shots!' Josh calls.

'Coming!' he yells back. 'By the lake? In, like ... ten minutes?'

'I'll be there,' I say.

And this time I mean it. I won't mess this up a second time.

There's nobody by the lake when I get there, just the moonlight rippling off the water, the stars twinkling in the night sky above. I walk down the wooden jetty that juts out over the surface and sit on the end. I let my feet dangle, kicking them idly as I wait for Cameron. My heart is fluttering. Is it finally gonna happen?

Kellen seems so certain about what this repeated day was for, at least for him. But I'm not so certain. Prom definitely hasn't gone anywhere near as badly as yesterday, but even so something still feels wrong. I pull out my phone and look at the time: 11.55 p.m.

I replay the events of last night in my mind over and over, trying to find a clue to confirm the identity of the person who kissed me. I remember the touch of their lips and try to imagine them belonging to Josh or Cameron. It could have easily been either of them.

'Zach?' a voice calls.

Cameron. He's early.

I get up to turn around but then quickly realise it's not him. The wrong twin *again*. Ethan is walking down the jetty towards me.

'I was hoping to find you,' he says.

'Huh?' I say, confused. 'Why?'

He shuffles his feet. 'This whole leaked photos thing. I think I know who did it . . .'

'OK,' I say. 'But what's that got to do with me?'

'I need to show you something,' he says. 'Come with me?'

And that's when the penny drops. He's trying to set me up. Just like he did Chase.

'Wow,' I say, refusing to take the bait. 'You really think I'm that fucking stupid?'

He hesitates for a second, as if contemplating whether to continue the lie, but then his lips twist into a sinister smile. It's like he's been taking lessons from Tiffany. 'So you know then? Who told you?'

'Nobody told me anything,' I say. 'It's just obvious, isn't it? But why me? Why am I suddenly the target? What the hell did I do?'

'Snitches get stitches,' he says.

I can't help snorting. 'Because I told Madzikanda that you cheated?'

'Cheated?' He laughs. 'It was just a tactic, Zach.'

'Why did you deny it then?' I say. He doesn't answer that. 'So that's what this is? You could be enjoying prom, but instead you're trying to ruin mine? It's pathetic.'

'I'll tell you what's *pathetic*,' he spits, getting uncomfortably close. 'You thinking you have a chance with Cam. That *is* why you're out here, right?'

'That's none of your business,' I say, pushing past him.

'He's my brother,' he says. 'Of course it's my business. If you think he's into you, you're delusional. You do realize he tells me *everything*, right?'

'Whatever,' I say. I keep walking, trying to seem unbothered. But I am bothered. What did Cameron say about me?

'Know your place!' he calls after me. 'You're just like Kellen. A pair of gold-digging nobodies. You'll go after literally anyone with money.'

'Excuse me?' I spin back round to face him. I know I shouldn't let him get a rise out of me, but I'm so tired of his bullshit. Him and Tiffany are *made* for each other. 'That's all you rich kids think about, isn't it? I couldn't care less about your stupid money.'

'That's what they all say.' He laughs. '*I don't care about money*. But the truth is you only pretend you don't care because you don't have any.'

'Fuck you,' I snap, squaring up to him so we're face to face.

'Fuck me?' He smirks. 'You'd like that, wouldn't you? Had a wank over my pics yet? If you squint hard enough, you can pretend I'm Cameron.'

I think about taking a swing at him.

'Go on,' Ethan says, nodding down at his body suggestively. 'Have a feel. It's the closest you'll ever get.' He grabs my hand and presses it to his chest.

'Get off me!' I yell, pushing him, the first firework screeching up into the night sky.

But I push harder than I mean to. It feels like it happens in slow motion. He loses his balance and stumbles off the edge of the jetty. The blood-red explosions of the fireworks reflect in the black of the lake as he disappears beneath the surface.

Fuck. I didn't mean to do that.

Though maybe he deserved it. He *definitely* deserved it.

But he doesn't surface.

'Zach!' a voice yells. Cameron is running up to me. 'What are you doing?!'

'Huh?' I say, disorientated. 'I don't know – he started it.'

'He can't swim!' Cameron says, pulling off his suit jacket.

'What? But he's on the rowing team . . .'

'Move!' He pushes me aside. I've never heard him sound so serious. He takes a deep breath, dives in and disappears beneath the water.

I look on helplessly, the sound of the explosions overhead growing louder.

'Cameron?' I call, watching the ripples get smaller and smaller until the lake falls completely still. 'Cameron?' I yell again, my voice growing panicked now.

'Help!' I shout, hoping someone will hear me, but it's hopeless. Everyone's inside, the squealing sound of each firework drowning out my voice. 'Somebody help!'

But nobody hears me. Nobody comes. I'm all alone on the jetty.

'Fuck,' I say, tearing off my jacket and kicking off my shoes. I brace myself for the cold of the lake and leap in after them. I dive beneath the surface and reach around for them. But the water is far deeper than I could have imagined. It goes *down* and *down*, until I feel the pressure pushing on my eardrums. Since when has the lake been this deep?

The fireworks continue to explode above us, the muffled sound rippling through the water. I dive deeper and deeper, reaching for them in the darkness, until finally I feel something grip my arm. It happens so suddenly that it startles me, and I almost choke.

It's a hand, and it's pulling on me. I pull back, but it's like whoever it belongs to is stuck on something, unable to move. Their fingers squeeze, more and more frantic, and now I'm almost out of air too. I try to break free and go for the surface, but the hand grips me tighter and tighter. A silent pleading in the pitch-black of the lake.

I don't want to let go, but I have to. I can't hold it any longer. I feel water in my lungs and the blackness consumes me.

3

'Prom night, baby!'

I gasp for air, coughing and spluttering as I wake. Chase is standing over me, holding the pillow he just hit me with. 'Fuck, are you OK?' He's wearing the same blue baseball cap. The same Miami Dolphins shirt.

'Again?!' I gulp. 'You can't be serious!'

I get out of bed and hurry over to the window. The rugby team are throwing the ball around as always, completely oblivious to the fact this is the third time we've all been here.

'No, I'm not doing it,' I say, grabbing a T-shirt and a pair of shorts. 'Not again.'

'Doing what?' Chase says, looking at me in confusion.

'There's no point explaining because you'll just forget again tomorrow!'

'What's that supposed to mean?' He looks offended.

'It's nothing,' I say. 'Everything's fine, OK? I just need some air.'

'OK . . .' he says, sounding completely baffled. 'Here if you need me!' he shouts as I charge out of the room and

162

go straight up to Kellen's. There's a dirty sock on the door handle for some reason. I knock twice and open the door, to see Kellen straddling Rhys, both of them naked.

'Zach!' Kellen squeaks. Rhys just seems to find it funny.

'Sorry!' I yell, quickly shutting the door again.

I must say I'm a little surprised at how he's dealing with this. Third day in a time loop and the first thing on his mind is sex? Last night really must have gone well for them. Not that Rhys would remember, but something must have Kellen in a '*good mood*' this morning.

We need to talk, but hanging around listening at doorways isn't my style, so I turn and head back for the stairs. I'll figure this out myself and then when he's *finished* we can –

'Zach, wait!' Kellen calls.

I turn to see him standing in the open doorway. He's wearing shorts now and is pulling on a basketball jersey so big it must belong to Rhys.

'The fuck was that?' he demands, pulling the door closed behind him. 'Did you not see the sock?'

'The sock?' It's still drooping on the handle. 'Is that supposed to mean something?'

'It means we're *busy*.'

'Since when?' I swear he's making this up.

'Since *always*. Literally everyone knows that. They practically teach it in sex ed!'

'I must have missed that lesson. All *we* got at my last school was Baby Making 101 . . .'

163

'The heterosexual agenda working overtime as always,' Kellen says with a shrug. 'You know, it is weird, isn't it? That this *loop* situation is just happening to us, the gays?'

'Only the two of us,' I say. 'I don't think this is some gay/straight thing.'

'It just seems weird, though. Of all the students this could happen to.'

'I guess?' I say. 'But does it matter? I really don't think I can go through this again!'

'Well, we don't seem to have a choice . . .'

'You seem awfully calm about it.' *Infuriatingly so, actually.*

'First rule of a crisis,' he reminds me.

'Fuck the rules of a crisis!' I cry. 'Who really remains calm during an earthquake? When a plane starts plummeting? When a building catches fire? You really think people actually make their way calmly to the nearest exit?'

'Well, they should,' he says. 'Panicking doesn't solve anything.'

'Neither does immediately hopping on your boyfriend's dick!'

'Watch it.' Maybe he's right. Maybe that was uncalled for.

'Urghhh!' I run my hands through my hair in frustration.

'Zach, chill,' Kellen says, catching my hand to steady me. He fixes his eyes on mine and there's something about the way he does it that makes me find a moment of stillness. Everything is still on fire, of course, but he looks at me like he knows the way to the exit.

'What are we gonna do?' I ask softly.

'Well,' he says, 'you can start by telling me what happened at midnight. Was it the guy in the mask again? He kissed you just like last time?'

'Not exactly.' I groan. 'I pushed Ethan into the lake.'

'You did *what*?' Kellen exclaims. 'You know he can't swim, right?'

'No, I didn't know that! Why does everyone know who can and can't swim?'

'He's scared of water, Zach! He fell off the side of a yacht when he was a kid!'

Truly, only a Hawthorn could have a story of childhood trauma that involves a yacht.

'That's why it's such a big deal that he's captain of the rowing team,' Kellen continues. 'How do you not know this? They ran a story in the *Herald* and everything!'

'Must have been a slow news day,' I scoff. 'Does the *Herald* not have more important things to report? Are they really that obsessed with the lives of teenagers?'

I hear Harrington's car alarm in the distance.

'There's a story now! Students Vandalize Headmaster's Car!'

'I would read that story . . .' Kellen says. 'But OK, focus, Zach. Why would you push Ethan in the lake? Why does your day keep ending in disaster?'

'You mean yours doesn't?'

Kellen seems unwilling to answer that.

'It doesn't matter what happened,' I say, thinking back to that awful conversation with Ethan. Him forcing my hand over his body. I don't want to have to explain that.

'He was just being a dick, OK? Fear of water or not, I promise you he deserved it.'

'But he was OK, right?'

'I don't know,' I say. 'I jumped in after him. The last thing I remember was choking on the water. And then I woke up here all over again.'

'You mean you . . . *died*?'

'I didn't say that.'

Kellen chews on his lip for a moment. 'And no sign of the mystery boy?'

'He never showed,' I say. 'Still as much a mystery as ever.'

'Hmm,' Kellen says, thinking. 'You know, we've gone through prom twice now, and neither of us have seen anyone wearing anything like that gold suit you described –'

'I'm not crazy, Kellen. I know what I saw!'

'I know,' he says in that infuriatingly calm voice. 'But what if someone switched outfits? Halfway through the evening?'

'Exactly what I was thinking,' I say. 'But who? And why?'

'An accident?' Kellen looks thoughtful. 'Maybe someone spilled something?'

The realization hits me like a bucket of pig's blood. 'Josh and Owen! I ruined their outfits that first night!'

Kellen seems confused. 'You did?'

'With the pig's blood!' I must have forgotten to tell him that part. 'It's a long story . . . but *yeah*.'

Suddenly he looks more hopeful. 'So it has to be one of them, right?'

'I mean, it makes sense. Bec was convinced it was Josh who voted for me anyway.'

'And you guys have so much history.'

'We don't have *so much* history.' I sigh. 'We hooked up *one time*.'

'But you like him, right?'

I don't know how to answer that. 'I don't *not* like him,' I say. 'He's cute, yeah, but –'

'But nothing. It has to be him. It's either that or Owen is a closet case.'

I consider that for a moment. 'Do you think he . . . could be?'

'Absolutely not.' Kellen laughs. He doesn't even need to think about it. 'Even in his rainbow outfit, I have never seen someone so unbendingly straight. It's Josh. I'm certain of it. Maybe it's time for you two to have a little heart-to-heart?'

'I'm not good at those!'

'What are you good at?'

OK, *ouch*.

'All right, fine,' I finally say. 'I'll talk to him. But I'm not doing a "*heart-to-heart*". We'll just have a normal conversation. Like two regular guys.'

'Don't forget to say *no homo*.' Kellen rolls his eyes. 'You know you're allowed to talk about your feelings, right? You don't have to be this emotionless robot all the time.'

'Emotionless robot?' I say. 'I'm plenty in tune with my emotions!'

'You're about as tuned as a grand piano that just fell from the Empire State.'

I scowl, but I know that there's a little bit of truth in that. 'I'll talk to him,' I say. 'Just give me a couple of hours.'

'Take your time,' he says. 'I've got some business of my own to attend to.'

'Business?' I look at the dirty sock still hanging on the door. '*Oh* . . . business.'

'Let me know how you get on?' He turns back towards his room. 'We're in this together, Zach. Everything's going to be OK.'

'Hey, Zach,' Owen says as I approach him and Josh on the grass outside. My palms are already sweaty and I haven't even said anything yet.

'Hey! Good morning!' I say way too enthusiastically. *What are you doing, Zach?*

'Someone's excited,' Josh says. I remember him saying something like that in the shower.

'I mean . . . it's our last day, right? Of course I'm excited!'

Owen laughs. 'It's good to see this side of you, Zach. You normally walk around campus like some emotionless robot.'

OK, that's the *second* time I've been called that. How am I only just learning this is what they all think of me?

'Well, speaking of emotions . . .' I say. 'Mind if I steal Josh for a second?'

'That sounds ominous,' Josh teases. 'Not gonna confess your undying love for me, are you? If you wanna play the beast-with-two-backs again, then just say so!'

This is a nightmare. How am I supposed to have a heart-to-heart with the class clown? Even when we hooked up, he was making jokes during. Though I have to admit I did kind of like that. It eased the pressure a little. Made it seem a lot less serious.

'Please take him,' Owen says. 'I'm begging you. He's doing my head in.'

'He's just annoyed that the gay boy wants to talk fashion,' Josh retorts.

'I just want you to make a decision! He's being indecisive about tonight's outfit.'

'I'm not being indecisive! I'm being *thorough*.'

'Well, actually,' I say, 'that's exactly what I want to talk about.'

'Why didn't you say so!' Josh jumps to his feet excitedly. 'I'm always here to talk fashion! Intending to pull a look tonight, are we?'

'Not exactly,' I say, thinking of my plain white suit.

Owen lies back with his head in his hands and shuts his eyes, taking in the warm sunshine. He's pretending to be grateful for the peace and quiet, but I know he loves Josh really. Because that's how we all feel. We pretend to be annoyed by his stupid jokes, but I've even seen him make Tiffany crack a smile. Life at Oakbrook would be a whole lot less fun without him.

'So?' Josh says, once we're out of earshot. 'What fabulous outfits are we talking?'

'Yours,' I say. 'I know what you're wearing tonight. It's a jester's outfit, right?'

'Oh, that absolute gibbon.' He glances back at Owen. 'I told him not to tell anyone!'

'He didn't tell me anything,' I say. 'But there is another choice, right? Something else you were thinking of?'

'Yeah, but it's too *serious*,' Josh says. 'I think everyone's expecting me to do something a bit more fun.'

'Why, what is it?'

'I can't ruin the surprise!'

'But it's . . . important.'

'Oh yes, *very* important,' he says. 'Zach, what's really going on here?'

'It's complicated,' I say. 'But did you see the results of the leavers' poll?'

'Oh my God!' he says. 'Hottest boy! I knew it was you that voted for me!'

'Wait, what?' I say. 'I thought *you* voted for *me*!'

'Why would I do that?'

'OK, wow,' I say. 'Why don't you tell me how you really feel?'

He laughs at that. 'You already know I think you're hot, Zach. I didn't need to tell you in some anonymous poll. You think I give out love bites to just anyone?'

'I didn't want the love bite! That's how people found out!'

'You expect them to believe we went into the boathouse to do what – a jigsaw? Though I do like jigsaws.' He bites his lip. 'The way the pieces slot together so *effortlessly*.'

'Oh my God –' I groan – 'can you be serious for one second?'

'Hmm.' He thinks about it. 'No, I really don't think I can.'

I want to be annoyed, but I can't help but smile. Maybe this makes things easier.

'So you really didn't vote for me?' I say. 'It seriously wasn't you?'

'You would've been my second choice,' he says. 'But no, I voted for someone else. It was a wasted vote, really. I went for one of the straight boys.'

I glance across at Owen, lazing in the sunshine. 'You voted for him, didn't you?'

'I wasn't about to let my bestie get zero votes,' he says. 'These girls are *blind* if they don't see what a catch he is.' I think about Chase then, and regret not voting for him. 'But don't you dare tell him! I want him to think it was one of the girls!'

'OK, I promise. And your backup outfit?'

I need to know for certain.

'Why are you so obsessed with what I'm going to wear, Zach?'

'I can't explain why. I just need you to trust me.'

He looks at me, confused for a moment, and sighs. 'I really don't get why this could possibly be so important, but . . . I was gonna dress up as Obama.'

'*What?*'

'Michelle's husband.'

'Yes, I know who he is.' I laugh. 'Why on earth were you going to dress as Obama?!'

'It's a masquerade!' he says. 'You're supposed to come in disguise!'

'Yeah, but not like *that*! I thought you were worried about it being too serious?'

'He's a politician! That's ultra serious!'

'Oh my God!' Literally only Josh would come up with this.

'So you weren't going to dress in a gold suit then?'

'Ew,' he says. 'No, Zach. What on earth would possess me to do that?'

'It wasn't Josh,' I say, catching Kellen at the main door to the school. He was upstairs for so long that I'm surprised he's not limping.

'Are you sure?' he says, raising an eyebrow.

'Hundred per cent,' I say. 'He went the best-friend route and voted Owen for hottest boy. Wanted him to think one of the girls did it. And he doesn't have anything gold.'

'Huh.' Kellen frowns. 'I really thought it was him. But if not, that means . . . *Owen*?'

'It can't be Owen!' I protest. 'He doesn't raise so much as a blip on my gaydar.'

Kellen rolls his eyes. 'Gaydar isn't real, though, is it? It's just a bunch of lazy judgements based on stereotypes.'

'I think it's a bit more than that,' I argue. 'There's just that indescribable *something*. Take Rhys, for example. He's not exactly one with the fairies, but I absolutely knew he was queer before he came out. And I think you did too! That's why you pursued him! Gaydar isn't real when straight people claim they have it. But us gays? We know. We just know.'

'Well,' Kellen says, 'we should at least rule Owen out properly, right? He's the only other person with a reason to switch outfits. He's our only lead now, Zach.'

'I suppose so,' I say. 'But I can't have another *heart-to-heart* right now. Talking to Josh was one thing. We have *history* as you oh-so-coyly put it. How am I supposed to ask Owen if he's secretly gay *and* if he fancies me?'

'Well, good job I came up with a Plan B then, isn't it?' Kellen smiles smugly. 'If he *is* your mystery kisser, that gold suit should be hanging up in his wardrobe.'

I have to admit this is a really good idea.

'So you think we should break into Owen's room? What if we get caught?'

'The day's just going to repeat anyway! Consequences don't matter!' Kellen beams. 'Besides, we don't need to *break* in.' He holds up a key.

So he wasn't with Rhys the whole time. That's where he's been.

'How did you get that?' I say.

He grins. 'I have my ways. Come on. While everyone's still at lunch . . .'

'How do you know which room is his?' I ask as we climb the final flight of Hawthorn stairs, reaching the top floor. I honestly don't think I've *ever* been up here.

'I've been in *all* the boys' rooms,' Kellen says. 'I'm a social butterfly.'

'That's true. I remember you brought me a house plant back in first year.'

'You seemed homesick! I thought you might need a project.'

'You said our friendship would blossom as long as the plant did.'

Kellen raises an eyebrow. 'And how long did it take you to kill it?'

'A week,' I say. 'Me and plants do *not* get along.'

He laughs at that. 'Maybe we'd have stayed closer if you'd done a better job of watering it.'

'Are you really gonna blame a *plant* for us drifting apart?'

'No,' he says. 'We've just had very different lives here. I wish we'd stayed close, though. I honestly mean that.'

'Well, be careful what you wish for. What if we get stuck in this loop forever?'

'We won't,' he says, stopping by one of the dorm rooms. 'Every story has an ending.'

'Is this it?' I say, trying the door to see if it's already open. It's locked.

'This is it,' he confirms, taking the little key out of his pocket and holding it up. 'You wanna do the honours?'

'I guess,' I say, taking the key and unlocking the door with a click.

Doing this feels necessary, but I still can't help thinking that what we're doing is terribly *wrong*. I'd hate it if somebody went snooping around in my room – not that I really have anything to hide.

The room is altogether unremarkable, barely different from mine. The only thing that sets it apart is that it has a much better view. Unsurprisingly, Hawthorn have all the rooms that look out over the lake. Though I suppose, from the Sycamore side, we do get to watch the rugby team, so there are some perks . . .

'So, is Owen top or bottom?' I ask.

'I can't say I've given it much thought,' Kellen says, looking at me weirdly. 'There is a certain masc energy about him, but –'

'The bunks, Kellen!'

'*Ohhhh*,' he says. 'Bottom, obviously. Owen is a conventional neat-and-tidy person. Look, his bed's made perfectly, the corners tucked, the pillows fluffed. The top one, however . . .'

'Who's his room-mate?' I say, looking at the messy bunk.

'I dunno, one of the rugby boys?' Kellen shrugs.

I'm so glad I don't have to share with a straight guy. I really lucked out with that one. Things could so easily have been different.

Kellen nods to the wardrobe. 'Ready to find out if Owen is your mystery man?'

'I guess.' I sigh, walking over to grab the handles. 'I bet it's not him,' I say, flinging the doors open. 'See . . .'

We both fall speechless as the sun strikes an elegantly cut suit, setting it shimmering in the light. Gold fabric that looks way too familiar. By pulling open those wardrobe doors, we pull Owen out of the closet.

'That's it,' I say, reaching out to touch the fabric. 'I can't believe it.'

'Me neither,' Kellen says, but his voice is strained.

'Are you OK?' I ask. There's a flash of something on his face that suggests there's something he's not telling me, like his brain is working overtime.

'I'm fine.' He reaches for a familiar mask on the top shelf of the wardrobe. 'And this?'

'Yeah,' I say, taking it from him. 'That's it. It was actually Owen.'

'Maybe it's not as surprising as we thought,' Kellen muses. 'He's always been a bit of an outsider, always kept his cards close to his chest. The Hawthorn kids are constantly awful to him. Maybe he thought coming out would make things even worse?'

'Maybe,' I say. 'But something about this doesn't make sense . . .'

'Could it be that you're disappointed?' Kellen says cautiously. 'I mean, you were hoping it was someone else, right? You were still hoping it was Cameron?'

'Maybe,' I say. 'Owen isn't exactly my type . . .'

'Well,' he says, 'perhaps that's all you need to know? Just because Owen kissed you, Zach, that doesn't mean he's *the one*.'

'True,' I say. 'But I kinda thought figuring this out might . . . I dunno . . . break the spell?'

Kellen shakes his head. 'We're in this loop together. Surely whatever we have to do to get out of it has to be something to do with both of us, right?'

'I suppose,' I say, feeling more lost now than ever. At least before I had an objective – uncover the stranger, secure true love's kiss. But that's not going to work now. Not with Owen. I can't just force myself to like him like that.

'Do you wanna go down and join them?' Kellen says, pointing out of the window. The rest of Sycamore are heading towards our base. 'Ethan won't get by us a *third* time.'

'Can we just skip it?' I say. 'Hawthorn are only going to win anyway.'

Kellen grins. 'I was kinda hoping you'd say that.'

'You were? But everyone will be wondering where we are.'

I take out my phone. There's already a load of **Where are you?** messages from Chase.

'Does it matter?' says Kellen. 'The day's just gonna loop over again anyway.'

'Do you really think so?'

'I don't know,' he says. 'But there's truly nothing I'd rather do less than play Capture the Flag for a third time. Do you trust me? I have a much better idea.'

'Two–one to Hawthorn!'

Miss Madzikanda's distant voice booms over the loudspeaker. The game is going ahead and our not being there has made absolutely no difference. The scoring is the same as always. Our team are no worse off without us.

'I've always wanted to do this,' Kellen says, opening the door to the boathouse. It smells like old wood and sawdust, with a hint of teenage sex. Though I wonder if I'm imagining that part. The reputation of this place precedes it.

'I'm not having sex with you,' I say, peering in.

'You should be so lucky,' he shoots back as we slip inside.

'So what are we doing?' I ask, looking around the racks of racing boats.

'Isn't it obvious?' he says, going over to a little wooden rowing boat bobbing up and down in the water. 'I always wanted to join the rowing team . . .'

'And yet you didn't,' I say.

'Because they take all the fun out of it. Correct posture . . . synchronization . . . health and safety . . .'

'Because nothing says fun like drowning.'

'It's just a little rowing boat,' Kellen says. 'What's the worst that could happen?'

'You do remember I almost drowned twelve hours ago, right?'

I remember the horrifying feeling of being trapped underneath the water.

'Of course,' he says, peering into the lake. 'Only you could drown in something so shallow.'

I look down, and in the sunlight I can see right to the bottom. Kellen's right: it's no more than a metre deep. Weird. I could have sworn it was far deeper than that last night.

'Besides,' Kellen continues, 'if you fall in, I'll jump in to save you.'

'My hero,' I say sarcastically, reluctantly climbing into the boat.

I sit facing him, watching as he grapples with the oars for a few moments.

'You have no idea what you're doing, do you?'

'I've seen this *plenty* of times,' he says. 'You just sort of have to . . .' He sticks his tongue out with concentration as he tries to get the boat to move, and eventually, with great difficulty, he finally pushes us out from the boathouse on to the water.

'See?' he says. 'It's easy!'

'And yet you make it look so difficult,' I tease as we begin to glide over the water, sunshine dappling across the rippled surface, reeds swaying in the gentle wash of the boat. I hate to admit it, but Kellen is right: it would have been a shame to leave school having never done this.

'It's hot out here,' he says, pausing to take off his shirt. Beads of sweat glisten on his skin, and I feel myself staring. As annoying as Kellen is, he's cute. You'd have to be blind not to see that. Maybe if him and Rhys hadn't ended up together . . .?

I watch as he fiddles with his phone for a moment before sighing and shoving it back in his pocket.

'Everything OK?'

'It's nothing,' he says.

What is he hiding?

'I'm so sick of these nails,' he says, changing the subject. 'If I'd known I was gonna be stuck with them *forever*, I'd have done a better job. See?' He holds his hand up so I can get a better look. 'This one's already chipped.'

I take his hand in mine as I study it. We make eye contact for a moment before I quickly pull away. *Get it together, Zach. He has a boyfriend.*

'So what do we do now?' I say as we reach the other side

of the lake. There's a little wooden platform that juts out over the water from the edge of the woodland, the trees swaying gently in the breeze.

'Nothing,' he says, tying up the boat and climbing out. 'We do absolutely nothing.'

'I don't understand.'

Kellen sighs. 'I don't know what the hell is going on here, but I'm starting to suspect that us being at prom just makes everything worse.'

'What do you mean?'

'Think about it. Everything bad that's happened has happened because of one of us. The pig's blood on the yearbook. Ethan in the lake. That embarrassing proposal. We're the reason everything keeps going to shit. I think we just need to stay out of the way. Stop messing everything up. It's like the butterfly effect. One tiny change can completely alter the course of history! You go back in time, tread on the wrong leaf, and suddenly humans have three eyes and can breathe underwater.'

'Why would we have three eyes just because you trod on a leaf?'

Kellen sighs. 'I think you're missing the point.'

'I see what you're saying,' I say. 'But have you not noticed how everything seems to want to run the same way, no matter what we do? We can ruffle a thousand butterfly wings and yet we wind up having the exact same conversations with our friends –'

'Another point to Sycamore!' Madzikanda's voice booms. 'Two–two!'

'— you see? Even the game is going the same way without us.'

'So what's your point?' Kellen says.

'Well, if we can do whatever we want and it doesn't have an impact, it means we're free of consequences, right? Like, if we do something awful but nobody remembers it, does it even matter? We could become supervillains and inflict pain on everyone, and then wake up the next day like saints!'

'Should I be worried that you went from zero to *supervillains inflicting pain on everyone* in the space of about three seconds?'

I huff. 'I'm not saying I *want* to inflict pain on everyone. But we could, right?'

'Well, no . . . because *we'd* remember, wouldn't we? We'd have that on our conscience forever. And, even if we didn't, I think karma would catch up with us eventually. Karma remembers, even when people don't.'

'Karma isn't real, though,' I say. 'It's just a nonsense concept people use to make themselves feel better about their choices. Look at all the worst people in the world getting away with stuff – murderers and dictators and Elon Musk. Where's their karma?'

'I don't know,' he says. 'But maybe it's still coming to them. How can you say karma is nonsense when we're stuck here living in nonsense? If this loop is real, then who says karma isn't? Or heaven and hell? Or whatever else people choose to believe in. "There are more things in heaven and earth, Horatio, than are dreamt of in your philosophy" – and we're quite literally living proof of that!'

I shake my head. 'There's a scientific explanation for everything. Maybe we're just dreaming all of this? What if it's a joint hallucination? Or how do I know that you're even here at all – you could be a figment of my imagination?'

'You really believe that?' Kellen scoffs. 'You really think this is just some dream.'

'I dunno.' I shrug. 'I'm just saying that there's probably a rational explanation. Just one we haven't figured out yet. Maybe the planets are just ... fucking with the timeline.'

'I'm sorry, did you just say *the planets are just fucking with the timeline*?'

I laugh. 'Shut up!'

Kellen holds his hands out in front of him, turning them over, as if examining them. 'Do you think we're getting older?'

'Huh?'

'While we're stuck here, repeating.'

'It's only the third day. I don't think the signs of ageing are gonna show just yet.'

'But do you think we're three days older than we were?'

'I don't know,' I say. 'That would mean I'm, like, two days from turning eighteen.'

'I'd forgotten you're not eighteen yet,' Kellen says. 'July twentieth, right?'

'Right.'

'So let's pretend we *are* stuck here for years. Do you think we'd actually start ageing? Like, we'll suddenly be middle-aged men and our friends won't notice?'

'I dunno,' I say. 'But I really don't want to think about being stuck here for years, Kellen.'

But Kellen isn't listening. He's pulled forward the waistband of his shorts and is peering into his underwear.

'*What* are you doing?'

'Just checking to see if it's grown.' He shrugs. 'Maybe if we stay here, we'll both end up really well hung.'

'I can't believe that's where your mind went.'

'You can't say you hadn't considered it!'

'I really hadn't.'

Madzikanda's voice erupts in the distance. 'Looks like we have our winners!'

'I'm sure Tiffany is thrilled,' Kellen says with a roll of his eyes.

'Three–two to Sycamore!'

Both of our mouths fall open.

'This is a joke, right? Sycamore wins when we're not playing?' I say. 'Come on! We're not *that* bad!'

'This is what I'm saying, Zach. We really kind of are . . .' Kellen glances down at his phone again. 'I think if we stay out of everyone's way today, then everything will be fine. It's not like we're missing anything – and it's not like anyone's missing us . . .'

'Why would you say that?' I bridle. 'Of course people are missing us.'

'They'll get over it,' he says. 'I think we should hide out for a bit. It's for the best. We've already had our prom *twice*, Zach.'

'You aren't seriously suggesting we skip prom?' I say, amazed. 'What about Rhys? You can't stand him up without a date. And what about the prank? We can't just sit by and let them do it again. They're gonna go after *someone*.'

'Just send out a few warning texts. Put a post up on Instagram.'

'But doesn't that still count as interfering? Even if we aren't there?'

Kellen huffs in exasperation. 'So don't then. I don't know . . .'

'It just doesn't feel right,' I say. 'Skipping everything. We can't just opt out of life.'

Kellen thinks for a moment. 'What if I told you we can keep an eye on prom without being there?'

'Like secret cameras?' I raise an eyebrow.

'No,' he says. 'Not like secret cameras, you weirdo . . .'

'What then?'

'Do you trust me?'

'Absolutely not.'

'That's what I thought. Come on.'

'This is ridiculous.'

We're hidden behind one of the bushes that fringe the lawn out in front of the school building. Everyone else is gathered by the fountain, admiring each other's outfits. Josh is doing twirls in his jester costume for Bec and Chase.

They seem happy, and it feels wrong to be hiding here rather than celebrating with them. I sent a message to the group chat with a lie about having to leave due to a family emergency, then a follow-up to say it was a false alarm, but that I couldn't make it back in time for prom. This day very well may continue to loop, but I didn't want them worrying about me and spoiling their fun tonight. Even if tomorrow they have no memory of any of this.

'I can't believe he's been secretly gay this whole time,' Kellen says, pointing out Owen in the crowd. 'He's dressed like a Pride flag and somehow we didn't see it.'

'I honestly *still* don't see it,' I say. I guess my gaydar wasn't as accurate as I thought. 'I just can't believe he's had feelings for me this whole time and never said anything?'

'Is the pot calling the kettle black?' Kellen raises an eyebrow.

'It's different with me and Cameron!' I say. 'It's more complicated.'

'Because you're making it complicated,' he replies flatly.

'Just make it go away!' Tiffany yells then, stomping up and down as she furiously begs her father to save Ethan from the humiliation of having his pictures leaked.

'Do you not think he seems just a little bit *too chill* about this whole thing?' Kellen whispers, watching him. I look across at Ethan. Just like the first time, and the second, he really does seem unbothered. 'I hate to say it – like, I don't wanna blame the victim, but . . .'

'You think he might have leaked them himself?'

Kellen shrugs. 'It's possible, right? All he cares about is boosting his social-media following. And we know this will do that.'

'Then why is Tiffany making such a big deal about it?' I say.

'Because she thinks it'll ruin *her* reputation. She doesn't care about Ethan.'

'That tracks,' I say. 'But I don't know if I believe Ethan would do it himself. There are other ways to grow his profile. Those pictures are on the internet forever.'

'I'm not sure he's thinking that far ahead,' Kellen says. 'But if he didn't do this? And this was someone's revenge plot? I think it's safe to say it's backfired.'

We stay hidden, listening to Harrington's droning speech, until everyone has gone inside. Once the coast is clear, Kellen leads me through a side door, up a winding staircase and down a long, narrow corridor. The last of the sunset disappears through the arched stained-glass windows as nightfall descends upon us. There's so much of this place I've never explored. I guess I thought I'd get round to it, and now we're out of time. Well, sort of.

'Do you ever think about how many secrets there must be within these walls? How many hundreds of people have studied here? And I bet every single one of them was hiding something.'

'What kind of secrets?' I say, struggling to follow Kellen's train of thought. Is he still talking about Ethan?

'The usual kind,' he replies, spinning round on his heel and walking backwards so he can face me. 'Because humans are predictable. It's always about love. Think about it: you can go back thousands of years, pick literally any time, any place, and the stories are all the same. Ancient Egypt or Mesopotamia, the first days of Babylon or the last moments of Pompeii. People were still acting out their silly love stories while they were dying of bubonic plague. Think about Hadrian: he's the perfect example. Did you know he was gay?'

'The guy with the wall?'

'The greatest Roman emperor to ever live, Zach. But yeah, sure, "*the guy with the wall*". He was madly in love with a hottie called Antinous. So much so that when the poor boy drew his last breath Hadrian plunged the entire empire into a state of mourning. All that power and he used it to mark the loss of the man he loved. They say that love conquers all, but I don't think it does. I just think humans are hardwired to be unable to think about anything else. The greatest battles, the greatest technological advancements, every single thing that has happened always comes back to one thing – the endless pursuit of love.'

'OK,' I say. 'But what's your point? What does any of this have to do with us?'

'I'm just saying that we could probably spend a decade trapped in this same day and there'd still be more secrets to uncover here. We all think we're unique. Whatever love story we have going on, we convince ourselves we're the first person to have ever experienced it.'

'But we *are* the first people to experience this,' I say. 'There are literally no records, throughout all human history, of anyone *ever* being stuck in a time loop.'

'Because anyone that ever told that story would have been written off as a whack job. In the past, they'd have probably burned them as a witch!'

'So, wait, you think this has happened before?'

'Yeah,' Kellen says. 'I mean, if it's happening to us, why not someone else? We're really not that special, Zach. In tens of thousands of years of humanity, you really think we're the only two to experience this? Do you know how unlikely that is? You'd be more likely to be hit by lightning while holding a winning lottery ticket and standing on one leg.'

I frown. 'I still don't understand where you're going with this.'

'I don't know,' he says. 'I just think this place has secrets.'

'Like whoever leaked those photos of Ethan?'

'Exactly!' he says. 'And I bet there's at least *one* secret romance going on right under our noses. You just know that somebody's secretly in love with their best friend. Someone else carrying a torch for an ex. Even the teachers probably have their secrets. Imagine what Harrington gets up to!'

He takes another left and we come to a dead end – there are no windows here, just a quiet corner in the shadows.

'So what exactly are we doing?' I say, looking at Kellen in confusion.

'Everyone has secrets,' he says. 'And this is one of mine.'

He points up at the ceiling. I hadn't noticed it, but there's a small hatch above us, and, as I lift my hand towards it, I can feel the faintest draught creeping through from outside. It must lead out on to the roof.

'How did you find this?' I say as he reaches up to push the hatch open, a cool breeze rushing through the gap.

'Honestly? I went looking for it. I'd always hoped that an old building like Oakbrook would have some secret dungeon or hidden door tucked behind a bookcase. A place where a forbidden club used to meet in the 1850s. A time capsule left behind and forgotten.'

'And you do realize this is real life, not some fantasy novel? Secret dungeons don't really exist, Kellen. Every building has a blueprint – there's no way you could hide something like that. It's like in *Casper the Friendly Ghost* when they "find" the secret chamber, and it literally has these gigantic windows that would be completely obvious from outside. Did they never just think to take a lap round the building? It's *ridiculous*.'

'Wow, remind me *never* to go to the movies with you, you killjoy,' Kellen says. 'Anyway, you're wrong.' He gestures to the opening. 'Because here's our secret door.'

'It's not a *secret door*,' I say with a laugh. 'It's just a maintenance hatch. Somebody's gotta get up there to clean the leaves out of the gutters.'

'I could have shared this with someone else, you know . . .'

'Fine. It's a secret door. You're not really gonna go up there, though, are you?'

'No, *I'm* not,' he says. '*We* are.'

'There's no way,' I say as Kellen pulls himself up and scrambles through. 'Have you got a death wish or something?'

'Course not,' he says, peering back down at me. 'It's not like we can die anyway.'

'What?' I say, taking a little step back from him. 'Why would you say that?'

'We're stuck in a time loop,' he replies cheerfully.

'That doesn't mean we can't die,' I say. 'Where would you get that idea?'

'It just makes sense,' he says. 'The day starts over no matter what. Besides, you drowned in the lake, didn't you?'

'I didn't drown!' I protest. 'I was in the process of drowning.'

'What's the difference?'

'I was still alive when the clock struck midnight!'

'Are you sure?'

I hate to say that I'm not.

'See,' he says, noting my silence. 'We definitely can't die.'

'We don't know that!' I protest. 'We don't know anything!'

'Am I going to have to prove it to you?'

'Don't you dare!'

'Well then, you'll just have to come up and stop me,' Kellen says, disappearing from view. 'I'll give you to the count of ten.'

'This isn't funny!' I call back, but he ignores me.

'Ten . . . nine . . . eight . . .'

'Stop it,' I say, and even though he can't see me I cross my arms to make it very clear that I'm not playing his little game.

'Seven . . . six . . . five . . .'

'Kellen, this is ridiculous,' I say. 'Don't even joke. You can't risk your life just because of something you saw in a movie.'

'Four ... three ... two ...'

'OK!' I say, jumping up and trying to lift myself through the opening. I struggle, and sort of expect Kellen to grab me and pull me up, but he doesn't. I scramble for a moment, and all I can see is the black slate of the roof offset against an endless canvas of twinkling stars. I can't see Kellen anywhere. I start to worry he might have –

'What took you so long?' His hands grip me from behind and pull me up.

'Don't do that,' I say, hitting him as I sit on the cool slate. 'I thought you'd jumped.'

'And miss the look on your face?' He grins.

'I'm serious,' I say. 'If anything happened to you ...'

'Nothing's gonna happen to me,' he says. 'But you must be at least a little bit curious? The rules of time and physics have gone out the window. Aren't you even slightly interested in what would happen?'

'If you died?' I say. 'No. Funnily enough, not even in the slightest.'

Kellen laughs at that. 'Chill. It's not like I'm suicidal or anything. I just can't help wondering what would happen if we pulled a Thelma and Louise. If we *"keep on driving"* and both jump off the roof right now, this second?'

'Kellen,' I say, 'don't even joke. Maybe you're right; maybe the day would just start over. But are you *really* willing to risk it?'

'Well, what if it was just one of us? Then the day would still have to restart, right?'

'I don't want to talk about this,' I reply, 'and honestly you're making me wanna get down from here. The roof isn't the place to discuss this . . .'

'All right, all right. It's not like I was gonna do it!'

'Good,' I say sternly. 'Because I'd rather be stuck here indefinitely than see something happen to you!'

'Aw,' he says, smiling. 'You like me.'

'Oh, whatever! I'd feel the same if it was Tiffany! I just don't wanna see you splattered all over Huckleberry. And what if the fall didn't kill you? It'd take *forever* for an ambulance to get here! What then? You'd be stuck writhing around with two broken legs!'

'You worry too much,' says Kellen. 'Here, chill out. Let me show you something.'

'Where are you going?' I say, watching him climb the pitch of the roof.

'Just trust me,' he says, disappearing over the top.

'Can you slow down?' I call. 'You're like Spider-Man.'

'But which one?' he asks, his head popping up over the ridge.

'Miles Morales, obviously.'

'Because I'm Black?'

'No,' I say with a laugh. 'Because he's the best one!'

'Hmm,' he says. 'Well, you are right about that. I'm just surprised, honestly. I would have pegged you for an Andrew Garfield kinda guy.'

'Nah,' I say. 'Morales is the real hero.'

'Well, I'm glad we agree. Guess you're not as basic as I thought.' He disappears over the roof again as I nervously try to follow. On all fours, of course. I'm not risking anything.

'Where are we going?' I say, cautious with my footing.

'Here,' he says. 'Look.'

I climb over the ridge to see what he's pointing to.

It's the giant skylight over the dining hall. We can see right down into prom.

'Wow,' I say, marvelling at the view. Tonight the hall is decorated entirely in blue and white – Sycamore's colours. It looks incredible. Way better than the tacky red and gold.

'This way we can keep an eye on everything, make sure nothing goes awry.'

'And if things *do* go awry?' I ask.

Kellen shrugs. 'We'll cross that bridge *if* we come to it,' he says.

I see him searching for Rhys in the crowd. He watches him longingly for a few moments: I can tell he wants to be down there with him. Is hiding up here really the best course of action?

I look for my friends. They're by the yearbook, and Bec is already writing something. Taylor Swift lyrics undoubtedly. Even from up here, Chase's reaction confirms it. I can almost *hear* him just by watching his hand gestures. '*I just thought maybe you'd write something more meaningful.*'

I watch her thrust the pen at him. '*Come on then, Plato, your turn.*'

Something about watching them act out this silly little play stings a little. I should be down there with them. I still have FOMO, even if I have done this twice before.

I look around the crowd again. I can't help but search for Cameron.

'You really like him, don't you?'

Kellen must have noticed me staring. I don't answer.

'You know it's not too late, right?'

'I just don't wanna get my hopes up again . . .' I say. 'Owen is my secret admirer. And Ethan said Cameron isn't into me anyway.'

'Ethan is full of shit.'

'Then why did he say it?'

'To get into your head! To ruin your chances with his brother! He hates that me and Rhys are a thing. Imagine how he feels about the idea of you being with Cameron?'

I sigh. 'I just don't know what to believe any more!'

'Well,' Kellen says, 'I don't know what's going on inside Cameron's head. But, for what it's worth, I think you're a catch. He'd be an idiot not to like you.'

'Wow,' I say. 'I think that's actually the nicest thing you've ever said to me.'

'Well, don't get used to it!' He laughs, lying down on the slanted roof.

I lie down next to him, and we don't say anything more for a moment. We just stay there in companionable silence, looking up at the stars. If you listen carefully, you can just about make out the music from the DJ below. It's muffled, like someone playing music in the next room.

'What is this song?' Kellen says as if reading my thoughts.

'"Baba O'Riley",' I say, air-drumming along with the beat. 'It's a seventies song. From one of my all-time favourite movies.'

'Oh yeah?' Kellen says. 'Is it an animated movie by any chance?'

'I do watch other things, you know.'

'You could have fooled me!' he teases, putting on a mock accent to mimic mine. '"The Fox and the Hound *is the saddest film ever made!* Pocahontas *deserved more than one Oscar!* Avatar *ripped off* FernGully!"' He grins. 'All you ever talk about is animated movies!'

'Well, this one isn't animated. *The Girl Next Door.* It's about a teenage porn star.'

'Of course it is,' he says, rolling his eyes. 'I'm just surprised it's not *The* Boy *Next Door.* That sounds more up your street, Zach.'

'It's not like that,' I say. 'It's sex positive. It subverts the audience's expectations. But, more than anything, it's beautifully romantic.' I reach across and put my hand on his heart. 'It gets you right here.'

'Sounds intense,' Kellen says. I feel his heart quicken.

'Yeah, well . . .' I hesitate, withdrawing my hand. 'Maybe you should watch it.'

'Maybe *we* should watch it,' he says. 'It's been a while since we had a movie night.'

'Sure,' I say, looking across at him with a smile.

The song rolls through its closing bars before shifting

through to an eighties track. I think the DJ is deliberately pulling music from all eras. They're obsessed with the past at this place. Oakbrook is always about looking back. Never about looking forward.

I glance back at Kellen to see that he's shut his eyes. His head is gently bopping from side to side as he listens to the music.

I shut my eyes too and breathe in the cool night air. Kellen's right. It *is* nice to take a moment of peace, away from everything. I let myself enjoy it for a minute or two. Even if we are going to have to go back round again tomorrow. Right here, right now, it almost feels like everything is back to normal.

That is until I hear the sudden sound of a crack. I open my eyes to see Kellen on his feet. But he's not *just* on his feet: he's standing on the skylight.

'Kellen?' I say, scrambling to stand up. 'What are you doing?'

'I wasn't sure if it could hold my weight,' he says, taking another tentative step forward. 'But I think it can. Look, it's fine.'

'I heard it crack,' I say. I can't see anything, but I *definitely* heard it.

'You worry too much,' he says, walking along the glass. Who knows how thick it is? But it's the only thing between him and a twenty-metre drop. I'm not the only one who's noticed either. Some of the students below are looking up now and pointing.

'Kellen, come off there!' I say. 'What happened to not

interfering with prom? This is *definitely* interfering with prom!'

'How is it interfering?' he says with a laugh. 'Zach, it's fine, look –' He jumps, and I feel my heart stop as he bends his knees and lands.

His eyes go wide as we both hear the distinct sound of another crack.

I expect the glass to break beneath him, but it doesn't. It actually seems to be holding his weight. He blows out his cheeks with relief.

'Told you,' he says, taking another step forward just as the whole thing shatters.

'Kellen!' I yelp, rushing forward to try to grab him.

'Zach!' he calls as his hand slips through my fingers.

I hear the deathly screeching of students below as glass rains around them. The sound of a table breaking. Looking through the broken skylight, I see the yearbook on the floor. Kellen lies beside it.

'Kellen!' I scream down at his motionless body.

It's OK. He can't die. He said so . . . He's fine, he has to be.

And that's when I see a Sycamore banner go up in flames. One of the candelabras has been knocked over as people run in all directions.

Flames begin to engulf the room, chaos ensues and –

'Zach?' Kellen says, shaking me awake. 'Are you having a nightmare?'

'Huh?' I say, disorientated. We're still on the rooftop. 'What happened?'

'You fell asleep.' He chuckles. 'You were out for, like, an hour and a half.'

'I was?' I say, rubbing my eyes. 'But that all felt so real.'

'What did?' he says, tilting his head, intrigued.

I look across at the skylight. 'You weren't planning on standing on that, were you?'

'On the glass?' he says. 'Zach, that's like a twenty-metre drop – do you think I'm insane?'

'No,' I say. 'Good, I mean . . . I'm just glad you're OK.'

He smiles. 'You missed the crowning ceremony. Tiffany and Ethan again.'

'No surprises there,' I say. 'So nothing's *gone awry*? The pig's blood?'

'It's still hanging,' he replies, searching it out. 'So far so good.'

But then he looks down at his phone again, as if expecting something. He's been doing this all day. There's something he's not telling me. I decide to face it head-on.

'What's up? You seem kinda distracted.'

'Huh?' He looks back up from his phone. 'Distracted how?'

'You keep checking that like you're expecting something.'

'Oh,' he says, clicking his phone to lock it. 'It's nothing. I guess it's just this whole situation. Sometimes I think I wouldn't mind if we were stuck here forever.'

That takes me aback. 'Why would you say that? What could possibly make you want to stay here? We should already be graduates!'

He pauses for a moment. 'You know how people say love is unconditional?'

'Yeah?' I have no idea where he's going with this.

'Sometimes I wonder if that's really true.' He leans back on his hands and stares up at the sky. 'Because life is full of conditions, isn't it? And when those conditions aren't met? People leave, people walk out, people change their mind.'

'Is that something that happened to you?' I ask as delicately as I can.

'Nobody walked out on me,' he says. 'But Dad's no longer with us.'

'I'm sorry,' I say. He's never spoken about this before. 'I never had a dad. My mum adopted as a single mother. Rare at the time. Rare even now. But she did it.'

'What was that like?' he says, turning towards me.

'Honestly? Mum was more than enough. I guess I never knew any different.'

'I was too young to really remember much about my dad. But he definitely left a hole. I still miss him. And that's what I'm saying. Maybe it's better to be stuck here because, whatever happens, we won't lose anyone we care about.'

'You're not gonna lose anyone, Kellen.'

'But what if I am?' he says, his voice cracking. 'Look.'

He hands me his phone. There's a new message.

I see the words *It's not you, it's me* and don't need to read anything more.

'Rhys?' I say.

Kellen doesn't say anything, just nods, barely holding back his tears.

'This isn't the first time this has happened, is it?'

'I just thought if I could stay out of his way, not give him any reason to leave.'

'That's why you wanted to avoid everyone today? You thought you were going to do something that would make him want to break up with you?'

'The whole proposal thing? He said I embarrassed him in front of everyone. I know it was cringe, but I didn't think it was reason enough for him to leave me . . .'

'And yesterday? After you got your crowns? You looked so happy.'

'We were,' he says. 'But then he ended it when the night was over. While you were out by the lake. Said I was suffocating him. Not giving him enough space.'

'So that's what this is? Giving him space? But what about this morning? When I walked in on you guys, you seemed to be, um . . . enjoying each other's company?'

'He's been pressuring me into, you know, *doing it*. I just thought if I could keep him happy . . .'

'Oh,' I say. That part doesn't sit right with me. How dare Rhys make him feel that way? But I can't go on the attack; he's not ready to hear that yet. 'You know you should never feel you have to –'

'I know,' Kellen says. 'I was honestly glad you walked in on us. It gave me a reason to stop. It's not that I don't wanna have sex with him, I'm just . . .'

'Not ready yet?'

'I don't know,' he says. 'I think it's more than that. I saw this TikTok about guys who don't like to top *or* bottom. Guys who just prefer to do other stuff. It's called being a *side*.'

'And you think you might feel that way?'

'Maybe,' he says. 'I don't know. I just want to experiment at my own pace. Not be rushed into it. I feel like the second you come out as gay, you have to choose your team. What if I don't want to do that? What if I don't know where I fit in yet? I feel like everyone looks at me, sees the nails and the heels, and just thinks *bottom*. They don't give me a chance to figure it out for myself.'

'Well, I never thought that,' I say. 'And, for what it's worth, it wouldn't be a dealbreaker for me. Top. Bottom. Side. I don't care. I'd be fine with doing whatever.'

'You say that now . . .'

'I mean it,' I say. 'You don't need some meathead pressuring you into doing something you don't wanna do.'

Kellen bristles. 'Don't call him a meathead.'

'Sorry,' I say. *Dial it back, Zach.* 'All I'm saying is that sex is supposed to be fun. Don't let him or anyone else ruin it.'

'I know you're right,' he says. 'Sometimes I honestly don't even know if I wanna be with him anyway.'

'You don't?'

'It's like there's two versions of him. When it's just me and him, he's kind and funny, and he makes me feel as if the only thing that matters to him is keeping me safe. But then there's this other side of him. The one that never texts me back, or notices when I'm sad. The one that gets angry when the smallest thing doesn't immediately go his way. It's like I mean the whole world to him, until I don't.'

'If you feel that way, why on earth did you propose to him?' I really can't get my head round that.

'Because I could feel him slipping away from me . . . and I wasn't ready for that. I thought if I could just keep him, for a little while longer, that we could work things out.'

'But you deserve better than that,' I say. 'You deserve someone who treats you like you're the most important person in the room, not just some of the time but *all* of the time. If Rhys really loves you, that's how he should make you feel . . .'

'You know he's never said it?' Kellen admits. 'That he loves me?'

What?!

'Really?'

'Never,' he says with a sigh.

A screeching sound startles us then as a firework shoots up into the sky. The night has flown by and prom is almost over.

'I don't wanna do this again, Zach.'

'Then we'll fix it, we'll find a way . . . I promise.'

'OK,' he says hopefully. 'And what if this is it? What if we wake up tomorrow and it's actually *tomorrow* tomorrow?' Kellen looks down at his watch. 'One minute.'

'Then I guess I'd be grateful for this,' I say. 'Sitting here with you. It's not exactly the prom night I imagined, but I have to admit this *was* pretty special.'

'I think so too,' he says, the fireworks reflecting in his eyes as he stares intently into the night sky. They look even more incredible from up here, illuminating the school grounds around us. 'Ten seconds.' He checks his watch again and sighs. 'You ready?'

'Do I have a choice?'

'I guess we'll find out. See you on the other side?' He offers me his hand.

'Yeah,' I say, taking it. 'See you on the other side.'

4

'Prom night, baby!'

I wasn't surprised when Chase hit me with the pillow this morning. In fact, it was everything I was expecting. It's confirmed that Kellen and I are indeed trapped here, even if we don't understand why. I thought about going straight up to his room but, after that conversation last night, I thought he might need a little time to himself. Or to be with Rhys. I don't know. Having his boyfriend break up with him every night, just to wake up right back there in his arms seems an especially cruel torment, like something out of a Greek myth. I think I'd rather have my liver pecked out, quite frankly.

Bec and Chase are running through their usual script at lunchtime – how they can't believe school is nearly over, yada yada – and I'm playing along with it. Kellen hasn't come down yet, but Rhys is sitting with the other Hawthorns, looking grumpier than usual. It makes me wonder if Kellen said something. Could he have actually broken it off with him? Like some sort of pre-emptive strike?

'I've been thinking,' I say, interrupting Bec and Chase as we take our usual seats. 'Imagine you were stuck in a day that looped over and over. What would you do in that situation?'

'Well, that came out of nowhere,' Bec says, surprised. 'But you mean like in the TV show? Like a real-life *Russian Doll*?' It still pains me that they haven't seen *Groundhog Day*.

'Yes.' I sigh. 'Exactly like *Russian Doll*.'

'I guess I'd work on a new skill?' Chase says. 'Like learn to speak Japanese or get really good at roller skating.'

'You realize you could do those things any time?'

'Yeah, but it's different when you have an *eternity*.'

'OK, nobody said *eternity* – let's not get carried away.' I shudder inwardly at the thought. 'Let's say the day was repeating, but it was only, like, Day Four.'

Chase laughs. 'Well, if it was only Day Four, I'd still be freaking out! Figuring out the rules, still hoping that tomorrow might actually be tomorrow?'

It's as if he's reading me like an open book.

'Day Four doesn't sound very fun,' he continues. 'But Day One-Hundred-And-Four . . . you could have so much fun on Day One-Hundred-And-Four!'

I groan. 'Let's just stick to Day Four. What would you do, Bec?'

'Well, I think I'd try to help out other people? You'd be able to see all their problems – solve everything! So I guess I'd try to do that? Make the world a better place.'

The fact I hadn't already thought of that makes me feel incredibly self-centred.

Bec looks at me suspiciously. 'Why all the questions anyway?'

'Oh, I'm . . . writing a book,' I say. *Smooth, Zach. That's totally plausible . . .*

'You're *writing a book*?'

'Think fast!' Ethan yells, standing up from his seat, but he freezes before he throws the ball. Something else has caught his attention.

'*Oh. My. God*,' says Chase. If his jaw was any lower, it would be resting on the table.

'What's going on?' Bec says, and I turn to see Kellen standing on the far end of our table. Only he isn't wearing any clothes. He's totally naked, cupping himself for *modesty*.

'Good morning, classmates!' he calls, beginning to stride the length of the table. 'Happy prom! Today is the first day of the rest of our lives. So let's all live a little, shall we?'

Josh cheers and stands up to give him a round of applause. He's the only one.

'Kellen, what are you doing?' I say as he approaches. I can't decide if this is the worst thing he's ever done, or the best. 'You do realize I will remember this tomorrow?'

'I think we'll *all* remember this tomorrow,' Chase says, clueless.

'Oh, but my sweet lamb,' Kellen says, leaning down so the two of them are face to face, 'that's just it. You won't. None of you will. Isn't that right, Zach?'

There's some murmuring as people look at me now, trying to figure out what the hell is going on and what I have to do with it.

You know what? Fuck it.

'Right,' I finally say.

There's no point in fighting it. He's correct: nobody will remember this tomorrow, so what does it matter?

'Do you trust me?' He offers me the hand he was cupping himself with, leaving him free as a bird. I don't take it. I've just seen where it's been.

'Absolutely not!' I laugh. 'Kellen, this is *crazy.*'

'Come *onnnnnn,*' he says. 'Let's cause some trouble.'

'Fine,' I say. 'But put some clothes on first.'

'You're the boss.' He winks, going to fish his clothing off the floor.

Chase is completely speechless.

'Are you gonna explain what the hell is going on?' Bec says.

I see Rhys storm across the room towards Kellen and grab his arm. 'What are you doing?' He tries to keep his voice lowered, but we all hear it.

'I'm just having fun,' Kellen says, pulling his arm free.

'You're humiliating me,' he says. 'In front of *everyone.*'

'I was thinking about myself,' Kellen replies. 'For once.' He sees that everyone is looking. 'We're done. I already told you that. We're finished.'

Oh my God! He actually ended it with him . . .

'Nah,' Rhys says. 'You're not the one ending this. I am.'

'Too late,' Kellen says, turning away. 'Show's over, boys – get a good look while you can!'

He turns on his heel and heads for one of the side doors, leaving Rhys and the rest of the room speechless.

I get up and follow. I catch him in the hallway, still only half dressed.

'Well, that was . . . something.'

'Why, thank you,' he says, taking a little bow. 'You might even say "magnificent"!'

'Not exactly the word I was looking for,' I say. 'But you actually broke up with him?'

Kellen shrugs, almost like he's completely unbothered. 'I realized we've been going about this whole thing the wrong way, Zach. Like, we've been trying to *escape* this day, but what if it's actually a blessing? A gift! We can do whatever the hell we like, right? None of the normal rules apply any more. When has anybody ever been so lucky?'

'I suppose . . .' I say. 'Though there is still the horror of being trapped here.'

'There's no need for dramatics, Zach,' Kellen replies. 'Are you coming?'

'Where?'

'To steal a car, of course!'

'Pardon?' I say, following after him.

'You heard me.' He grins as he stops at the door of Miss Madzikanda's office. 'She never locks this,' he says, going to open it and finding that his theory is entirely incorrect. 'Huh, well, whaddya know?'

'What do you want to steal a car for anyway?'

'To escape the "horror of being trapped here"?' he says. 'We have the power to do *anything*, to go anywhere, Zach! We can streak naked down the high street and nobody would remember it!'

'What is it with you and wanting to strip naked?'

'You're telling me you don't?'

'Funnily enough, no.'

'Huh,' Kellen says. 'Kinda figured that was what *everyone* wanted . . .'

'Nope, literally just you.'

'So,' he says, trying the door again, 'can you pick the lock?'

'*Can I pick the lock* . . .? I'm sorry, have you got me confused with someone else?'

'Well, it's either that or we kick the door down.'

'OK, let me just hop on Grindr and find someone masc real quick . . .'

'You're masc, Zach.' he says, looking me up and down. 'Kind of.'

'What do you mean *kind of*?' The absolute cheek.

'I mean *kind of*!'

'Well, I guess we could *try* picking the lock?' I say. 'Have you got a paperclip?'

'Why would I have a paperclip?'

'I don't know!' I say. 'What else am I going to pick the lock with? In the movies, they just sort of shove it in and jiggle it about a bit.'

'Maybe we really do need to get on Grindr,' says Kellen, giggling.

'Will you stop talking about Grindr!'

'Oh, this is so stupid.' Kellen pushes me aside, takes a step back and rams the door with his shoulder. I think Kellen is as surprised as me when it actually bursts open.

'Masc,' he says, checking his nails.

'I can't believe that actually worked . . .'

'Never underestimate me, Zachary.' Kellen crosses to Madzikanda's desk. 'Jackpot!' he says, opening the drawer and pulling out her car keys.

'And you're really sure about this? There must be a better way to get out of here.'

'It's, like, twenty-five miles to the nearest town, Zach. It's this or start training for a marathon. And you know how I feel about sport.'

'OK!' I say. 'But you know what you're doing, right?'

'Of course not. Whatever gave you that idea?'

'What are we *doing*?' I mutter to myself as Kellen unlocks Madzikanda's car.

She's down on the playing field, getting the rest of the students ready for Capture the Flag. Really not all that far away, considering what we're about to do. Hopefully, she's focused on the game because if she looks over she's definitely going to catch us.

'Like, never in a million years did I think I'd be carjacking a teacher . . .'

'Really? I sort of always knew this was on the cards for me,' Kellen says sarcastically.

I hear Chase's voice in my head. *We're talking about kissing a boy, Zach, not stealing a car.* If only he could see me now!

I hop in the passenger side. Kellen gets into the driver's seat and . . . opens TikTok.

'*How to drive a car*,' I read as he types it into the search bar. 'You can't be serious?'

'Well, how else are we gonna learn?!'

'I sort of thought you already knew the basics . . .'

'How would I know the basics?'

'I dunno. Maybe your parents taught you or something?'

'Yeah, my dead dad was the perfect instructor!'

'Shit . . . sorry.' *You're an idiot, Zach. You literally just had that conversation!*

'And Mum had *loads* of time to teach me between working multiple jobs. Most of the time we were just driven around in a limousine, though. *Obviously*.'

'All right, I get it,' I say, rolling my eyes.

'It'll be fine,' Kellen says, studying the video that's now playing. 'Seems pretty simple. You just sort of have to . . .' He fumbles with the keys as he puts them in the ignition. 'See?' He beams as the car grumbles to life. 'I'm getting the hang of it already.'

'You're going to get us both killed.'

'I already told you we can't die!'

'And I already told you that *you don't know that*!'

'Oh ye of little faith!' he says, releasing the handbrake.

'OK, we're not doing this,' I say, trying to reach across for the keys.

'It's not rocket science, Zach!' Kellen declares, just as I spot Madzikanda heading in our direction. *Fuck*. She must have heard the engine.

'Floor it!' I say in a panic as she furiously blows her whistle, the shrill shriek sounding right across the school grounds.

'What do you mean *floor it*?'

'Drive! Accelerate!'

'How?!' he says, fiddling with the gear stick.

He slams his foot down on one of the pedals and the car jolts backwards.

'Abandon ship!' I say, getting tangled up in my seat belt as I try to release it.

'What in God's name are you doing?!' Miss Madzikanda shrieks, racing towards us, but it's too late because Kellen's figured it out, and we're actually moving forward.

With a squeal of tyres, the car flies out of the car park, down through the open gates and on to the road that snakes down through the woodland that surrounds the school. Oakbrook and Miss Madzikanda disappear in the rear-view mirror, and we drive until there's nothing but nature surrounding us.

'I can't believe we're actually doing this.' Kellen finally exhales, his hands clamped firmly on the wheel, not daring to take his eyes off the road for even one single moment. I can tell he's scared but exhilarated because that's exactly how I feel too.

'OK, I hate to admit it,' I say, winding down the window and letting the wind rush in, 'but I think maybe you were right?'

'See,' Kellen says. 'Only good things can happen when you put your trust in me.'

'Is that so?' I laugh, the leaves of the overhanging trees rustling in the breeze. 'You know, we're really lucky we're stuck in a perfect summer's day. Imagine if we had to live through a blizzard?'

'Sounds romantic,' Kellen says. 'We could build snowmen, cosy up by the fire.'

'Get soaking-wet socks . . . frostbite . . .'

'You really don't like winter?'

'I hate winter!' I say. 'Besides, what could be more romantic than this?'

I fumble with the cable and plug in my phone. I have a playlist of my favourite movie soundtracks that's perfect for the occasion. It would turn even the most simple drive into something cinematic. The forest practically comes alive as the score begins to play.

'So this is a romance now, is it?' Kellen says. 'Don't get your hopes up, Zachary. Whatever our relationship is, I assure you it's strictly platonical.'

'Not a word.'

'Huh?'

'Platonic,' I say. 'There's no such thing as *platonical*.'

'Same difference.'

'Besides,' I say, 'there can be romance in friendship too, you know? There's romance in a road trip. Romance in a summer's day!'

'Didn't realize you were such a softie.' Kellen smiles, taking his eye off the road for longer than is sensible.

'Please watch where you're going,' I say. 'What if the police pull us over?'

'Do you see any police?' He gestures to the empty road ahead of us. 'Or anyone, for that matter? Anyway, a Black kid without a licence in a stolen car? I'm sure they'll be *just fine* with it.'

'Does it even matter if we get arrested?' *Am I really saying this?!* 'Like, we've got a get-out-of-jail-free card as soon as the clock hits midnight.'

'True, but knowing our luck this will be the day that sticks. Can you imagine? Stealing Madzikanda's car and then the day doesn't reset?'

The car actually slows as the realization of this possibility dawns on Kellen.

'It'll be fine.' I laugh. 'But maybe let's try *not* to get arrested. Just in case?'

'Deal! What's the speed limit here anyway?'

'I dunno. Thirty?'

'We're never gonna get anywhere going thirty.' He puts his foot down.

'Yeah, but just don't crash the car, OK? I don't even know CPR.'

'Wait, what?!' Kellen says, slamming on the brakes. Only my seat belt stops me from being thrown through the windscreen. 'You seriously don't know CPR?'

'No?' I say.

'What is that mother of yours teaching you?' he demands. 'Get out.'

'Huh?'

'Get out!' he repeats, unbuckling his seat belt and opening the door.

Against my better judgement, I do as he says.

'What are we doing?' I ask.

'Lie down,' he says, gesturing to the space in front of the vehicle. 'There.'

'I'm not lying down in the road, Kellen!'

'There's nothing coming!' he says.

'Even so!'

'Ugh, fine. Let me put the hazards on.' He leans back into the car before quickly reappearing. 'How do I put the hazards on?'

'How should I know?' I laugh. 'Why don't you ask TikTok? I'm not lying in the road.'

'You need to learn CPR,' he says. 'What if we crash and you need to save me? I don't even have a licence!'

'Exactly why we shouldn't be driving!'

'What happened to the "romance in a road trip"? Just when I thought you were lightening up a little!'

'I just don't want to see you getting hurt!' I say, remembering the vivid dream I had. Kellen's body lying on the stone-cold floor of the hall. People running and screaming around him.

'Well, do you wanna *walk* back to school?' He gestures to the road behind us.

I don't say anything to that.

'Just lie down, Zach.'

'OK, fine!' Reluctantly, I lie down in front of the car.

'Here,' he says, straddling me.

'I thought you said this wasn't a romance?'

'Oh, shut up,' he snaps. 'Just be a corpse.'

'Sexy.'

'Zach.'

'OK, OK,' I say. 'I'm a corpse.' I roll my eyes and go perfectly still.

'*Ah, ah, ah, ah … stayin' alive, stayin' alive,*' Kellen sings as he puts his hands together on my chest and presses down in time with the words. 'The Bee Gees!'

I can't help laughing. 'OK …' I watch him intently, his skin glowing under the dappling sunlight, the branches of the trees swaying above him.

'I'm being gentle,' he continues. 'But, in an emergency, don't be afraid to put some real pressure on.' He pushes a little harder so I can feel his whole bodyweight. 'You're better off breaking a rib than having them die on you.'

'And then what?' I say, meeting his eyes.

'Then …' he says, hesitating as he stares back down at me.

'Yeah?'

'And then …' He clears his throat. 'Then you give them the kiss of life.'

'The kiss of life?'

'. . . Yeah.'

I swallow hard.

Neither of us say anything.

'But obviously I'm not going to do that!' Kellen finally breaks the silence.

'Obviously!' I laugh nervously. 'Not that I'd let you!'

'You should be so lucky!'

He climbs off me.

There's another awkward pause.

'Just don't stop, Zach. Whatever you do. Even if you think they're gone, don't stop until the ambulance gets there. That's the most important part.'

'Thanks,' I say.

It's actually shocking that I didn't know any of this.

'I really appreciate the lesson.'

'Course,' he says, then gestures back to the car. 'So where to now?'

'I thought you wanted to streak down the high street?'

'Only if you'll do it with me.'

'You're not serious!'

'I'm one hundred per cent serious.'

I laugh at that. 'How about we keep our clothes on and just go for iced coffee?'

'Sounds boring,' he teases. 'But sure, I could do with the energy boost.'

We climb back into the car, and Kellen hums along to the music with that sweet voice as he clumsily tries to start it again. I catch myself staring at him.

What are you doing, Zach? Snap out of it . . .

The engine comes alive, and he looks up with a huge smile, the sun shining on his face. When we set off once more, he glances over at me from time to time as we roll through the woodland. And I don't know if it's just this messed-up situation we're in, or if it's something more than that, but it's, like, for just a moment, I see him in a different light.

'Kellen?'

I don't even know what I'm going to say.

'Yeah?'

'I just wanted to, um . . .'

'Yeah?'

'It's just –'

And that's when it happens.

I feel the seat belt slam against my chest as we hit something full speed.

5

'Prom night, baby!'

You have to be fucking kidding me.

The pillow hits me before the windscreen does. I snatch it out of Chase's hand and throw it back at him. 'I swear to God, if you hit me with this one more time . . .'

'All right, chill!' He laughs, holding his hands up in surrender.

I reach up to touch my face, checking for injuries, but I seem to be completely fine. So Kellen must be OK too, right? *Right?*

'Kellen!' I shout, jumping out of bed. I don't even bother to put on clothes. I run up the stairs two at a time, in nothing but my underwear. 'Kellen! Are you OK? Kellen?!'

'Zach!' He appears at his door. He's still touching his face as if checking for injuries. He looks me over too. 'What the hell happened?'

'We hit something,' I say.

'But there was nothing in the road.'

'I know,' I reply. 'It was like . . . an invisible barrier or something?'

'An invisible barrier,' Kellen echoes. 'That's *insane*.'

'All of this is insane! That doesn't mean it's not real.'

'What are you two talking about?' Rhys asks, appearing behind Kellen, towel wrapped round his waist and frankly ludicrous abs on display.

Kellen waves him away. 'Just go back to bed.'

'Not until you tell me what's going on.'

'All right, fine! I'll tell you exactly what's going on!' Kellen snaps. 'We're breaking up, OK? That's what's going on.'

He slams the door in Rhys's face, and, even though I know this isn't the first time he's dumped him, it's a shock to see it happen in real time.

'Come on,' he says, taking my hand and quickly leading me down the corridor. Rhys starts yelling after us, but Kellen doesn't even flinch. It's like he doesn't hear him.

'Do you not think that was a bit harsh?' I say, once we find a quiet corner.

Kellen's eyes go wide. 'So you're taking his side now?'

'No,' I say. 'It's just that –'

'It doesn't matter, Zach! We're just going to go round again tomorrow.'

'I don't believe that. Not forever. There has to be a way to break the cycle. There's always a way out! We should try stealing the car again.'

'What's the point?' Kellen says with a shrug. 'It didn't work the first time.'

'Well, that's just *Tom and Jerry* logic,' I say.

Kellen gives me a confused look. '*Tom and Jerry* logic?'

'The cat and mouse!'

Kellen rolls his eyes. 'I know who they are, Zach . . . But what in the fuck is *Tom and Jerry* logic? What is it with you and cartoons?'

'Well, Tom comes up with all these plans to catch Jerry, right? And some of them are actually pretty good. Some of them would even work if he just tried them a second time. But, whenever a plan goes wrong, he immediately gives up and tries something else. Stupid, really.'

'Are you telling me you were rooting for Tom?'

'Of course I was rooting for Tom.' I don't understand why everyone thinks he's the villain.

'He wanted to *murder* Jerry!'

'That's a very strong word,' I say. 'A lion doesn't *murder* an antelope. It's the circle of life! Did you not watch *The Lion King*?'

'Yeah, enough times to know that Scar is very much the bad guy.'

'Scar did what needed to be done.'

'He killed his own brother!'

'He overthrew an unelected official!'

'Oh my God . . .'

'Besides, if Tom's owners fed him properly, maybe he wouldn't be so hungry.'

'Wow, I bet you were such fun to watch cartoons with.'

'Well, anyway, I'm telling you it's a thing – *Tom and Jerry* logic!'

'Is it a *thing*, or is it a *Zach thing*?'

'A *Zach thing*,' I admit. 'But tell me I'm wrong.'

'Why not Wile E. Coyote logic? Or the logic of Elmer Fudd?'

'The Logic of Elmer Fudd sounds like a Netflix documentary where they dive into his tragic past and discover that he was just deeply misunderstood.'

'For wanting to shoot Bugs Bunny?'

'He's a hunter; he's got a family to feed. And Bugs is *massive*. He's *taller* than Elmer Fudd! Imagine the meat on him!'

Kellen laughs at that. 'Well, this is ridiculous, but I see your point. *Tom and Jerry* logic. The logic of Elmer Fudd. Maybe we *should* try again . . .' He looks us both up and down. 'Though maybe we should get dressed first?'

'Want to borrow an outfit?' I offer, just as Harrington's car alarm starts blaring. 'So you don't have to go back and face Rhys again?'

'Please,' he says. 'Just make it something cute.'

We don't waste any time. We go straight back to Madzikanda's office while everyone else is at lunch. Kellen is wearing a pair of my shorts and one of my T-shirts. They're a bit tight on him, and I can't really explain it, but I kinda like seeing him in them. Chase was a bit confused when we came back together, but he didn't ask too many questions after Kellen told him he'd broken things off with Rhys. He just gave him a hug and left us to it.

This time, I decide I want to take a turn at breaking down the door. Kellen must be stronger than he looks, though, because I have to ram it a good five times before it finally bursts open. The bruise to my ego hurts more than the one on my shoulder.

'You drive this time,' Kellen says, fetching the keys from Madzikanda's desk. He twirls them round his finger before tossing them over, expecting me to catch. My hands slap together pathetically as they drop to the floor in front of me.

'You know I can't do sport!' I groan, leaning down to pick them up.

'Ah yes, competitive key-catching: goes all the way back to the first Olympics.'

'They used to wrestle naked in Ancient Greece,' I say. 'I think I'd be better at that.'

'You really think so?' Kellen says, raising an eyebrow.

'Depends who I'm wrestling.'

'All right,' he says, pulling his T-shirt off in one swift motion. 'Right here, right now.'

'You wouldn't stand a chance.'

'Wouldn't I?' He goes to take off his shorts.

'OK, OK,' I say, covering my eyes. 'You win. Put your clothes back on.'

'It's cute you pretend you don't wanna look.' He smirks as he puts his T-shirt back on. I suppose he's not entirely wrong. He does look good topless.

'Can you imagine if Madzikanda walked in to see us wrestling naked on her carpet?'

Kellen laughs. 'I think it would be enough to force her into early retirement.'

'I sometimes feel kinda bad for her. Can you imagine having *us* as your year group?'

'I don't know,' Kellen says as we exit her office. 'I heard she was pretty rebellious when she was a student. You know Harrington was headmaster even back then?'

'That can't be right,' I say, following him down the corridor, trying to do the maths on my fingertips. 'He'd have to be, like, a hundred years old.'

'He was a young headmaster. Apparently he used to be less miserable then.'

I snort. 'I find that hard to believe.' I'm pretty sure that man came out of the womb scowling and ready to give out detentions.

'Besides,' Kellen says, 'I'm sure we're not the worst she's had!'

'Kellen, we're literally about to commit grand theft auto.'

'You don't need to be so dramatic,' he says, laughing. 'It's just one little vehicle.'

I unlock the car. 'Petite theft auto then?'

'Petite theft auto it is.' Kellen grins, climbing in the passenger side. 'I'm glad I get to play passenger princess today.' He drums on the dashboard like an excitable child.

I can't believe I'm about to do this. Kellen driving was bad enough, but me? As I just proved with the keys, I have zero hand-eye coordination. I can't even win a game of *Mario Kart* with the difficulty set to easy. At least we don't need to worry about getting caught this time. Everyone is still inside at lunch. We can take it slow. There's really no need to rush.

'What the *hell* are you two doing?!'

'Shit!' Kellen says, turning to see Madzikanda running out of the building. She must have gone to her office and seen we'd swiped her keys. 'Drive!'

'I'm not ready!' I say, fumbling with my seat belt.

'Forget the seat belt!'

'What do you mean *forget the seat belt*?!'

'Just drive! She's coming!'

'Don't rush me!'

I shift the car into gear and slam my foot down on the accelerator. The car lurches forward way faster than I expect, crashing straight into Harrington's. The alarm blares noisily. That's the second time today. I try to reverse, but that's when Madzikanda pulls open the door to stop me.

'Have you lost your damn minds?!'

'I can explain!' Kellen says.

'Save it,' she snaps. 'I know exactly what's going on here.'

'I don't think you do,' I mutter.

Madzikanda scoffs. 'There's only one reason you'd be doing something this stupid.' She glances back and forth between us.

'Could it be that you're stuck in a time loop?'

Miss Madzikanda doesn't say anything else until we're inside her office with the door closed. Except it doesn't close properly because I smashed it in while pretending to be masc.

'So which one of you is it?' she demands, looking back and forth between us.

'It's . . . both of us,' I say meekly. I'm still in shock. I can't believe she knows about this. What else hasn't she been telling us?

'Interesting . . .' She drums her fingers on her chin.

'But how did you know, miss?' Kellen asks.

Madzikanda takes a deep breath and sighs. 'Every prom night something happens that doesn't make any sense.'

'But time loops, miss?' Kellen says. 'No offence, but isn't that a bit far-fetched?'

She raises an eyebrow. 'Says the boy quite literally stuck in one?'

'No, I know,' he says. 'But how on earth did you work that out?'

'Because I was stuck in one too.'

'What?!' we say in unison. She can't be serious!

'At the time, I thought I was the only one,' she tells us. 'But then, after I graduated, I started hearing stories. Other things that didn't add up. And I knew – I just *knew* – that there must be more of us. I had to find out so I applied for a job the next year.'

'Wait, wait, wait,' I say. 'Slow down, miss. I have *so* many questions.'

'This whole situation –' she gestures to the space around us – 'it happens every year. Or at least most years anyway. Usually there's something that gives it away, but sometimes it's harder to tell. Sometimes the day is as plain as the nose on my face.'

'So you're trying to tell us we're at a *magic school*,' Kellen says. 'That's ridiculous.'

'And yet here we are.'

'So now we've found you, and figured it out, does that mean this is it then? You know the way out of this? Time will carry on normally now?'

'I should bloody hope not after you smashed up my car, Zach. Honestly, I've only known of one other student to do something so stupid!'

'It's not *that* stupid . . .'

'It's incredibly stupid!' she says, getting up to pace around the room. 'Can either of you idiots even drive?'

'We learned from TikTok,' Kellen says. 'It's surprisingly informative.'

She looks at us with utter disbelief. 'It's so strange, knowing I won't remember this conversation tomorrow. I know I've been in this situation with students before – they've told me about it afterwards, but I can't remember any of that. All I ever remember is the day that finally sticks.'

'Is it really the time for a mid-life crisis, miss?'

'An *existential crisis*, Kellen. This has nothing to do with me being middle-aged.'

'What's the difference?'

'A mid-life crisis is when a straight white man runs off with his secretary. An existential crisis is . . . well . . . *this*.' She looks back and forth between us. 'So how many days then? How many loops? What are we talking here?'

'Five,' I say, counting on my fingers. 'It's been awful.'

Madzikanda laughs.

'Sorry, what's so funny?'

'One hundred and eighty-six,' she says, sinking back into her chair. 'That's how many days it took me. One hundred and eighty-six.'

I feel the breath rush out of me.

I groan. 'I can't do this a hundred and eighty-six times.'

'One time, a boy looped closer to five hundred. Said he lost count in the end. Another student did it in just three – though she always was a bit of an overachiever.'

'So what did you have to do to get out, miss?' Kellen asks.

'I had to make up with a friend I'd fallen out with.'

'That's it?'

'That's it,' she says. 'Though it didn't seem that simple at the time. World-shattering, actually. Teenage emotions are a lot to deal with.'

I try to think who Kellen and I have fallen out with. Ethan and Tiffany perhaps? Surely this doesn't have anything to do with them? They're literally monsters. We can't be expected to buddy up with them. Not after the heinous things they've done.

'It's always different, though,' Madzikanda continues, almost like she could hear my thoughts. 'Sometimes the solution is about friendship. Sometimes it's romance. Sometimes it's about reconnecting with family or self-realization. One year it was about overcoming addiction. I'm glad I don't remember the *many* iterations of that one.'

'So you're saying you don't know what we need to do?'

Madzikanda shakes her head. 'Nope. But this is the first time I've seen it happen to two people simultaneously.' She glances between us as if something has occurred to her, but she doesn't want to say it out loud. 'Some years I don't even notice anything unusual, and it's impossible to say whether the day looped or not. Other years the students talk to me afterwards – tell me that I helped them – but obviously I don't remember. Sometimes I wonder how many times I've looped round, year after year.'

'Maybe that's why you're such a wise old owl,' Kellen says.

Madzikanda frowns. 'That's the second time you've called me old.'

'It was a compliment!'

'I'm sure you *thought* it was a compliment . . .'

'But how long has this been happening?' I ask. 'This school is *ancient*.'

'Hard to say.' She shrugs. 'But you should read the yearbook – there are some very cryptic messages. Somebody in 1926 wrote about the prom they "*never thought would end*". But perhaps I'm reading too much into it. Maybe it was just a particularly rough night.'

'Wait, I saw that!' I say. 'It was the first entry that jumped out at me!'

'What about the other teachers?' Kellen says. 'Is Harrington in on it?'

'He doesn't have a single clue. None of them do. I've hinted at it over the years, but they're all completely oblivious. It's frustrating, really. They're teaching fractions while the fabric of reality tears down the seams on a regular basis.'

'And yet here you are teaching PE, miss,' Kellen says with a twinkle.

'Do you really think that's why I'm here? To watch you lot puffing around the playing field? I'm here because there's something special in these walls. Something that's never been documented. I want to stick around and see it.'

'You should make a Netflix documentary!' I say. 'I'll help you with it. Just wait until I graduate from film school. Imagine the money we'd make!'

She chuckles at that. 'It's a nice idea, Zach. But who's ever going to believe us?'

'We can find proof,' I say. 'Interview everyone who's been through it! Find receipts to back up their stories! There has to be a way to prove it, right?'

'I've yet to find one,' she says. 'But I'm open to ideas.'

'And it's always prom night?' Kellen asks.

'It's *always* prom night. Just be glad you're not stuck in the Covid year . . .'

'Oh my God,' I say, imagining endless days of social distancing and wearing masks. And not the fun masquerade kind. What a terrible prom that must have been.

'Shaaba Singh,' Madzikanda recalls. 'Always said she wanted to be a doctor. She actually convinced herself that the way to break her loop was to stop the pandemic.'

'You're joking!' Kellen gasps.

'I'm one hundred per cent serious. Eighty-six days she spent trying to find a solution. Apparently everyone around her thought she was *insane*.'

'And did she help to stop it?' I ask. Was she the secret mastermind behind Pfizer?

Madzikanda nods. 'Yes, she single-handedly created the first vaccine.'

'Really?!' Mine and Kellen's jaws drop in perfect synchronicity.

'Of course she bloody didn't! She was seventeen, Zach.'

'Well, I don't know!' I say defensively. 'I don't know what to believe any more!'

'She realized she wanted to be a dancer,' Madzikanda explains. 'That was always her true passion, deep down. It was calling her parents to tell them that finally did it.'

'That's all it took? A phone call?' Kellen shakes his head. 'And she was busy playing scientist? Actually trying to stop Covid?'

'It always sounds easier than it really is,' Madzikanda says with a comforting smile.

'Maybe I should call my mum?' I say. I haven't spoken to her once through all this.

'I'm sure she'd appreciate that, Zach, but you can't just try to copy someone else's solution. What happens here is always unique to the individual. Or individuals . . .'

Kellen groans. 'I still have so many questions!'

'Well, don't go trying to steal any more cars, OK?'

'So you'll give us the keys then?' I ask cheekily.

'No, I'm not giving you the keys. You can't leave. The loop won't let you.'

'The barrier!' I exclaim.

Madzikanda's eyes widen. 'You stole my car already, didn't you?'

'*Maaaybe*,' says Kellen.

She shakes her head. 'So you already *know* you can't leave then. You're stuck here until you do whatever it wants you to.'

'"*It*"?' Kellen says. 'What's "*it*"?'

'The loop, or whatever causes it,' Madzikanda replies. 'Believe me, I tried *everything*. There's no way out. The second you breach that perimeter, you wake up back at the start of the day.'

'But what if there's another way? Something you didn't think of?'

'Such as?'

'Going through backwards!'

'Tried it.'

'Tunnelling under?'

'Tried it.'

'Flying out by helicopter?'

'Do you have a secret helicopter hidden away on the school grounds that you're not telling us about, Zach?'

'No.'

'And do you know how to fly a helicopter?'

'No.'

'Then I think we can probably put a pin in that one then, can't we?' Madzikanda folds her arms.

'What if you got a helicopter for us?' Kellen suggests.

'I'm not getting any helicopters! You make it sound like ordering a pizza . . .'

'I could go for a pizza right now,' he replies.

Madzikanda squeezes the bridge of her nose.

'Listen, just trust me, OK? You can't cheat. You can't escape. You've got to do whatever it wants you to do. The only way out is through.'

I puff out my cheeks in frustration. Beside me, I sense Kellen is just as annoyed. 'So how much longer do you think we'll be stuck here?'

'I don't know, Zach. But I'm always here if you need me. Just say the codeword.'

'The codeword?' Kellen asks. She's acting like we're in a sci-fi movie.

'Huckleberry.'

Kellen scratches his head. 'Like the dog?'

'Like the dog.'

'You said that to me before, miss,' I say, remembering. 'Though I didn't understand why at the time.'

'I did?'

'The very first night, after I threw fake pig's blood all over the yearbook.'

'You did *what*?'

'It was an accident,' I say. 'Harrington expelled me, chucked me out of prom, but you came after me. Said you wanted to talk about Huckleberry. Honestly, I thought you'd lost it.'

Miss Madzikanda laughs at that.

'You were trying to help,' I say. 'Thanks, miss.'

'Of course,' she replies with a smile.

'So,' Kellen says, 'if we really *are* stuck here, and we're going to just loop again tonight, do you think we could *actually* get some pizza?'

Madzikanda sighs in disbelief.

'I'm serious,' he says. 'We haven't solved anything, so today isn't going to stick, right?' He leans across the table and whispers something in her ear.

Madzikanda glances back and forth between us, as if trying to figure us out.

'Pepperoni?' she finally says, picking up the phone.

Kellen beams.

'Pepperoni.'

'I can't believe she just cancelled Capture the Flag,' Bec says as we sit on the front lawn, where several dozen pizzas have just been delivered to the school. When it comes to Italian cuisine, Madzikanda knows how to commit. 'Someone said it's the first time since the Second World War. There must be something she's not telling us!'

'Who cares about house rivalry when there's gooey cheesy goodness?' Chase says.

'But what about the food in the hall?' Bec replies. 'It's all gonna get thrown away.'

I'd normally agree, but I'm not sure food waste is an issue in a never-ending day.

'Don't worry about it,' Chase says. 'It's really not our problem. God bless Madzikanda is what I say! Do you think she was always planning this for the last day?'

'I think it was more of a spur-of-the-moment thing,' I murmur.

'Apparently Old Man Harrington is furious and he's threatening to fire her,' Kellen says, coming over. 'Mind if I join you?'

'Course not,' Chase says, though he does sound a little surprised.

'Thanks,' Kellen says, sitting down. We exchange a knowing look.

'So you really broke things off with Rhys?' Bec asks.

'Yeah.' He shrugs. 'I still care about him. It just ... wasn't working.'

'Well, for what it's worth,' Chase says, 'I always thought you were too good for him. And I've missed having you sit with us. You don't belong with Hawthorn.'

'Thanks,' he says. 'I just wish they wouldn't treat me like the enemy ... Break-ups happen ... It's not like I'm the *villain*.'

I glance over to where Cameron and some of the rugby team are sitting. Rhys is actually *glaring*. I wish they'd just eat their pizza and mind their own business, but Tiffany is loudly declaring that she's not having any because 'no carbs before prom'. She has to take the fun out of literally *everything*. If only she knew that those carbs won't even matter. Kellen and I should find a way to get more junk food. A healthy lifestyle is one thing we don't need to worry about.

I keep thinking about what Madzikanda said. The solution could be *anything*. This whole thing did start with a kiss, so what if the answer really is a romance? Not between me and Owen – but between me and someone else? I glance over to where Cameron and the rugby team are sitting. I can hear him complaining about someone taking the last slice.

'I'll be right back,' I say, grabbing a slice and heading over. I don't know where the sudden spurt of confidence comes from – maybe the fact that I know this won't stick? Even if I embarrass myself, it doesn't matter. So it's worth a shot, right?

'Hey, Zach,' he says as I approach. The sun is in his eyes so he squints while he looks up at me. Even with his face all crumpled, he's still cute.

'Hey,' I say. 'I overheard you needed an extra?'

'My actual hero!' he says. 'You sure you guys have enough?'

'We've got plenty,' I say. 'We swiped, like, four boxes.'

'Well, thanks,' he says, taking a bite, the cheese dripping down his chin. Somehow he even makes that look sexy. 'I was going to come over and talk to you, actually,' he says. 'There's something I've been meaning to ask you.'

'Oh yeah?'

'Cameron has a *crussshhhhhh* . . .' one of the other rugby boys sing-songs.

Cameron turns bright red. 'Shut up!' he says. 'Ignore them, it's nothing like that.'

I feel myself turning red too. 'I mean . . . yeah . . . course not . . .'

A rugby ball hits Cameron in the head.

'OK, ow,' he says, throwing it back. 'Maybe talk later? Away from these idiots?'

'Sure.' I smile as the ball hits him a second time.

'I swear to God, I'm gonna kill you, Dan!' he growls as I go back to join the others.

Chase is the first to raise an eyebrow.

'What?' I say. 'I was just taking him a slice.'

'Mmm-hmm,' he says, giving me *that* look. 'And how many *spicy movies* start with a hot boy delivering pizza . . .?'

'It's nothing like that,' I say, secretly hoping that it is. Maybe this really is the solution. Could getting together with him be what I need to do to break the loop? Clearly, finding the identity of the masked stranger was just a distraction. A red herring to throw me off! Though I still feel bad that Owen has unrequited feelings for me. I can't believe he's been secretly gay this whole time. Maybe that's a part of this too.

I look over to where he's sitting with Josh. I wonder if he's told him, at least? They've been best friends since forever. Maybe there's something I'm missing?

'*Yasssss!*'

Josh's voice is unmistakable, his gloved hand snapping furiously at Kellen who's just made his grand entrance. The hateful muted black outfit is gone and he's wearing something so much more Kellen – a flowing outfit in fiery shades of orange and striking accents of red. His mask is the shape of curling twisting flames, and he has on these scarlet cowboy boots that pull the whole look together. Finally I understand why he painted his nails red for that first night. This is always what he wanted. I'm glad he's finally wearing it.

Josh runs over to hug him, positively bubbling with excitement.

'You're on fire!'

'Ready to set this prom ablaze,' Kellen says, twirling so we can all get a good look.

'You had this all along?' I say, marvelling at the fiery design.

'It was my backup outfit,' he says with a shrug.

'This was the *backup*? Kellen, that's *ridiculous*.'

'Well, I know that now,' he says. 'So you like it then?'

'I love it,' I say, holding eye contact with him.

'I can practically feel the heat coming off you,' Bec adds.

'Ten out of ten,' Chase agrees, smiling.

'Just make it go away!' Tiffany screeches, right on schedule. The news about Ethan must have broken. 'I don't care, Daddy! I swear to God, if I see *anything* about this in the *Herald* . . . !' She violently hangs up the phone.

'What's happening?' Chase says.

'Oh God,' I say, watching as Tiffany scans the crowd for suspects, then starts furiously marching in our direction. But Chase didn't mess with the poll results today, or do anything to rile her. Why's she suddenly trying to pin this on him again?

'I know it was you!' she says as she approaches. 'Do you really think we're that stupid? That we wouldn't figure it out?'

'Leave him alone,' Kellen snaps. 'Chase had nothing to do with this.'

'Chase?' she says. 'I'm talking about *you*!'

'What?'

'Drop the act!' she snarls. Everyone's looking now. 'Don't even try to deny it!'

'Why the hell do you think it was me?'

'I don't *think* it was you,' she says, 'I *know* it was you . . . Pretending to like Rhys just to get close to us? Just so you could swipe Ethan's phone and steal his photos?'

'Sorry, what the actual fuck are you talking about? That's the most ridiculous thing I've ever heard. Seriously, Tiffany? This is a new low. Even for you.'

'I'm not the one going around leaking naked photos of underage boys!'

'He's eighteen, Tiffany.'

'And that makes it OK, does it?'

'Oh my God,' Kellen says, shaking his head. 'This is ridiculous!'

'Is it?' she says. 'You realize my family knows *everyone* in publishing, right? We'll have proof soon enough.'

'OK then.' He rolls his eyes. 'I can't *wait* to see it.'

'Oh, you will,' Tiffany growls, stomping away from us.

'She doesn't actually have any proof, right?' Bec says.

'Of course not!'

'I don't think it matters if she actually has proof,' I say. Everyone's still looking in our direction. They're whispering. Furiously typing in their phones. This was her plan all along. Fabricate a story and then get everyone to believe it.

'But who actually leaked the photos then?' Chase says.

'I was wondering that too,' Kellen says. 'But it's obvious, isn't it?' He looks at me, wondering if I've figured it out. 'I don't know why I didn't see it sooner.'

We all look at him blankly.

'It was *her*.'

'Do you really think this is a good idea, Kellen?'

Prom is in full swing. Since there was no game of Capture the Flag, the hall has been decorated in a combination of Hawthorn and Sycamore colours. You'd think they would clash, but they actually complement each other quite nicely. Maybe they should have just cut the toxic competition and done this in the first place?

'I don't *think* it's a good idea,' Kellen says. 'I *know* it's a good idea!'

We're watching Tiffany from up on one of the balconies.

'But if she catches us trying to steal her phone . . .'

'Then what?' He shrugs. 'What's the worst she can do? Everything is temporary! The day's just gonna loop anyway.'

'But what if exposing her is our objective? What if this actually works . . .?'

'Then we're free and we can worry about the consequences later!'

'I don't like the sound of that,' I say. 'Are you really sure about this?'

'Absolutely,' he says. 'Whatever happens, tomorrow is not going to be *tomorrow*. I'm certain of it. Do you want me to prove it? I'll streak right across the dance floor naked!' He pulls a string on his costume and it opens to reveal his chest. 'That's how sure I am!'

'Why is your answer to *everything* that you're going to get naked?'

'Why isn't it yours?' Kellen says with a grin.

'I'm just not sure this is the best plan anyone has ever hatched,' I say. 'It's not exactly *stealthy*.'

'It doesn't need to be stealthy! Because it doesn't matter if we get caught!'

'What if someone stops us? What if Ethan attacks us? He already hates you, Kellen. If he thinks you're the one who leaked those photos . . .'

'He'll be distracted!' he says. 'I'm telling you, this plan is *infallible*!'

'Famous last words,' I mutter as the music dies down and Mr Harrington approaches the stage. He begins his extremely long-winded speech, and I watch closely as Tiffany moves through the crowd like a shark. She does exactly what we expect her to do – what we *know* she's going to do – forcing her phone into Owen's hands so he can stream her big moment. It almost seems too easy, like taking candy from a diamanté-studded baby.

'Bingo,' Kellen says. 'You ready?'

'As I'll ever be,' I reply, following him down the stairs and into the crowd.

Mr Harrington seems to be speaking even slower than usual, but that's good because it gives us a little more time. We snake through the crowd until we're standing on either side of Owen. I don't love using him like this, but there's no other way we can get Tiffany's precious phone away from those manicured claws.

'And so, without further delay,' Mr Harrington says, 'it's my honour to announce this year's Prom King and Queen.'

'Prom Royalty!' Kellen yells in sync with Josh. 'It's gender neutral.'

'Oh . . . erm, yes,' he says. 'This year's Prom Royalty . . .'

The crowd groans as he fumbles with the envelope.

'Tiffany White and Ethan Clark!'

The live stream is already rolling. We watch as Tiffany and Ethan climb up onstage. We wait until the confetti canons burst and gold rains all around us and then . . .

'Now!' Kellen whispers, pretending to fall forward into Owen, knocking him off balance. I snatch the phone from his fingers and tuck it into my jacket, disappearing back into the crowd before he even realizes what's happened. That was far too easy.

'Oh my gosh, I'm so sorry!' I hear Kellen saying from the crowd behind me, pretending to slur his words. 'What *did* they put in that punch?'

'Wait . . . where's the phone?' Owen says.

'What phone?' Kellen replies as I quietly slip out of the side door. It's incredibly tempting to stay and watch the chaos that's about to unfold – you haven't seen a woman scorned until you've seen Tiffany White separated from Instagram – but I've got a job to do.

There's nobody out here – everyone is inside watching the crowning ceremony.

The phone is still unlocked. I quickly cancel the live stream before I incriminate myself and go straight into her emails. It has to be here, it just has to be.

I click into her outgoing mail. The moment of truth. But there's *nothing*.

I check her deleted folder – because of course she'd cover her tracks – but there's nothing there either. What the hell? She can't be innocent. She just can't be.

I think of checking her photos to try to find something else incriminating – it must be *full* of things we could use against her – but hesitate because that feels like crossing a line. I'd hate it if someone went through my photos, and if I did that then I really would be no better than what she's been accusing us of.

I keep tapping on the screen, careful not to let it lock on me, as I walk to the edge of the lake. There must be something in here, something I'm missing.

'You got it?' Kellen calls, appearing through the same side door.

'Yeah,' I say, holding up the phone. 'How did you manage to shake them?'

'I said I saw her phone slide underneath the stage,' he says with a cute evil laugh. 'She's in there screaming at Harrington, telling him to take the thing apart. Madzikanda said it can wait till tomorrow, and I swear Tiffany was about to rip out her throat.'

I can't help but laugh at that.

'So anything juicy?' He gestures to the phone.

'No,' I say. 'Nothing.'

'Have you checked the deleted folder?' Kellen demands, taking the phone from me.

'I've checked everything,' I say. 'It's clean.'

'Hmm,' he says, tapping around for a few moments, the same disappointment on my face reflected on his. And then . . . '*Aha!*'

'*Aha?*' I peer at the screen hopefully. 'You found something?'

'She's got a second account on here!'

'You're kidding?'

'Oakbrook.anonymous@gmail.com.'

'That has to be it!'

He taps around for a few more moments, his eyes lighting up. And then, suddenly, his face drops.

'What time does the loop restart?'

'Eleven fifty-nine a.m.,' I say. 'That's when I wake up anyway.'

'Same for me. Fuck. We can't stop her, Zach.'

'What do you mean?'

'It *was* her who leaked the photos,' he says, showing me the email. 'It's all here. But she sent them at eleven fifty-eight a.m. One minute before either of us wakes up . . .'

'That can't be a coincidence,' I say. Maybe her sending that email is what set this whole looping day in motion? Maybe exposing her *is* the solution.

'Wait,' Kellen says, looking at the phone again. He taps around for a couple of moments before his eyes widen. 'Zach, there's another email here.'

'Another?'

'Sent a year ago . . . It's about Chase.'

'Oh my God,' I say. He doesn't even need to explain the contents. I already know exactly what's in there. 'So it *was* her! I fucking knew it!'

I take the phone and read the email. It's exactly what we'd suspected: Tiffany pretending to be one of the male students, voicing fake concerns about feeling 'uncomfortable' in the bathroom. It's clever – that's the thing that's most insidious about it. The language is subtle and manipulative, incredibly well written, designed to sound reasonable enough to make others side with her bigotry.

'So what do we do with this? We have to expose her . . .'

'We will,' Kellen says, taking the phone back. 'We just need to –'

'Hey, guys!'

Josh comes up behind us, followed closely by Owen. As soon as he sees them, Kellen panics and tosses Tiffany's phone into the lake.

Oh my God, what did you do that for?

'What was that?' Owen says.

'Um . . . skimming stone!' Kellen squawks.

'Well, that's the worst technique I've ever seen,' Josh says, crouching down for a flat stone. He takes one between his fingers and effortlessly sends it bouncing across the lake. 'See, it's all in the wrist.' He does the jerk-off gesture.

'Tiffany is absolutely losing her mind in there. She's gonna kill me,' Owen says.

I see the fear flash across his face, and feel bad for setting him up like this.

'She'll have to go through me first,' Josh says, putting his arm round Owen's shoulder. 'Besides, it's the last day. What's the worst she can do?'

'Are we talking about the same Tiffany?' Owen groans.

'It's fine,' Kellen says. 'It's my fault. Not yours. If she wants to take it out on someone, she can take it out on me. She already hates me for breaking it off with Rhys.'

'Break-ups happen!' Josh says. 'She can't hate you for that.'

Kellen shrugs. 'I'm sure there's already a plan in place to drown me in pig's blood.'

'But Harrington's forbidden the prank this year,' Owen says.

'Do you really think that's gonna stop her?' Kellen replies. 'Just watch out for buckets over the stairs. Rumour has it she's already planted one.'

'Noted,' says Owen, nodding.

Josh tries to reassure him. 'Nothing's gonna happen to you. Zach will keep you safe, won't you, Zach?'

'Me?' I say, confused.

'Yeah.' Josh grins. 'Me and Kellen have some business to attend to.'

'What business?' I say, looking at Kellen, unsure.

'There's more to my masterplan,' he says with a grin.

'Huh?' I say. I don't like the sound of that. We never talked about any of this.

'Just trust me,' he says. 'You ready, Josh?'

'You know it,' he says as the two of them walk away from us.

What are you up to, Kellen?

Doing something without me makes me think it's something I wouldn't approve of. If he's going to exact revenge on Tiffany, this will end badly . . .

'Do you have any idea where they're going?' I say to Owen.

'Not a clue.' He shrugs. 'But let's try to stay out of Tiffany's way, eh?'

'Yeah,' I say. 'Let's.'

Tiffany is on Ethan's phone by the time we get back inside. She's logged him out of his Instagram and is now using the phone as if it's hers. I doubt he had any say in the matter.

'Everything is going so well,' I say, finding Miss Madzikanda in the middle of the hall. 'Kellen has split with his trashy boyfriend, Cameron is *actually* flirting with me, everyone got a pizza party –'

'You crashed my car . . .'

I laugh. 'Apart from that bit,' I say. 'It maybe feels like we've solved it?'

'You'd better *not* have solved it,' she says. 'If you think I can actually afford all those pizzas on a teacher's salary, then you are *deeply* mistaken.'

'I'm sure we can find a way to pay for them!'

'And for my car?' she retorts with ample side-eye.

'I just don't know what else there is to fix.'

'Well,' she says, 'if there's one thing I've learned from all this, it's that when it's the end, you'll *know* it's the end. Is that how it feels right now?'

'Maybe?'

'So that's a no then.'

'Ah, come on, it can't be that cut and dried.'

'I'm just saying be careful. There's still time for everything to go pear-shaped.'

'Yeah, yeah,' I say. I think Madzikanda has got this whole thing wrong. I'm not really listening any more anyway. I've spotted Cameron over by the punchbowl. 'You better start figuring out a payment plan for those pizzas!' I call, slipping away from her.

'Hey, Zach!' Cameron lights up as I approach him. 'I've been looking for you.'

'So you keep saying.' I smile. 'I think I know why too. It's what your friends said earlier ... about your *crush*, right?'

'Kinda. How'd you know?' He's blushing again. He looks so cute when he blushes.

'Well,' I say, taking a step closer, 'maybe I can make it a bit easier for you?'

'Oh yeah?' he says, perking up a little.

'Yeah,' I say, holding eye contact. 'I've wanted to say something for a while, but never built up the courage. I have now, though.'

Cameron swallows. 'What do you mean?'

'I mean ... I like you,' I say. 'I *really* like you.'

'You do?'

'Yeah,' I say.

'Zach ...'

'It's OK, you don't have to say anything.'

'No, I kinda really do . . .'

'Huh?'

'Zach, I . . . *Fuck*, this is awkward.'

I look at him blankly. 'Why is it awkward?'

'I think you're a great guy, I *really* do,' he continues. 'But the crush I was talking about . . . isn't on you.'

'What?' I say.

Hello, pear-shaped thing Madzikanda tried to warn me about. I want the ground to actually swallow me up.

'Then why did you want to talk to me?'

'I thought you might know if the feeling was mutual. To save me humiliating myself.'

'Like I just did . . .' I groan. 'So who is it then? Josh? Chase?'

He looks down at his feet like he can't bring himself to say it.

'It's not Owen, is it?'

'Owen? No, Zach. It's Bec.'

'Bec?!' I splutter. 'But you're *gay*!'

'I'm not gay, Zach.'

'What?!' I protest. 'There's a rainbow flag in your bio! You've *always* been the queer twin! That's literally your USP.'

'Yeah, exactly,' he says. '*Queer.* I'm bisexual, Zach. I thought you knew that . . . I thought *everyone* knew that.'

How the hell did I not know that?!

'Well, now I feel like an idiot.'

'It's fine. It's not *your* fault. Everyone always forgets the B in LGBT. You come out as bisexual and everyone just refers to you as *the gay kid*.'

'So you like girls then?'

'And guys,' he says with a laugh. 'That's kinda how the whole "bisexual" thing works.' He meets my eyes. 'For what it's worth, I did use to like you too, you know?'

'Use to?' What does he mean *use to*?

'Back when you first got here. I thought you were ultra cute. I wanted to make a move, but then I got shy. Then you and Josh started dating and –'

'We were never dating!' I exclaim. 'We hooked up *one time*!'

'Well, whatever.' He laughs. 'Josh was my friend. I wasn't gonna try and steal you away from him, so I kind of ruled you out after that. I still think you're cute, but . . .'

'Your heart is elsewhere.' I follow his gaze over to Bec. She's by the yearbook, no doubt furiously scribbling down the immortal words of Ms Swift.

His eyes light up as he looks at her. How did none of us see this sooner? I feel like this should bother me more – my crush liking my friend more than me – but I don't know: it weirdly feels like a silver lining. Maybe my heart is elsewhere too.

'Do you think she might feel the same?' he asks hopefully.

'I honestly couldn't say,' I answer. Bec has never openly expressed an interest in Cameron, but then maybe she also thought he was gay? 'I could go over and play Cupid if you like?'

'No,' Cameron says, taking a deep breath. 'I've done enough pussyfooting around. I'm a big boy. I can talk to her . . .'

But, just as he says it, the lights go out.

The music stops too. And now all that's left is the sound of alarmed voices and candles flickering in the darkness. *This can't be good . . .*

'All right, settle down!' Mr Harrington shouts from somewhere in the hall. 'It's just a power cut. I'm sure it'll be fine in a minute.'

But there's never been a power cut before . . . this is brand-new territory. I try to find Kellen in the darkness. He must be responsible. *What have you done, Kellen?*

'Look!' Cameron says, pointing to the top of the stairs. I half expect to see someone drenched in pig's blood, but instead there's something that actually makes me smile.

It's Kellen, holding a birthday cake, as he slowly starts to sing. People usually rush through the lyrics of 'Happy Birthday', but he holds them, slowly and tenderly, his voice like sweet caramel as it cuts through the silence and reverberates round the hall.

'*Happy birthday to you,*
Happy birthday to you,
Happy birthday, dear Zachary . . .'

Cameron turns to look at me. 'It's your birthday?'

I'd completely forgotten about it in all the chaos, but Kellen's right. If time had continued to move along as normal, today would, in fact, be my eighteenth birthday. I can't believe I almost missed it.

'Sort of,' I reply as Kellen approaches.

'*Happy birthday to you!*'

Kellen holds the cake up for me to blow out the candles. 'Happy birthday, Zach. You didn't think I'd forget, did you? What do you think the pizza party was about?'

'That was for *my* benefit?'

'Why do you think I asked Madzikanda for it?'

'So that's what you were whispering!' I say, trying to find her in the crowd.

'This is very cute,' Chase says, finding us. 'But, um, it's not Zach's birthday.'

'It wouldn't be a surprise if we celebrated on the exact day!' Kellen replies.

Chase opens his mouth, and I can see he wants to tell Kellen that's the stupidest thing he's ever heard. But he doesn't. I guess he doesn't want to take this moment away from me.

'Come on,' Kellen says. 'Make a wish. I haven't got all day.'

'That's *all* you've got,' I joke.

You'd think I'd want to wish for this day to finally come to an end – and maybe that's what I *should* wish for – but seeing Kellen standing there in front of me, doing all this for me even when so much in his own world has spiralled out of control, reminds me that he deserves better than the half-hearted relationship Rhys has given him. He deserves to find so much happiness, and so I close my eyes and, with one swift breath, I wish for exactly that.

'Well, as lovely as all this is,' Miss Madzikanda says, appearing from the darkness, 'did you actually switch off the power just to pull this little stunt?'

'Oh, er ... maybe ...' Kellen says. 'But it doesn't matter, right? We can do whatever we like, totally free of consequences! That's what you said, right?'

'Why would she say that?' Chase asks, bewildered.

'I don't know how you took that from what I said. Don't start getting reckless now.' And, just as she says it, everything suddenly goes wrong.

'Fuck!' a voice exclaims from the stairs as someone trips, staggering into one of the flickering candelabras. From there, it all seems to happen in slow motion – the candelabra topples, and in a flash one of the trailing Hawthorn banners goes up in a fiery blaze.

'Stay calm! Stay calm!' Miss Madzikanda yells as everyone immediately descends into panic, practically climbing over each other to get out of the way as the fire begins to spread. The flames curl and twist, and black smoke starts to billow. Another banner catches, and then another. It's happening at such an alarmingly rapid pace, it's almost as if somebody has doused the whole room in petrol.

This all happened before, but it was just a dream. I close my eyes and open them, expecting everything to be fine, but it's not fine. I'm not dreaming; this is actually happening for real. In no more than thirty seconds, the whole room is consumed by flames, along with everyone's ability to *stay calm*!

'Fuck, fuck, fuck,' Kellen says, still holding the cake. 'It's OK, right? The day is just gonna start over.'

I look at my watch. 'Not for another ten minutes ...'

'Now is not the time!' Madzikanda says. 'Everyone out! Now!'

'Fuck,' I say, reality dawning on me.

What if this *is* real? What if this sticks?

The rope suspending the pig's blood must have caught fire because it comes swinging down, spattering half the student body. Now it really is like we're in a Stephen King movie.

While everyone scrambles for a way out, Madzikanda is checking corners and alcoves, making sure that absolutely nobody is left behind. The other teachers are too – and they have *no idea* that this day may potentially loop. It's impressive, really. Harrington is the *only* one to go for the exit – which says it all. Everyone else stays.

'I think that's all of them!' one of the teachers calls.

The hall is really fucking hot now, the smoke is getting thicker, and it's getting harder and harder to breathe.

'Boys, out!' Madzikanda yells as she sees the two of us lingering. 'Come on, move!'

By the time we get outside, people are coughing and spluttering, and flames have burst through the upstairs windows, licking the night sky. At least everyone is out safely.

'Josh?!' Owen yells suddenly.

'Huh?' I say, scanning the crowd Madzikanda is trying to headcount. 'Where is he?'

'Oh my God,' Kellen breathes, the horror dawning on him. 'He was in the basement. He's the one who tripped the power.'

'Oh no,' I say.

'We need to get him!' Kellen cries.

'Don't you dare!' Madzikanda snaps, but it's too late because Owen is already sprinting towards the building, disappearing into the thick black smoke that's billowing through the doorway. A deep red firework explodes above the school, as the timed pyrotechnics kick off. 'Owen!' she booms, going after him.

Some of the students actually scream as the two of them disappear inside. Kellen and I look at each other helplessly. I feel like we should go after them, but what good would that do? We're standing there, paralysed by fear and confusion – and that's when I spot him. Josh. Coming round the side of the building, coughing.

'He's already out!' I yell after Owen and Madzikanda, but I know they can't hear me over the sound of the blaze. 'He's already out!' I try again, louder now. 'Josh is here!'

I look back at the crowd of students, all of them stunned with fear.

I have to go in after them, but Kellen realizes this before I do, and he's already running towards the building, one with the flames as his fiery outfit disappears between the doors.

'Kellen! Wait!' I yell. 'Kellen!'

'Don't!' Cameron says, grabbing me and dragging me backwards. 'Zach, don't!'

'Get off me!' I scream, trying to push him away, but he holds me down. 'Get off me!'

'You're gonna get yourself killed!' he shouts, pinning my arms down. I try to fight him, but he's too strong.

'Get the fuck off me!'

'Zach, stop!' he yells. 'Just stop!'

'Kellen!' I scream again, and that's when I see him and Madzikanda reappear, Owen unconscious between them. People actually start cheering.

They did it! They're out!

And that's when it happens.

Above them, weakened by the fire, the ornamental door frame shudders and creaks.

Repetitio Est Mater Studiorum.

Repetition is the Mother of Learning.

With a final groan, it collapses and all three of them disappear in a cloud of fire and smoke.

'Kellen!' I scream, my vision blurring.

And then everything is suddenly black.

6

'Prom night, baby!'

'Kellen!' I scream, pushing Chase out of the way and running for the door. 'Kellen!'

I sprint up the stairs, but this time he doesn't appear in his doorway. Instead, I hear Rhys. The unsettling sound of his desperate cries for help. Some of the other students rush out into the corridor as I burst through into Kellen's room.

Kellen is lying on the floor, Rhys crouched next to him, frozen.

'I don't know what . . . I don't know what happened . . .' he says, looking up at me. He's white as a sheet. 'I just woke up and he's . . .'

'Move!' I shout, pushing him out of the way. Kellen is lifeless, his skin ashen.

Pressing my hands to his chest, I frantically start giving him CPR, exactly as he taught me.

'Call a fucking ambulance!' I yell at Rhys, who is still just frozen to the spot.

I know it'll take too long to get here, but what else am I

supposed to do? I continue the compressions on his chest, but he isn't responding.

'Kellen!' I bawl, pushing harder now.

You're better off breaking a rib than having them die on you . . .

I hear his words clear in my mind.

'*Ah, ah, ah, ah . . . stayin' alive, stayin' alive.*'

My voice is fraught as I push harder and harder.

'There's no service!' I hear Chase in the corridor, trying to make the phone call.

'*Ah, ah, ah, ah* – Someone get Madzikanda!'

Kellen, wake up . . . Wake the fuck up!

I think of us driving along the road, me in the passenger seat, the summer air breezing through the open window; us lying on the roof; him struggling with the rowing boat; the birthday cake; the way he smiles from one side of his mouth; the way he brings light to every room he walks into.

The thought of waking up every day without him dawns on me now. The thought of never again seeing the light in those deep brown eyes . . .

Kellen! Please wake up!

Ah, ah, ah, ah . . . Don't you fucking die on me!

Ah, ah, ah, ah . . . Don't leave me here alone in this!

Ah, ah, ah, ah . . . And I'm crying now because it's not working.

He's not waking up.

'Kellen . . .'

'He needs air,' Rhys says, finally snapping out of his daze and pulling me off Kellen. 'You're not doing it right.'

I watch helplessly as Rhys leans down to breathe into his mouth, then continues the compressions.

Please be OK, Kellen. I need you to be OK.

But nothing. It doesn't work. His heart has stopped. He's completely lifeless.

Rhys's shoulders slump. I can see him giving up. But then I remember Kellen's words:

'Even if you think they're gone, don't stop until the ambulance gets there.'

'Keep going!'

'He's gone, Zach . . .'

'He's not gone!'

I push Rhys out of the way and climb back on top of Kellen. I keep the compressions going, desperately pushing on his chest, willing him to take a breath.

Come on, Kellen. Wake up! Please, just wake up!

This time, I lean down to breathe into him myself and, the moment my lips touch his, I feel an electric shock that jolts me backwards. A weird feeling. Something I've felt before. Kellen lies still for a moment. Everything is silent.

And then, suddenly, he starts gasping for air.

'Kellen!' I choke through tears as I grab him and pull him into me.

His whole body is trembling.

'Zach . . .?'

'Yeah,' I say, squeezing him. 'It's me.'

'Did I . . . *die*?' he says. 'Zach, did I just . . . *die*?'

'You're OK,' I say, letting him go to give him some air. 'You're OK.'

'Kellen . . .' Rhys says. He looks like he's seen a ghost.

'Rhys . . .'

Rhys rushes forward and throws his arms round Kellen.

'I love you, Kellen. I love you so fucking much.'

And there it is. It only took his boyfriend dying to get him to say it.

'Are you sure you're OK?'

'Yeah,' Kellen says, though he still sounds shaky.

We're back in Miss Madzikanda's office, having already explained that this is a Huckleberry Situation.

'You need a hospital,' she says. 'Just to be on the safe side.'

'You know I can't leave,' Kellen replies. 'Besides, what's a doctor going to do? They can't treat me for an accident that hasn't happened yet!'

'*We can't die*,' I say, repeating Kellen's words back to him. 'You're such an idiot. I can't believe you thought we couldn't die . . .'

Madzikanda digs her fingers deep into her Afro. 'Of course you can die! Why the hell do you kids always think you can't die?! I swear to God, I could kill you both myself!'

'For the record, I *always* thought we could die,' I say.

'Well, did you think of telling him?' She points at Kellen. 'What the hell happened?'

'Prom caught fire.'

'Again?!'

'What do you mean *again*?!'

'Prom *always* catches fire! Every bloody year! In my year, it happened *twice*.'

She reaches into her desk for the yearbook, the weight of it slamming down in front of us.

'Why do you have that out of its case?' I ask. 'Harrington's going to flip.'

'Oh, let him.' She dismisses the idea with a wave of her hand. 'I need you to see this.' She leafs through until she lands on 1978. 'Look,' she says, pointing to one of the entries.

'"*To a scorching-hot prom*,"' I read aloud.

'Well, that's just in bad taste,' Kellen says.

'So which one of you idiots was it then? Who's the pyro out of the two of you?'

'That would be me,' Kellen says. 'I cut the power and –'

'Why would you cut the power?'

'Because it was Zach's birthday! We were doing candles!'

She looks across to me. 'It's your birthday?'

'Yesterday was my birthday.'

Madzikanda shakes her head. 'Yesterday as in today, or yesterday as in yesterday?'

'Yesterday as in five days' time.'

'I don't follow.' Madzikanda sighs. 'Every year I think I have this figured out. And every year you kids find new ways to surprise me.'

'Why didn't you tell us before that prom *always* catches fire?' I ask. Kinda seems like an important detail that she somehow failed to mention?

'I don't know, Zach, because I don't remember what conversations we have and haven't had. But my guess is that I didn't want to put ideas in your head. You kids are all the same. I tell you *not* to set prom on fire, and you go straight out and buy a box of matches . . .'

'We can't go to the shop, though, miss. We can't leave. But Kellen *did* manage to convince you to order us all pizza.'

'Pizza?'

'Pepperoni . . .'

She looks at us in disbelief before burying her head in her hands.

'I need you to understand,' she says after a moment, 'that this day has a way of *speeding you along*, if you know what I mean. The second you get distracted? Start wasting time? Ordering pizza? That's when bad things start to happen.'

'Why did you let us order pizza then?' I protest.

'I don't know *because I wasn't there*!'

'Well, you *were* there . . .' I grumble.

'I swear to God . . .'

'What do you mean *bad things*?' Kellen asks. He actually looks scared now.

'Fallen trees, crashed cars . . . One kid swore blind they were attacked by a bear.'

'We don't have bears in this country,' I say automatically.

'Well, I didn't think so either!' Madzikanda snaps back.

'Told you.' Kellen smirks.

'The longer you stay in this day,' she says, 'the less things start to make sense. There's no reason the building should *keep* going up in flames, and yet someone knocks the tiniest candle and it's like a match has been lit at a petrol station.

You're right, Zach, there are no bears in this country . . . until suddenly there are.'

'So you're saying that this place has the ability to distort reality?'

I think of the black smoke billowing from the school. The car slamming into the barrier that wasn't there. The never-ending depths of a lake that's barely a metre deep. Even the vividness of that dream, of Kellen falling through the skylight. It all felt so real. As real as anything else that's going on here.

'So you're telling us anything can happen?' Kellen asks. 'We might get attacked by a poltergeist . . . bitten by a vampire! Chased by an enormous fire-breathing dragon?'

Madzikanda squints at him. 'I think we can safely rule out ghosts, vampires and dragons. But if it can happen in the real world, it can definitely happen here.'

'Gotcha,' Kellen says sarcastically. 'Coming back from the dead is just fine, but we draw the line at dragons.'

'You're just lucky you're blessed with such good weather.' She peers out of the window. 'One poor kid's prom night was in the middle of a thunderstorm, so you can imagine how that went . . .'

'They got hit by lightning?'

'No, but just about *everything else* did.'

'So you're saying the loop is malicious then? Like it has *thoughts*? Bad intent?'

'Only if you ignore it.'

'You're making it sound like it's sentient!'

'Honestly, sometimes it seems like it might be.'

'So it's evil?' I say. 'You're telling us we're stuck in a real-life horror movie?'

Madzikanda shakes her head. 'I don't think it's malevolent. If anything, I think it's trying to help you.'

'Help us?' Kellen looks at her in disbelief. 'By trying to kill us?'

'It's just giving you a little . . . push.'

'Off a cliff?' Kellen says.

'I know it's probably difficult to hear this right now, but everyone who's gone through this experience came out the other side grateful for having done so.'

'Yeah, I'm *really* grateful. Just love it when my heart stops,' Kellen grumbles.

'Personally, I can't get enough water filling my lungs,' I chip in.

'Look,' she says, 'I know it doesn't sound that way now. If somebody had said that to me when I was in the loop, I'd have probably punched them. But trust me, it'll all make sense in the end.'

'Yesterday you told us that we had an objective,' Kellen says. 'Something we had to figure out? I'd given up on trying to get Rhys to try and stay with me, but then this morning he said he loved me. Could that be it, miss? Is all this really about me and Rhys?'

'You tell me,' she replies.

'But he's an asshole,' I protest. 'You said it yourself!'

'I said that because I thought he didn't want to be with me . . .'

'He *doesn't* wanna be with you!' I say. 'He was just in shock!'

'Wow . . .' Kellen says. 'Jealous much?'

'Jealous? Why would I be jealous?!'

'He tried to save me, Zach! You said it yourself.'

'Tried and failed,' I mutter.

'You're being a dick.'

'I'm telling it how it is. This isn't about Rhys. Crawling back to him would be an astronomical mistake. You heard what Miss said – we need to stop wasting time.'

'*Wasting time?*' he says. 'I've done enough of that the past few days with you.'

'Excuse me?'

'You're excused,' he snarls, storming out of the door, slamming it behind him.

'What an asshole,' I say.

'Because you handled that so well yourself?' Madzikanda frowns. 'You two do see what's happening here, right? Like, you can't be that oblivious?'

'What do you mean, miss?'

She gives a long-drawn-out sigh. 'If you and Kellen don't start being honest with each other, I think you're gonna be stuck here a *while*.'

'Being honest with each other? What's that supposed to mean?'

She stands up and goes over to the door.

'I'm going to go and make some bad decisions because Lord knows they won't stick. Tell the others Capture the Flag is cancelled. Come and find me when you've figured it all out, though, won't you? I'd quite like to be there for the finale.'

'Let's get out of here,' I say, finding Bec and Chase in the dining hall.

'What about the game?' Bec asks, confused. 'What's going on, Zach?'

'It's cancelled,' I say. 'On account of Kellen's injuries.'

'He seems fine to me . . .' Chase says.

I look across the room and see Kellen and Rhys already playing the happy couple. I can hear Rhys telling a highly exaggerated story about how he 'saved' him. Kellen isn't even bothering to correct him. What an absolute fucking joke.

'You know Tiffany's already made a call to her dad?' Bec says. 'They're running a story painting Rhys as the *Hawthorn Hero*. They're saying he saved Kellen's life . . .'

'Rhys did fuck all,' I snap. 'But let them say whatever the hell they want. I'm so far past caring.'

'But it's a lie,' Chase protests. 'Whatever happened to the integrity of journalism?'

'*The integrity of journalism?*' I squint at him. 'I think that ship has sailed, Chase. Just look at what they wrote about you! Where was the integrity of journalism then?'

'Exactly why you should set the story straight!' he says. 'Though I still don't understand how you realized something was wrong. You ran out of the room screaming his name like you already knew he was in trouble.'

'I just sensed something wasn't right,' I lie. 'Call it a gut feeling.'

'*A gut feeling?*' Bec says. 'Are you telling us you're psychic, Zach?'

'You wouldn't believe me if I told you.'

'Try us,' Bec says. I look back and forth between them. My two best friends in the whole world. They didn't believe me last time, but maybe I just didn't explain it right. Maybe I *can* convince them. Maybe I should try a second time. *Tom and Jerry* logic, right?

'Look over there,' I say, nodding towards Owen. 'Any moment now, Ethan is going to stand up and throw that ball at him.'

'What?' Chase says, looking at me puzzled.

'Just watch,' I say as it all plays out in real time.

'Think fast!'

I feel bad for Owen, humiliated again. But I had to prove it somehow.

'How did you know that was going to happen?' Chase says, confusion painted across his face just as Owen's lunch is sprayed across his shirt.

Bec looks equally puzzled. 'Are you *actually* saying you're psychic?'

'Not exactly,' I say. 'But if I tell you, do you promise this time you'll believe me?'

'What do you mean *this time*?'

'Come on,' I say. 'I'll show you.'

We're sitting outside on the grass, the yearbook open in front of us. Mr Harrington would lose his mind if he saw us, but Madzikanda was right – there really are so many clues in here when you know what you're looking for. You have to read between the lines, but it's undeniable that some of these kids must have gone through the same thing as me and Kellen. Despite whatever hardships they may have faced, they seemed to come out the other side better for it. They all seem grateful for what happened. Just like Madzikanda said.

My favourite is an entry from someone called Jacob in 1984. Orwell's year. I try to imagine what he might have looked like. Unsurprisingly, I imagine him being really cute.

Glad for every iteration
For showing me the way
Through this never-ending story
On this never-ending day.

Barely even cryptic. He might as well have just written *BY THE WAY, FOLKS, THIS IS A MAGIC SCHOOL.*

'I think he's just referencing a movie,' Chase says, holding up his phone. 'Look, *The Neverending Story* came out that same year.'

'Give me that,' I say, taking his phone and looking at the Wikipedia entry. 'It was released in the United States in 1984. Didn't come out in the UK until 1985. He couldn't have seen it!'

'Because aeroplanes didn't exist in the eighties?' drawls Chase. Why is he determined to poke holes in this? 'He probably saw it in America, Zach.'

'That's a bit of a stretch, don't you think?'

'You're asking me to believe you're trapped in a real-life *Groundhog Day*, but a kid getting on a plane is absolutely unfathomable . . .'

I sigh. 'I knew you wouldn't believe me.'

'I didn't say that. I'm still processing.'

'This evidence is all a bit circumstantial, but it's still really convincing,' Bec agrees. 'But what else? You've been looping round in circles for what? Nearly a week now? There must be something else you've uncovered, something else we didn't know about before.'

'Well,' I say, racking my brain, 'something *bad* is gonna happen.'

'Something bad?' Chase says. 'Worse than Kellen suddenly dropping dead?'

'Just before prom,' I say. 'When we're all gathered by the fountain, everyone finds out Ethan's private pictures have been leaked all over the internet.'

'Really?' Bec sits upright, a look of concern spreading across her face.

'I wouldn't joke about this,' I say. 'They're gonna go majorly viral. Tiffany will make a scene. She'll call her dad and scream at him, begging him to *"make it go away!"* But it's all an act. The person that leaked the photos? It was her.'

'What?' Bec says. 'You're not serious?'

'Deadly,' I say. 'It's going to happen. And there's nothing we can do to stop it.'

'But why would she do that?' Chase says. 'It doesn't make any sense.'

'Doesn't it? All publicity is good publicity – that's what she always says, right?'

'But leaking her own boyfriend's nudes? That's bleak. Even for Tiffany . . .'

'And Ethan?' Bec asks. 'How does he take it?'

'Surprisingly well,' I say. 'Not that it makes it OK.'

'But why can't we stop it? If you already know it's gonna happen . . .'

'She sent the email this morning, before I even woke up. We got into her emails and found everything. It's not the only one she sent. There's one from last year . . .'

'Oh my God,' Chase says. I don't even need to finish the sentence. 'This whole time? Despite every time she's denied it? It was her? You're absolutely certain?'

'I'm positive,' I say. 'We had the evidence right in our hands, but . . .'

'The day reset?'

'Well, yeah, but Kellen also threw her phone in the lake . . .'

'What? Why?' Bec sighs. 'This is a lot to take in, Zach.'

'I know,' I say. 'I don't expect you to believe me. You didn't the first time. But I'm not sure I even have the capacity to make something like this up.'

'You *do* watch a lot of movies.' Chase frowns. 'And this low-key sounds like the plot from one of them. But . . . I think I might actually believe you.'

I feel instantly lighter just hearing him say that.

'Me too,' Bec says. 'Is there anything else we should know?'

I think about telling them about the pig's blood and what happened to Chase that first prom, but I don't think he needs to know that right now. Instead, I settle on something more positive.

'Well,' I say, 'there is *one* other thing. You know how I've always had a crush on Cameron?'

'Oh my God!' Bec exclaims. 'Did you and him actually . . . ?'

'No.' I laugh. 'I *wish*.'

'So what then?'

'He told me he has a crush on someone else.'

'Ouch!' Chase winces. 'That must have stung.'

'You'd think so,' I say. 'But then he told me who it was and it softened the blow a little . . . Bec, he was talking about you.'

I don't think I've ever seen her look more stunned. 'Me?'

'Yeah, I know you don't feel the same, but —'

'Whoa, whoa, whoa,' she interrupts. 'I didn't say that.'

'Huh?'

'I never said I didn't feel the same.'

Now it's my turn to look gobsmacked. 'So you're telling me you *do* like him?'

'Kinda . . .'

Maybe Kellen was right when he said that *everyone* is carrying secrets.

'Then why didn't you say something? Because you thought he was gay?'

'What? I've always known he's bi, Zach. I didn't say anything because I knew *you* liked him. There's plenty of other boys at this school, but he was the one you really fancied. I wasn't about to get in the way of that.'

'This whole time?'

'This whole time,' she says. 'It's not a big deal.'

'It kind of is, though.' Talk about selfless. 'I don't know what to say . . .'

'You don't have to say anything,' she says, laughing. 'Except that you wouldn't mind if I . . .'

'Of *course* not!' I exclaim. 'If there's one good thing that comes out of this, please, for the love of God, let it be at least one of us seeing him naked!'

Bec shakes her head. 'OK, I didn't say we were going to get naked. I was thinking more like going for tapas.'

'Tapas and then tap that ass!' Chase says.

'Go *immediately* to jail,' she says, laughing again.

Prom is in full swing by the time I finally have the two of them caught up. If they had any doubts, they don't once they see Tiffany screaming for her father to '*make it go away!*' Their jaws drop in perfect synchronization as they watch it happen in real time. I just wish this wasn't all going to reset again at midnight; it's nice to have them clued in for once.

The hall is once again decorated in both Sycamore and Hawthorn colours. I could tell that annoyed Tiffany when she got up onstage to be crowned Prom Queen. She must have given Owen clear instructions not to get any Sycamore banners in shot because this time he streamed her win from the most awkward angle.

Bec and Cameron are standing together, and I think they may finally be making progress. I definitely sense a spark between them. I think they just need that little extra push. I make a mental note to try to play Cupid later, but I'm still confused about what it is exactly that I'm supposed to be doing to break the loop. Bec and Chase have thrown out some compelling suggestions, but I think they're too preoccupied with the outside world rather than what's going on right here.

That's something I've come to understand – this isn't about *winning the lottery* or *finding a cure for Covid*. It's about something that is happening within the walls of this school. I look across the hall at Kellen awkwardly dancing with his boyfriend. He's convinced that this was all about saving his relationship, but I'm certain he's got that wrong. This isn't about *them*. Whatever is going on here, it's about *us*. It has to be. Why else would we *both* be stuck here? Rhys is just one great big oversized distraction. I'm not bitter. *Honest.*

But then there's still Owen. On that first night, when everything went so disastrously wrong, he was the one to come after me in that dazzling gold suit. He's probably the nicest and most gentle person I've ever known, a real-life Prince Charming. I hate that I don't reciprocate those feelings, but maybe I'm just not looking hard enough. Maybe there is something there ... something I'm missing? Could this be our love story? Am I just too stupid to see it? It can't be a coincidence that this was all started by that kiss. Maybe if we could just recreate it – kiss a second time – then maybe those feelings would come?

With the intensity that Kellen is kissing Rhys, you'd think he was working on a similar theory. It's like he thinks the solution to this problem is in the back of Rhys's throat and the only way to get at it is with his tongue. It's so intense that it's clearly making people uncomfortable. So much so that if it was a pair of straight students that were doing this they'd definitely be asked to stop. Nobody wants to say that to the gay kids, though. What if someone yells homophobia? I look around for Madzikanda. She's the only member of staff who *really* understands that equality is about treating everyone exactly the same.

Watching them kiss is starting to turn my stomach, so I resolve to go looking for Owen. I'd rather kiss him than spend even one more second watching Kellen and Rhys.

I find him and Josh sitting out by the lake. They look like they're having a heart-to-heart, so I hang back for a moment and pretend to be busy on my phone. It must be hard for them, having built this incredible friendship, knowing that it won't be the same after tonight. That's something we all have to deal with: life won't be the same once we finally cross midnight. At least me and Kellen have endless opportunities to make sure we get this right.

Owen shakes his cup, signalling that it's empty, and Josh stands up to go and get them some more drinks. This is my opportunity and so I take it. Owen is definitely not *unattractive*. In fact, he's kind of handsome in his own soft, dorky kind of way. On paper, he's boyfriend material. Kissing him wouldn't be *that* bad. I just need to reprogramme my stupid brain into fancying him. How hard can that really be?

'Hey,' I say, approaching. 'I'm not interrupting, am I?'

He chuckles. 'Yeah. I was deep in conversation with my imaginary friends.'

I take that as an invitation to sit down.

'So?' Owen says, reading me perfectly. 'You've gone all serious, Zach . . .'

'Yeah,' I admit.

Where do I even start? How am I supposed to make a move on a guy that I'm not even attracted to? 'I just don't really know how to do this.'

'Do what?'

I hold eye contact for a moment, thinking about the past two years we've spent together. He's always sort of faded into the background, but could it be . . .?

'It's our last night,' I say, moving my hand a little closer to his leg. 'And I honestly don't know what I'm supposed to do. I don't even really understand how I feel any more.'

'OK?' Owen says. I can tell he's confused, but he's listening like he really cares.

'You've always been so nice to me,' I continue. 'You're nice to everyone. That's what makes you Owen. And yet somehow you're always single, never dating anyone . . .'

Owen shrugs. 'Dating isn't everything, Zach. I can find happiness in other ways.'

'I know,' I say. 'But what if you didn't have to find other ways? What if happiness was right here in front of you the whole time. What if you just couldn't see it?'

Owen's face turns serious now too. Like he suddenly understands what I'm saying.

'Do you not think it's worth giving happiness a shot?' I ask, holding eye contact. I look at the stars reflecting in his eyes, hear the sound of the water lapping beside us. This might actually be it. We're finally going to have our moment.

And so I take a deep breath and lean in . . .

'Whoa!' Owen says, withdrawing. 'What are you doing, mate?'

'It's OK,' I answer. 'There's no one here. I know you like me.'

'What?' he says. 'Zach, what are you talking about?'

'It's hard to explain,' I say. 'But you don't need to hide it. I *know*.'

He withdraws further. 'I think you're confused . . . Where is this coming from?'

'Your wardrobe,' I say. 'Don't be mad, but me and Kellen kinda broke into your room. We had our reasons, I promise. And, well, we went in your wardrobe, and –'

'You did *what*?'

'It's not what it sounds like!'

'Well, it sounds like you went rummaging through my things . . .' He doesn't seem angry, he seems hurt. 'And you found something that makes you think I'm gay?'

'The suit,' I say. 'The gold one . . .'

'You think I'm gay because of a sparkly gold suit? It isn't even mine, Zach.'

'Wait. It isn't?' I'm so confused. It was in his room. Who else would it belong to? And then the realization hits me. 'Your room-mate . . . So wait . . . you're not gay?'

'You're an idiot, you know that, Zach?'

'Yes, I know, but your room-mate . . .' I say. 'Who is it?'

Owen just shakes his head in disappointment. 'I'm gonna take a walk.'

'Owen, wait!' I say, but he's already on his feet, and my phone starts ringing.

I look down to see it's Kellen. I'm surprised he managed to unstick himself from Rhys's face. I want to ignore it, but what if it's important? What if 'something bad' is happening all over again?

'What do you want?' I reluctantly answer, barely disguising my annoyance.

'Zach.' I hear his muffled voice. 'I . . . I got it wrong.'

'Huh?' I say, softer now. 'Why, what's wrong? What happened?'

I automatically imagine the worst.

'Everything was fine,' he says. 'Everything was perfect . . .'

'And then?'

'Just out of nowhere . . .'

'He broke up with you again?'

There's just silence on the other end of the phone.

'I could kill him!' I swear. 'Where is he? I'm gonna actually murder him!'

'Forget about him, Zach,' he says meekly. 'He's not worth it. I'm such an idiot.'

'You're not an idiot,' I say. 'He's just a fucking asshole.'

'I can't do this any more,' he says. 'I can't wake up with him again tomorrow. We have to get out of this, Zach. There has to be a way out of this!'

'Where are you?' I say, already heading for the building.

'Out front,' he says. 'With Huckleberry.'

'Meet me inside? I'm coming.'

'OK . . .' he says, hanging up just as a firework goes shooting into the sky.

I look at the time. It's already 11.58 p.m.

Fuck, I think, rushing in through the side door and into the crowded hall. If I can just get to him, maybe we can stop this day from resetting. I know what we need to do now. I think I've known deep down for a while. In every fairy story, it's always the same thing that breaks the spell. A kiss. Just before midnight. It's been a Cinderella story all along.

'Hey, Zach!' Cameron says, clutching me by the shoulder. 'Have you got a sec?'

'I'm kinda busy,' I say, trying to get round him.

'It's about Bec . . .'

'I know,' I reply. 'She likes you, Cameron. You just need to make a move.'

'Huh?' he says. 'How did you –'

'Just go and make a move! It'll work, I promise. We'll talk later, OK?'

'Is everything all right?'

'Everything's fine!' I say, looking at my watch. It's already ticked past 11.59.

And that's when I see Kellen appear at the top of the stairs.

Even from here, I can see his eyes are puffy from crying.

'Kellen!' I call over the crowd of heaving bodies. 'I'm coming!'

'Zach!' he calls back, rushing down the stairs towards me.

Everything feels like it's moving in slow motion. This is the movie moment we've been waiting for. The moment where we reach each other at the very last second. He's just a couple of metres away now. Almost within my grasp. He reaches out his hand, and I reach mine out too. Our fingers finally touch.

'I can't do it again, Zach.'

'You don't have to,' I say softly, looking down at his lips, his fingers wrapping round mine. We make eye contact. The clock's ticking down to midnight. This is finally it. We both know what's coming, and all eyes are on us now.

I take all of him in, those beautiful eyes, that perfect smile.

I don't know how I didn't see it sooner.

I close my eyes and lean in. He leans in too, and, as the fireworks explode above us, there's this static charge between us, pulling us closer.

For just a moment, it feels like everything is exactly how it should be. Like the spell's about to be broken. Like the two of us are finally free.

And just as our lips touch . . .

7

'Prom night, baby!'

No, it can't be . . .

I think of Kellen, one floor above, waking up next to Rhys. My stomach sinks as his words replay in my mind: *I can't do it again, Zach.*

'Are you OK?' Chase says, noticing my mood and sitting down on the bed next to me. 'I thought you could do with a wake-up call. You missed breakfast.'

'I know,' I say. 'Thanks.'

I can't stop thinking about Kellen. I'd convinced myself in those last moments that this was our love story, but maybe I was wrong. What else are we still missing?

And that's when there's a knock at the door.

'I'll get it,' Chase says, going over and pulling it open. 'Kellen?' he says, seeing him standing there wearing nothing but a pair of oversized basketball shorts. They're so big on him that he's having to hold them up with one hand.

'Hey,' he says. 'Is Zach there?'

'Yeah,' Chase replies, stepping aside and letting Kellen into the room.

'I grabbed the first thing I could find,' he says, pulling on the waistband of his shorts.

I smile at that. 'But you're OK?'

'I am now,' he says. 'You were right, Zach. You were always right. Rhys *is* an asshole. And I made sure to tell him that.'

'Wait,' Chase interrupts. 'So you and him . . .?'

'We broke up.'

'Oh,' Chase says. 'Shit. I'm so sorry.'

'Don't be,' Kellen says. 'We were over a while ago, really. We've just been going round and round in circles.' He shoots me a wink as he says it.

'Well, for what it's worth,' Chase says, 'I always thought you could do better.'

'Yeah . . . I *definitely* can,' he replies. 'That's why I'm here, actually. I was kinda hoping you'd be here to witness this.'

'To witness what?' Chase looks utterly lost.

'Me asking Zach to go to prom with me.'

'Huh?' I say stupidly as Kellen turns in my direction.

'I know you felt it, Zach. Last night, when we . . .'

'Last night?' Chase shakes his head. 'Zach was with me and Bec all night.'

'There's a lot I need to explain,' I say.

'So . . .' Kellen says. 'Would you? Be my date?'

'Of course,' I reply. 'I'd love to.'

The car alarm sounds from outside, almost as if in celebration.

Chase looks back and forth between us for a moment and smiles.

'Well,' he says, 'I am *so* confused, but also completely on board with all of this. Me and Bec were starting to think you two idiots would *never* figure this out.'

'What do you mean?' Kellen asks.

'Zach has had the *biggest crush* on you for ages!' Chase laughs.

'I haven't!' I protest, but then I hear the sound of Kellen's laugh, and I realize how completely and totally right Chase is. There's no point in denying it any longer. Of course I have a crush on Kellen. How could I *not* have a crush on Kellen?

'Well, I feel like you two lovebirds could do with a minute,' Chase says. 'So I'm gonna get some lunch. Can I tell Bec? I can't wait to tell Bec!'

'Sure,' Kellen says. 'As long as you're OK with that, Zach?'

'Yeah,' I reply as Chase slips out of the room, clicking the door shut behind him.

'So we're really doing this?' I ask as the two of us are finally alone.

'It's just a date,' Kellen says, coming to sit next to me, his hand brushing against mine. 'It's what Madzikanda said, right? We have to give the day what it wants?'

'But if this really was about us, then why are we still here? If we already . . . kissed?'

'We're not counting that as a kiss. Your lips grazed mine for about half a millisecond, Zach.'

'So you think we should do it again then?'

'I'm not that easy!' He jumps up before I can get too close. 'A date. That's what we're doing. We're not rushing through this just to break some spell. Yesterday was a mess, Zach. Maybe it just wants us to do it properly? To have the perfect day? Together? Madzikanda said we'd know when it was the final day, right? And I feel that now. Deep down, I know that this is it. Don't you?'

'Honestly?' I hesitate. 'I don't think I do . . .'

'Oh . . .'

'No,' I say. 'It's not that I don't want this to be our final day. Of course I do. Being asked to prom by you, Kellen? That was perfect. It's just . . . I don't know if I feel it yet? That feeling you're describing. It's like everything doesn't quite make sense. Almost like I still have unfinished business?'

'OK,' Kellen says. 'I'm listening . . .'

'I still don't know who kissed me. On that first night. The person in the mask.'

'So you figured out it wasn't Owen then?'

That brings me up short. 'You mean . . . you *knew*?'

'I wasn't sure.' Kellen sighs. 'Not a hundred per cent anyway. But yeah, I suspected. It . . . it was his room-mate, right? That's who the suit belonged to?'

'I think so,' I say. 'But I still don't know who that is.'

Kellen gives me a tight smile. 'Think about it, Zach. Really think about it. How come I had a key to their room? Why would I have that?'

'I don't know,' I say. 'I just assumed you swiped it.'

He shakes his head. 'You know how Rhys usually sleeps in my room?'

'Yeah?'

'Where do you think his *actual* room is?'

'Oh my God,' I say. 'You mean . . . No, it can't be . . .'

'It is, Zach. I suspected it from the very first time we went in there.'

'Then why didn't you say something?!'

'Because if I said it out loud, that would have made it real.'

'So it was *Rhys* who kissed me?' I wipe my mouth with disgust. 'But why? Why the change of clothes? Why any of this?'

'That first night? When he broke up with me? I was so upset that I threw the entire punchbowl all over him. Completely *ruined* his outfit.'

Now he says that, I do remember seeing the bowl on the ground just before the pig's blood incident. I didn't think anything of it until now.

'So he went to change, then ran into me on the way back down? And thought what? That he could use me as his rebound? This whole time I thought it was some big romantic moment? And it was just . . . *this*?'

'I don't like it any more than you do, but *yeah*.'

'Kellen, I'm so sorry. You know I would have *never* –'

'I know, Zach. But *he* would. In fact, I think he's always secretly had a crush on you.'

'What makes you think that?'

'How could he not? Have you seen yourself, Zach? You're beautiful. Josh. Cameron. Rhys. I think Chase is just about the only queer kid at this school who *hasn't* had a crush on you.' He takes out his phone. 'There's also this. The school poll. Someone voted you for hottest boy, but it wasn't Cameron, or Josh, or Owen. It was Rhys. It had to be.'

'How can you be so sure?'

'Because look,' he says, scrolling through the results.

Kellen Thomas – 0 votes.

'He never loved me, Zach. And you know what? I'm fine with that.'

I pause to take this all in.

'Well, for what it's worth,' I finally say, 'I should have voted you for hottest boy. And if I could go back and change my vote, I'd do it in a heartbeat.'

'You could get Chase to change the results again?'

I groan. 'Don't even joke.'

'I'd quite like to change my vote too,' he says. 'Voting for Rhys? It seems silly now.'

'It's not silly,' I say. 'You were in love.'

'Nah,' he says. 'I don't think I was, actually. Not really. I was in love with the idea of him. Of being in a relationship with the hottest guy in school. But real love? I think that's something different. We're just starting out, but ... I was kinda hoping we could maybe try to find it together? It's you I want, Zach. I only wish I hadn't waited until the last day of school to realize that. We might get out of this mess today. But even if we don't? Even if we have to go round a hundred more times? I don't care if we're stuck here forever because I get to be stuck here with you.'

'Mind if we join you?' I ask as Kellen and I approach Bec and Chase at lunch.

'So it's true!' Bec says. 'You two are *actually*? I almost didn't believe him . . .'

'Why would I lie?' Chase laughs.

'I don't know,' Bec says. 'You *are* prone to exaggeration . . .'

'What's that supposed to mean?'

'You know *what that's supposed to mean*,' she says, raising an eyebrow. 'Sorry about Rhys,' she adds to Kellen. 'You really are better off without him, though.'

'I know,' he says, looking at me and smiling.

'Well, for what it's worth,' Chase says, 'I'm glad you've come back. From the dark side, that is.' He nods over to Hawthorn. 'We've missed you sitting with us.'

'You have?'

'Course,' he says, tapping the seat next to him.

As Kellen sits, I spot Owen across the room. He's oblivious to what's about to happen. He's been silently putting up with Hawthorn's bullshit this whole time, letting them walk all over him. No wonder he feels like he can't stand up to them. And what's worse is that nobody has stood up for him either.

I see Ethan whispering to the rest of Hawthorn, and I know what I need to do.

'Think fast!'

Ethan is standing and taking aim, but I'm prepared this

time, and I'm already running across the hall. As he hurls the ball towards Owen, I manage to intercept it just in time, smacking it down with my outstretched hand. Maybe I *can* do sport after all! The ball goes crashing back into their table, sending food spattering over the entirety of the Hawthorn Elite. Tiffany screams as if she's had *actual* pig's blood thrown over her.

'I'm gonna fucking kill you!' Ethan says, slamming his fist down on the table, his face dripping with carbonara.

My fight-or-flight instinct kicks in and for some reason I pick *fight*.

'Let's go then!' I say, standing my ground as Ethan thunders towards me.

'Zach, what are you doing?' Owen cries.

'What I should have done a long time ago,' I reply, clenching my fists. I've never thrown a punch in my life, but everyone knows that bullies always back down if you stand up to them. That *is* what everyone says, right? At least that's what I'm banking on.

'You little prick,' Ethan says, grabbing me by the collar. Not much backing down going on here. I flinch and close my eyes.

'Get off him,' someone says, intercepting the blow. I open my eyes to see Cameron on his feet now too. 'I am so sick of seeing you pushing people around. Every fucking day it's the same. At least this time you had a taste of your own medicine.'

'Sit down, Cameron,' Ethan says. 'This is none of your business.'

'Isn't it?' he says, squaring up to Ethan. 'You made it my business when you chose to pick on people I care about.'

'What?' Ethan says, releasing my collar and staring at me and Owen with genuine bafflement. 'These two? That's who you're siding with? Over your own flesh and blood?'

'Being my brother doesn't give you a free pass to act like an asshole.'

The twins are face to face now, and a couple of people have taken out their phones to film the inevitable fight. Just when I think Ethan's about to throw a punch, Miss Madzikanda strides into the room.

'Whoa, whoa, whoa!' she says, immediately picking up on the tension and rushing over to separate the two brothers. 'What's going on here?'

'He's being a fucking prick, miss,' Cameron says. 'As always.'

'Language,' she says. 'You're not arguing about Huckleberry, are you?'

'What?' they both say in unison. It takes all my strength not to laugh.

'Never mind,' she says. 'Ethan, you're Hawthorn, Cameron, you're Sycamore, so whatever dick-measuring contest you have going on here, you can take it to the playing field.' She drops the box of bandanas down on to the table. 'How about team captains?'

Cameron and Ethan look at each other for a moment, as if unsure whether to accept. 'I'm down,' Cameron says, taking the blue bandana. Ethan grumpily takes the red.

'And two girls?' Madzikanda says.

Bec's and Tiffany's hands go up before she can even finish the sentence.

'Well, that's settled then,' she says.

And, just like that, we're back with our original team captains. Everything has come full circle. But this time something feels different.

This time something tells me we're not going to lose.

I want to hold Kellen's hand as we walk through the woods. It's all I can think about, his fingers just centimetres away from mine, but even after everything I'm still too nervous to do it. But just having him walk alongside me feels special. The birdsong seems louder than usual, and it's almost as if there's an added spring in Cameron's step as he leads us to our base. Bec is smiling as she watches him waving the flag. She's probably always looked at him that way – it seems obvious today – but it's only now I'm really noticing it.

'So I was thinking,' I say, once Kellen and I are finally alone, 'what if we just go and hide? Stay out of everyone's way? Remember that day out on the lake? Sycamore actually won without us being there.'

'Wait, wait, wait,' Kellen says. 'After Cameron stood up for you in front of the whole school, you wanna abandon our team and, what, go sunbathing?'

'*What?* No!' I say. 'I just think they have a better chance without us.'

'They almost definitely do,' Kellen says. 'We know they

do, in fact. But where's the fun in that? There's more to life than winning, Zach.'

'I thought you hated Capture the Flag?'

'Maybe it's grown on me.' He shrugs. 'Besides, I know how we can win this.'

'You do? How?'

'Isn't it obvious?' Kellen grins. 'We just need to stop Ethan from cheating.'

'But we've already tried that. It didn't work.'

Kellen chuckles. 'Well, that's just *Tom and Jerry* logic.'

'So you *do* listen to me.'

'You talk a lot of nonsense, Zach. But occasionally some sense.'

'So you really think we can win?'

'I dunno,' Kellen says. 'But we can at least have fun trying.'

'And then what?' I ask. 'Even if we beat them, all we get is a few lousy banners hanging in the hall. Tiffany still gets away with everything.'

'Not if I have anything to do with it,' Kellen says with a smirk.

'So you have a plan then?'

'Course. Don't I always? You just have to promise not to be all *Zach* about it.'

'Fine,' I say. 'Against my better judgement, I trust you. Just tell me what I need to do . . .'

'They're coming!'

It's Ethan, pretending to be his brother again. Kellen

and I are ready and waiting. 'They're coming!' he repeats. It's actually pretty comical seeing him acting out this whole charade again with us knowing everything. 'Their whole team.'

'What?' I say, doing my best job of feigning surprise. '*Their whole team?!*'

Kellen looks at me as if to tell me I need to work on my acting skills.

'Their whole team,' Ethan repeats, bouncing on his heels, clearly having not picked up on it. Kellen and I pretend to be distracted, and patiently wait for him to try and snatch the flag. I watch him out of the corner of my eye until . . .

'Yoink!' Ethan darts in to grab the flag, but this time I'm ready. I charge him at full speed, knocking him to the ground before he can run even half a metre.

'Got him!' I yell as Kellen stands over the two of us.

'Get off me, gay boy,' Ethan says, squirming away from me.

'Good job, Zach,' Kellen says, offering me his hand to help me up. 'That's what he gets for underestimating us.'

Ethan smirks. 'If a tree falls in the woods and there's nobody around to hear it . . .'

'What?'

'Nobody's ever going to believe you two managed to tag me.'

Kellen shrugs. 'And yet we did.'

'Did you, though?' Ethan snatches the flag and is up on his feet again.

'You're out,' Kellen yells after him. 'You can't do that!'

'Watch me,' he says, running for the treeline.

It's hopeless. I can't believe we're going to lose this game *again*.

At least that's what I think. But Kellen is running like I've never seen him run before. Like some kind of miracle, he tackles Ethan and rips the flag from his fingers.

'That's twice,' Kellen says, clutching the flag in his fist. He looks like he actually might swing for Ethan if he dares to try and take it from him.

Ethan grumbles something under his breath before sulking off back to the Hawthorn base.

'What was *that*?!' I demand. 'I've never seen you move so fast.'

'I have no idea.' Kellen laughs. 'I just couldn't let him get away with it. Not this time.'

'You're incredible,' I say, and I want to lean in and kiss him. But the butterflies are swirling so intensely in my stomach that I can't bring myself to do it.

'Come on,' he says. 'Let's get this flag back to base.'

We reattach the flag and stand guard, eyes like hawks as we scan the woodland for the enemy. We're in brand-new territory in this loop now; whatever happens, happens.

It's quiet for a while until Tiffany finally makes an appearance.

'You stopped Ethan?' She laughs. 'I'm actually embarrassed for him.'

'Don't think we won't stop you as well,' I say. 'Nobody is taking this flag from us!'

Just as I say it, someone runs out from the trees and snatches it.

For fuck's sake, I think. *Now I look like an idiot.*

But then something softens the blow a little. It's not Ethan. It's Owen.

'What are you doing?' Tiffany screeches. Evidently this wasn't part of her plan.

'I'm tired of sitting on defence,' he says, running past her. 'I'm just as capable as anyone else. I'm tired of you underestimating me.'

Wow. Go, Owen. I'm so impressed that I almost forget we should be stopping him. Then I remember, and run after him, but he's quick. Really quick, in fact. There's no way I can catch him. And, deep down, a part of me doesn't want to.

We reach the treeline and he sprints out into the open, heading for the hill. Blue bandanas appear to try and stop him, but he ducks and dives and manages to stay just beyond their reach. Out of breath, I give up chasing him, doubling over as I watch Josh barrelling down the hill, Hawthorn's red flag trailing in the wind behind him. It's Josh against Owen now, two best friends pitted against each other. Whatever happens, I'm seeing this as a win.

And that's when Ethan ruins it. Coming in fast from the left, he trips Josh and sends him toppling forward, and, just as he snatches back the Hawthorn flag, I see him stamp down on Josh's ankle. The yelp of pain from Josh is so harrowing it makes everyone stop in their tracks. I look for Madzikanda, she wouldn't let him get away with that, but she's way over the other side of the playing field. She didn't see anything.

I glance back at Owen, but he's also stopped in his tracks, a look of worry falling over him as he stares in Josh's direction. He's so close to scoring, just a few metres away.

'Fuck this,' he says, throwing the flag to the ground and running back to his friend.

'And that's time!' Madzikanda blows her whistle. 'We have ourselves a tie!'

'Any news on Josh?' I say as Cameron pushes into the locker room behind me. I didn't feel the need to avoid being in here with him today. I don't feel as awkward as I did before. That was just a few loops ago now, but so much has changed since then.

'Miraculously, nothing's broken,' he says. 'Though I swear I *heard* something snap.'

'Me too,' I say, recalling the sound of that ungodly yelp. 'And your brother?'

'They've let him off with a warning,' Cameron says sourly. 'I think Madzikanda suspected foul play, but he swears that it was an accident, and Harrington actually believes him.'

'Or chooses to believe him,' I say.

'Exactly.' He sighs. 'I quit the twinstagram, though.'

'Really?'

'Really, Zach. I don't want anything to do with it any more. I've been thinking about quitting for a while, and after seeing what Ethan did to Josh today? I don't know why I let myself be attached to him for so long.' He pauses and reaches into his pocket. 'And look.' He shows me his phone. 'I started my own account.'

I take the phone and look at the profile. There's just one picture of him smiling. Under his own name. No mention of being a twin.

'But what about all your followers?' I say, looking at the big fat o that shows he doesn't have a single one.

'They'll come,' he says. 'Or they won't. Who cares? I must admit that I don't like seeing that zero, though. Do you think you could fix it for me? Be my first follower?'

'I'd love to be,' I reply, taking out my phone and turning the o into a 1.

'Thanks.' He beams, watching. 'On my way to fame already!'

He pulls his T-shirt off and starts getting undressed. And it's weird because just a few days ago his bare torso rendered me practically unable to speak, but now it's different. I can still see that he's hot – I mean, you'd have to be *blind* – but without feeling the need to impress him, it's almost like I can relax.

'You OK?' he says, pausing before taking off his shorts. 'You look kinda spacey.'

'Sorry, I was just daydreaming.'

'Daydreaming, huh?' he says with a laugh. 'I get it. If I was in the girls' locker room, I don't think I'd be able to form sentences . . .'

'But you like guys too, right?'

'Yeah,' he says, looking directly at me. 'But it's different.

I've got used to you lot. Showering with a bunch of messy boys twice a day kinda ruins the mystique.'

'Right? That's what I keep telling Bec. She doesn't see the sweaty socks and the muddy towels. She thinks every time I step in here, I'm living every gay boy's fantasy!'

'Are you saying I'm *not* the fantasy?' He smirks and flexes, and, sweet Jesus, those abs, but . . .

'I used to think so,' I say, surprised by my own candour. 'But then . . .'

'Kellen?'

'Yeah,' I say with a smile. 'That boy has done a number on me.'

'I know how that feels,' Cameron says, exhaling and sitting down on the bench. 'I'm jealous, honestly. I've been trying to build up the courage to talk to someone for so long . . .'

'You mean Bec?' I ask, sitting down next to him.

He looks surprised. 'Is it really that obvious?'

'Nah,' I say. 'It was just a hunch. But I think I might be able to help.'

'Really?' His eyes light up.

'Really,' I say. 'You're just gonna have to trust me.'

'So you and Kellen?' Chase says as I walk back into our dorm room.

He's sitting in his usual spot on the window sill. I guess it's the first time we've really been alone together since the start of the day.

'Yeah,' I say. 'I know it all seems a bit sudden.'

'Not really.' He smiles. 'I'm honestly surprised it took you this long.'

'He was with Rhys.' I shrug. 'I wasn't about to go after a guy with a boyfriend.'

'I know,' Chase says. 'I'm just saying I'm glad it's finally happened. Truly.'

'Thanks,' I say. 'Me too.'

Chase peers out of the window. 'What on earth is Bec doing?'

'Huh?' I say, pretending to be surprised by the sight of her scaling the fire escape. She disappears from view for a moment and I wait for the sound of her knock.

'What was that? You're like an Asian Lara Croft.' Chase laughs, pulling her in. 'You're not supposed to be up here. What if someone sees you?'

'That's why I took the fire escape,' she replies. 'Anyway, what's the big deal? It's not like it's the first time I've been in the boys' dorm . . .'

'It isn't?'

I smile, remembering the first time we had this conversation. 'She hooked up with Jacob remember? And Kyle!'

'Exactly,' she says. 'At least Zach pays attention.'

'I do pay attention!' Chase protests. 'Anyone you've got your eye on this evening?'

'It doesn't matter. It's not like it's gonna happen. Apparently I'm too *intimidating*.'

'Who said that?' Chase looks annoyed again.

'That's what all the boys say about me. They call me the *praying mantis*.'

'The females eat the males after having sex with them?' I say, playing along.

'Exactly. They use them and then mercilessly rip them apart.'

'Well, as far as nicknames go,' Chase says, 'that *is* kinda iconic.'

'I guess,' she says with a sigh. 'But now none of them dares ask me to prom. Is it so much to ask for some guy to knock on the door with a big bouquet of flowers?'

As before, she looks at the door as if she expects it to happen.

Except this time there's the sound of a double knock.

Chase opens it to reveal Cameron standing there, holding a big bunch of freshly picked flowers. They're looking a little worse for wear, but it's the thought that counts.

'Typical,' Bec says with a laugh. 'Of course you get flowers, Zach! You see! The universe is mocking me!'

'I don't think they're for me,' I say. 'Cameron knows I'm with Kellen.'

'He's right,' Cameron says, shifting awkwardly from side to side. 'They're actually for you.'

'What?' Bec replies, confused, glancing across at me. She knows I'm with Kellen now, but I can see she's still hesitant after all the months I've been mooning over Cameron. I smile and give her a nod to tell her it's OK.

'You actually bought me flowers?'

'I picked them,' Cameron says, holding them up like a toddler who's proud of their art project. 'I got, like, thirteen bee stings, but it was worth it.'

'You braved the bees for me?'

'The whole hive.' He beams.

Bec laughs at that. 'But I'm confused. How did you even know I was up here?'

'Where else were you gonna be? You're *always* with these two.'

'He's not wrong,' I say, and then there's a slightly awkward pause. '*Sooo?*' I finally add, giving Cameron the gentle nudge he needs.

'Oh shit, yeah,' he says, like a true gentleman. 'So, Bec, do you wanna like ... go to prom with me?' Absolutely smashed it out of the park.

Bec's entire body seems to light up at the question.

'I'd love to,' she says. 'I thought you'd never ask.'

It wasn't exactly what I had been hoping for this morning, but walking into prom and seeing it decorated in both Hawthorn and Sycamore colours feels right. Everything just seems brighter, bolder, more magical now. Like everything is exactly as it should be. It took all my strength not to call out Tiffany while she paraded around, pretending to be angry about Ethan's photo leak. It was hard to listen to her screaming at her father to '*make it go away!*' – she deserves an Oscar for that one – but I have full faith that Kellen's plan will work. She's absolutely not gonna get away with any of it.

'I told you not to get any Sycamore banners in the background!' she scolds Ethan as she flicks through the six hundred photos he's just taken of her. 'Do them again!'

'Wow,' Bec says. 'She *really* cares about this, doesn't she? I honestly feel a bit bad for her. It's just a few bits of fabric . . .'

I laugh at that. 'You? Having empathy for Tiffany? Never thought I'd see the day.'

'I wouldn't call it *empathy*,' Bec says. 'More like . . . pity.'

'Well, whatever it is, it's more than she deserves.'

'Yearbook?' Kellen says. 'I wanna be the first to leave a message.'

'Sure.' I follow him. 'What are you gonna write? *Zach and Kellen 4eva*?'

'Forever? I was thinking this was more of a one-night thing,' he teases, picking up the pen and twirling it between his fingers.

I put a hand to my chest in mock outrage. 'So you're not going to get onstage and propose to me later?'

'OK, wow,' Kellen says. 'That was a low blow, Zach. Didn't know you had it in you.'

'There's a lot about me you don't know,' I say, plucking the pen from his fingers.

'Oh yeah?'

'Yeah.'

'Well, I know you hate breaking the rules, you like movie soundtracks better than pop music, and you've convinced yourself that the cat from *Tom and Jerry* is the victim . . .'

I laugh at that. 'You really pay attention.'

'Course I do,' he says. 'It's my superpower.'

'You would look good in a superhero outfit,' I say, my mind wandering as I imagine him in tight-fitting spandex.

'Just call me Miles Morales,' he says with a grin.

We *really* need to spend Halloween together.

'So go on then.' Kellan nods at the yearbook. 'Either write something or give me back that pen.'

I look down at the open yearbook, thinking for a moment before scribbling something down.

'*To a night that was fire,*' Kellen says, reading my message. 'You have such a twisted sense of humour, you know that? You do realize I *died*, right?'

'Oh, don't be so dramatic,' I say. 'I brought you back to life.'

'Fine,' he says, taking the pen from me.

'*To a prom that was to die for,*' he reads out loud as he writes.

'You're such an idiot.' I laugh. 'Do you not think maybe we should write something useful? Something that could help the next person?'

'Because all those before us were oh-so-helpful? Besides, where's the fun in that?'

'So this was fun, was it?'

'Are you telling me it wasn't? Madzikanda was right, Zach. I think this just might be the best thing that's ever happened to us. When else are you going to get to kick down a door? Or steal a car? Or streak naked in front of everyone!'

'For the record, I never streaked naked. That was entirely you.'

'It's not too late,' he says with a wicked little grin.

'I think maybe you're right, though,' I say, looking around the hall. 'Maybe we should have broken a few more rules . . .'

'Oh, *now* you want to break the rules! Where was this energy three days ago?'

'Well, it's not too late. Maybe we could go round a couple more times? Mess things up a little. I could drive a bulldozer into the building, set all the fireworks off at once . . .'

'Go and wrestle the bear?'

'There is no bear!' I laugh.

'Well, that reminds me,' Kellen says. 'Did you ever check what Madzikanda wrote?'

'No?' I reply, turning the pages. 'What year is she again? Like, 1972 or something?'

'Ninety-eight.' Kellen laughs. 'Take a look.'

I turn through the pages, scanning the various entries until I find it, the only entry without a signature, inscribed in her beautiful handwriting at the bottom of the page.

To joyrides, broken headlights and stealing the headteacher's car.

My jaw drops.

'She said there was only one student to ever try something so stupid,' Kellen says.

'And she gave us *such* a hard time for it!' I exclaim. 'Unbelievable!'

'I guess we have a lot more in common than we think.'

'Who do you have a lot in common with?' Owen says, startling us.

'Madzikanda,' I say. 'Apparently she was a real rebel back in the day.'

'Oh, because of the stolen car?' he says with a laugh.

'*What?*' I say. 'How could you possibly know about that?'

'I thought everyone knew that,' he says with a shrug.

Kellen laughs. 'Are you going to write something, Owen?'

'I want to,' he says. 'But I went near the book with my drink earlier and Harrington nearly had an aneurism. I'm honestly surprised he takes it out of the cabinet for even one night a year.'

'I might pretend to spill something on it,' I say. 'Just to get a reaction.'

'Don't even joke,' Owen replies. 'He'd expel you on the spot.'

'Don't I know it,' I say, remembering when that actually happened.

'Well, I'm running kinda empty anyway,' Owen says, the ice rattling around in his cup. 'You wanna get a refill, Zach? There's something I wanted to talk to you about.'

'Oh,' I say. 'I mean, sure. You don't mind, Kellen?'

'Course not,' he says, studying the yearbook. 'I wanna see what other secrets are in here anyway.'

'Aren't you bored of secrets yet?'

'Never,' he says with a wicked grin as I follow Owen to the punchbowl.

'Well, speaking of secrets,' Owen says, starting to fill up our cups, 'I haven't stopped thinking about what you guys did this morning. Standing up for me like that? I guess I never realized you actually cared.'

'Of course we care,' I say. 'People like Ethan shouldn't be allowed to just throw their weight around. Someone had to stand up to him. Besides, allyship goes two ways, you know? You've always had our back. We've definitely got yours.'

'I see that,' he says. 'You and Cameron? You were like a pair of queer superheroes.'

My mind wanders back to the spandex.

'Well, let's not get carried away.' I laugh.

'I guess the whole thing just got me thinking. Got me questioning a lot of things. Seeing the way you guys stick together? Stand up for one another? It made me wonder why I've been so scared ... why I've been hiding.'

'Hiding?' I say. 'What do you mean *hiding*?'

'I think you know what I mean ...' He looks down at his feet for a moment and takes a deep breath before he looks up and finally says it. 'I'm gay, Zach.'

'Owen ...' I say, feeling the joy spreading across my face. 'You're serious?'

'I'm serious,' he says with a tentative nod.

'Oh my God,' I say, pulling him into a hug. 'Owen, this is amazing!'

'It is?' he says, hugging me back.

'Of course it's amazing!' I say, releasing him. 'Though we're gonna have to start recruiting for a new token straight friend.'

Owen laughs at that.

'Who else knows?' I say.

'Just you,' he answers. 'I've never said it out loud before. Not even in the mirror.'

'You've really never told anyone? Not even Josh?'

'Not even Josh,' he replies. 'It seems silly now, being surrounded by all of you and still feeling like I had to hide it. I don't know, I guess I just thought that Hawthorn would never accept me if they knew. I don't know why I cared so much . . .'

'They'll never accept you because they're a bunch of assholes,' I say. 'It's nothing to do with you being gay. And I'm sorry they made you feel like that. You don't belong with them. You never have. After what you did in Capture the Flag today? You're an honorary Sycamore for life now. We're the queer house. They can keep Rhys, but you belong right here with us.'

'Thanks, Zach,' he says, and I can see his whole body relax a little. Like he's finally let go of a little bit of that tension. That thing that's always made him so rigid and wooden. 'I don't think I want to be in the closet any more,' he continues. 'I don't wanna go round telling everyone individually. I just wish I could tell everyone in one go. Put up an Instagram post or get up onstage and make a big announcement . . .'

'Do whatever feels right for you,' I say. 'Just don't feel like you need to rush.'

'But it's the last day. If I don't tell people now . . .'

'Tell them when you're ready,' I reply. 'And not a moment sooner.'

'OK,' he says. 'Thanks, Zach.'

I smile, looking up and down at his sparkling outfit. 'You really were hiding in plain sight with this,' I say.

'Maybe deep down I knew,' he says. 'A subconscious choice to wear a rainbow?'

'A rainbow?' I laugh. 'I thought it was more ... *iridescent.*'

'Nah,' he says, holding his arm up so it catches in the light. 'It's definitely a rainbow.'

I sit with Kellen on the edge of the jetty, looking out across the water. It feels like time is going slower this evening, like we're finally present in the moment. I pretend to yawn so I can put my arm round him, my heart racing as I do so.

'Whoa, easy there,' Kellen teases. 'Should I be worried? You're not going to push me in like you did Ethan, are you?'

'You had to ruin the moment, didn't you? You know I almost died that night?'

'Yeah, can't imagine how that feels ...' He places one hand on my leg and squeezes.

My curiosity gets the better of me. 'What *did* it feel like?'

Kellen hesitates for a moment, his gaze fixed on the stillness of the lake. 'It was like ... one moment I was there, and then the next I wasn't. But ...' He pauses for a moment and then, surprisingly, he smiles. 'It was actually kinda nice.'

'Nice?' I say. He can't be serious. 'You're saying you *liked* it?'

'Not exactly. I'm really happy to be here, Zach, but there was something about *that place*. Maybe it was just neurons misfiring in my brain, but it was so calm there. So still. It was like I was aware, but not exactly conscious? And everything was all just . . . dust. An eternity of endless glittering dust.'

'*Dust?*'

'I told you it's hard to explain. But being there, it felt like being . . . *atomic*.'

'Like a bomb?'

He laughs softly at that. 'No, not like a bomb. Like I was just atoms. Pulled apart in the most wonderful way. It's like I wasn't human, not any more anyway, but part of something bigger, something immeasurable and infinite.'

I think on that for a moment. 'Do you think maybe reincarnation could be real?'

'What makes you ask?'

'Well, you said you felt like you were being pulled apart. Maybe you were? Ready to be put back together into something different.' I look at the lake for signs of life, and then spot a glint of amber sparkling just above the water. 'Like a firefly, maybe?'

'A *firefly*?' Kellen splutters. 'Of all the things I could come back as, you're choosing an insect? Not a flying fox? A majestic moose? A beautiful Bengal tiger?'

'Most Bengals are born into captivity,' I say. 'At least as a firefly you'd be free.'

'Until someone ends me with a swatter!'

I shake my head. 'That's not how people react to fireflies, though. They make people happy. Nobody thinks, *Ew, gross, bug!* They think, *Oh wow, how magical!*' I point to the flashes of green and gold. 'You'd be bringing people joy. Seems kinda fitting.'

Kellen fixes me with a stern look. 'Zachary Evans, are you trying to get into my pants?'

'What? No!' I say, withdrawing. 'I was just saying that –'

'I'm teasing,' he says, pulling me back in close to him.

My heart is thumping. I look at him and I think this might be it. The moment we've been building to. I look down at his lips, and he does exactly the same.

'Zach! Kellen!' Bec calls, interrupting us. 'Stop jerking each other off!'

Wow, Bec, way to ruin the moment.

'Come on!' she insists. 'They're about to announce Prom Royalty!'

'Shit,' Kellen says. 'I completely lost track of time.'

'Me too,' I say. 'You're ready to do this then?'

'Born ready,' he says, leaning in to kiss me on the cheek. My skin tingles as if his lips are actually magic. 'Let's end the reign of Prom Queen.'

I stand with Kellen as the music dies down and the crowd start to murmur. It's time to carry out Kellen's plan. There's so much that could go wrong, but I am *utterly* confident it won't. I feel it in the pit of my stomach. Maybe it's what Madzikanda said about the last day of the loop feeling different, or, I don't know, maybe it's just indigestion – the brie and cranberry canapés were definitely not my friend. Can you imagine if this whole looping-day situation was just to figure out that I'm lactose intolerant?

Mr Harrington approaches the microphone and clears his throat before beginning his familiar speech. I can parrot it word for word by now. He clutches the same envelope as always, Tiffany and Ethan's names tucked inside.

'Ready, Zach?' Kellen says, squeezing my hand.

'As I'll ever be,' I reply with a smile. 'Let's do this.'

Tiffany is alone as we approach. She's ready to make her grand entrance, sipping a blood-red mocktail as she listens to Harrington's speech. She nods along as if deeply inspired by every word.

'Can I help you?' she says, keeping her eyes fixed on Mr Harrington.

'Oh, we just came to wish you good luck,' Kellen says with a smirk.

'I don't need luck,' she replies. 'So if you don't mind? I'm *trying* to listen.'

'Sure,' I say. 'But there is just one thing we need. Before you go onstage.'

'And what would that be?' she says, rolling her eyes.

'Your confession,' Kellen says, deadpan.

Tiffany laughs. 'And what exactly am I supposed to confess? Other than being the best dressed, of course.' She holds up her hideous bag. 'For that, I'm very much guilty.'

'Oh, I don't know,' muses Kellen. 'How you leaked your boyfriend's nudes, maybe?'

'And pretended to be a boy to file that complaint about Chase,' I add. 'Ironic, really, that you have such an issue with trans people, and yet you then pretend to be a guy yourself?'

'I don't know what you're talking about.' Her poker face is impeccable. She doesn't falter even slightly. Her gaze is fixed on that golden envelope, eyes forever on the prize. 'Why would I leak photographs of my own boyfriend anyway? Don't you think that's just a little bit far-fetched?'

'Oh, it's completely insane,' Kellen agrees. 'Absolutely batshit crazy.'

'But –' I place a hand thoughtfully on my chin – 'a *scandal* like this might drive up his profile. Yours too. *All publicity is good publicity* – that's what you always say, right?'

'Are you going somewhere with this?' Tiffany pretends to yawn.

'How many followers have you gained today? Like, ten thousand?'

'I don't pay attention to that.' She shrugs. 'Literally couldn't care less.'

'Funny because I saw you checking your follower stats earlier,' Kellen says.

'I'm sure you must be mistaken.' She smiles through gritted teeth. 'Is that really all the proof you have? That I gained some new followers? I literally called up the *Herald* to get them to kill the story. I stopped those photos from going viral.'

'And you did such a good job of doing that in front of *everyone*.'

A twitch of muscle beside her eye. 'What exactly are you insinuating?'

'The *Herald* was never going to publish the story, were they? Why would a national paper care about photos of a random teenage boy? Sure, he's got a fair few followers, but this is not national news, Tiffany. Even Daddy wouldn't do that for you.'

Tiffany doesn't say anything to that.

'So you took the photos to a competitor, didn't you? The trashiest gossip magazine you could find? And then made quite the fuss of publicly demanding that your dad "*make it go away*". The perfect alibi, right?'

Tiffany's smile is so tight it might snap. 'You really do have quite the active imagination, don't you?'

'Oh, without a doubt,' Kellen says. 'Vivid, actually. But these emails –' he reaches into his pocket to pull out his phone – 'don't require any imagination whatsoever.'

'What emails?' Tiffany's composure buckles as she glances down at Kellen's phone.

'The ones you sent to Blaze first thing this morning. From oakbrook.anonymous@gmail.com, right? We got Chase to break into your account.'

Tiffany swallows hard. 'That's a complete invasion of my privacy,' she bites.

'Just like leaking someone's private photos?' Kellen hits back.

She hesitates for a moment and then her lips curl upwards into a smile.

'I think you're forgetting one very important detail,' she says. 'Do you really think anyone is going to believe *you* over me? I've got our beloved headmaster right under my thumb. He'd expel you just because I said so. You're nothing, and you'd do well to remember that. You don't even pay for your tuition. Who cares if I leaked a few stupid photos? Ethan should be grateful. It's just like you said – his followers have doubled. I was doing him a favour.'

'Do you really think he'll see it that way?'

'It doesn't matter,' she says, 'because he's never going to find out.'

'Oh, but he is,' I say. 'Because, returning to our original point, you're about to get on that stage and admit to everything you've done.'

She snorts at the suggestion. 'And why the hell would I do that?'

'Because if you don't,' Kellen says, 'we're going to leak these emails to *everyone*.'

And that's when Tiffany snatches the phone out of his hand.

'No, wait!' he says as she drops it to the floor and stamps on it, the tip of her stiletto puncturing the glass screen.

'Fuck,' Kellen says. 'Well, I didn't see that coming . . .'

'That's your problem, Kellen, you *always* underestimate me.'

'Well,' I say, 'at least now we can get her for criminal damage as well.'

'*Get me?*' Tiffany laughs. 'The only thing you're getting, Zach, is expelled.'

'If you say so,' I reply. 'We didn't actually have any proof anyway. Chase has this moral code that prevents him from hacking into people's emails.'

'So you admit you made it all up then?' Her smile grows wider and wider.

'Just like you just admitted to everything you've done,' I say. 'But, before you go running to Mr Harrington, do you think you could do me a favour?'

'A favour? For you?'

'Yeah, if you could just smile for the camera. You're live on Instagram.'

'What camera?' she snaps, looking at my empty hands. 'Whose Instagram?'

'Your Instagram,' Kellen says, pointing behind her. 'You're live-streaming, remember?'

'What?' The colour drains from her face as she turns to see Owen – ever-obedient Owen – pointing her own phone at her, just as she'd wanted. He gives her a little wave.

'And so, without further delay,' Mr Harrington says, 'it's my honour to announce this year's Prom King and Queen!'

'Prom Royalty!' Kellen and I join in with Josh. 'It's gender neutral!'

'Oh . . . erm, yes. This year's Prom Royalty . . .'

'Not now, not now,' Tiffany mutters, turning to look around for an escape route.

'Tiffany White and Ethan Clark!'

The spotlights find them both, illuminating them for the whole room. Tiffany stops in her tracks, trying to regain her composure.

'What's the matter?' Kellen says. 'Don't you want your crown?'

Her jaw clenches as she forces an agonized smile and begins walking towards the stage. Some of the crowd are oblivious, smiling and clapping as she passes. Others are nudging each other and whispering. Word really travels *that* fast.

Tiffany reaches the stage, accepting her crown as she looks around for Ethan. But he's not moving. He's frozen in place, phone in hand, his face stony as he glares at her. She keeps the smile stapled to her lips, gesturing for him to join her. Phones start to appear, filming this, live-streaming this, documenting this all in glorious 4K. Ethan finally raises his hand and flips her off before turning on his heel and heading straight for the exit.

'Ethan!' she calls, but he doesn't stop. She grabs the microphone, shouting his name a second time, the speakers screeching with deafening feedback. She tosses her crown to the ground and chases after him, leaving Mr Harrington holding the other one.

'Right,' Mr Harrington says, setting the crown down again. 'Well, I suppose nothing to see here . . .'

He gestures frantically to the DJ, and the music comes back on as he swiftly leaves the stage. Gossip erupts all around us, and Kellen seizes me in the tightest of hugs.

'We did it! We actually did it!'

*

'The evil has been defeated!' Bec celebrates, coming to join me, Chase and Kellen out by the edge of the lake. She's got four cups topped to the brim with God knows what. 'I don't know how you two pulled that off, but I'm impressed.'

'Thanks,' Kellen says, taking a little bow. 'But do you think maybe it worked a little bit *too* well? Like, I didn't wanna ruin her whole life or anything.'

'She'll bounce back,' Bec says. 'Have you seen the sycophants on her Instagram? They're trying to argue that she's somehow the victim. They're using #Justice4Tiffany.'

Chase snorts. 'Yeah, I wouldn't feel too bad for her, Kellen. That girl has nine lives. You just took a swipe at one of them.'

'What about her and Ethan?' I ask. 'Do you think that's the end of them?'

'Nah,' Bec says. 'They'll soon realize that they're both as evil as each other. They'll be back together in a couple of hours. Ready to breed and make devil spawn.'

'What's this about breeding?' Josh says, bouncing over towards us, the bells on his jester hat jingling. His ankle seems to have made a miraculous recovery. 'Not planning an after-party without me, are you?'

'An after-party with you four?' Bec says. 'Well, that's one way to absolutely guarantee I won't get laid.'

'We'll invite Cameron as well,' Josh says with a twinkle. 'How are things going? Rumour has it that a couple matching your description was spotted earlier headed for the boathouse . . .'

'We were not!' Bec protests. 'We went for a *stroll* round the lake.'

'Is that what we're calling it now?' he teases. 'Well, I'm happy for you.' He looks at Bec and then at me and Kellen. 'Seems like everyone found their happily-ever-after.'

'You sound disappointed,' Chase says. 'You know, the clock has yet to strike midnight. Was there someone you had your eye on?'

'Maybe,' Josh replies. 'You guys really haven't picked up on it?'

'What do you mean?' Kellen looks across at me. Was there something we missed?

Josh looks between us before letting out a sigh. 'Owen. I really like Owen.'

'You have a crush on the straight boy?' Chase says. 'Oh, that's rough.'

I want to correct Chase, but I know it's not my place to out Owen. Even now, to his closest friends. I can't even tell Kellen.

'Wait,' I say. 'Where is Owen anyway?'

'He's with the banshee,' Josh says with a shrug.

'What?' Kellen demands. 'He's with Tiffany? Why?'

'I don't know,' Josh says. 'She said there's something *private* they need to discuss. She made it sound like it was super urgent.'

Oh my God. Not again. The prank!

'When did this happen?' I say, looking back at the school.

'Like, just now? A minute ago? Why?'

'Fuck,' Kellen says, already on his feet.

'She's going after Owen!' I cry, breaking into a run.

After everything we've done today, how could we be so stupid to think Tiffany wouldn't be out for revenge? Owen was the one who 'ruined' Capture the Flag, the one who live-streamed her demise. In her eyes, he's public enemy number one.

'What's going on?' Josh says, following us into the building. 'What's happening?'

'Pig's blood!' I pant, pointing to the top of the stairs. 'Owen is the target!'

'Shit,' he says, trying to push through the crowd of heaving bodies. It seems even busier than usual, almost like everyone's trying to get in our way.

I look to where the bucket is hanging, and there's Owen, standing directly beneath it, flicking idly through his phone. Tiffany must have planted him there and gone to release the bucket. Without Ethan's help, she's having to pull the whole thing off by herself.

'Owen!' Josh yells, finding a gap in the crowd and breaking through. 'Owen!'

But it's too late. I see Tiffany up on the balcony. She tugs the rope, and the bucket comes swinging down from the rafters.

'Look out!' Josh yells, pushing Owen out of the way. Owen stumbles to his knees as Josh takes the hit himself. He stands there, drenched, his jester's costume ruined.

My heart sinks. We've really fucked up this time. I might as well take a blowtorch and set this place on fire again. Speed things along a little. Just when things were going so well, now we're gonna have to go back and do it all over again. I understand now why Madzikanda looped so many times. Just when you think you have all the puzzle pieces slotted together, something else falls out of place.

But then something incredible happens and Josh starts to laugh.

He doesn't stop. He's literally shaking with mirth, the bells on his cap jingling in time with his heaving shoulders. Class clown right until the very end.

For a moment, Owen just looks at him, stunned. Then he starts laughing too.

'Oh my God. You look ridiculous,' Owen says, catching his breath. 'I can't believe you did that. You saved me!'

''Twas nothing,' Josh replies, wiping the viscous liquid from his eyes. ''Tis but a little beetroot.' He licks his finger. 'And perchance a hint of cornflour?'

'My hero,' Owen says. 'You know, I could actually kiss you.'

'Oh yeah?' Josh wiggles his eyebrows. 'Covered in this? I dare you . . .'

Owen hesitates for a moment, looking around at all the eyes that are on them. He'd told me he wanted to come out to everyone at once, but that's easier said than done. I'm not sure how he's going to get out of this one. And, it seems, neither is he.

Owen finds me in the crowd and gives me a little smile.

'Josh, I've wanted to do this since *forever*.'

'Huh?' Josh says, stunned as Owen takes him by the hand.

'Kiss me,' Owen says. and so they do, in front of everyone.

The hall is silent for a moment as everyone does the maths.

'*Wait, Owen is gay?*'

'*I knew it!*'

'*I thought they were already a couple?*'

And then someone starts cheering. And then somebody else does too. And, before we know it, the whole room is clapping for *them*. Chase grabs the two crowns that were left behind, and places them on their heads. Meanwhile, Madzikanda must have seen the whole thing because she triggers the rainbow confetti from somewhere behind the scenes.

'Love is love!' I yell as it rains down all around us. Josh was right. It *is* all about context.

And that's when I feel it. An electricity surging through me. The same feeling I felt when Kellen kissed me last night, but a thousand times more intense. I look across the room to find him, and, when our eyes meet, I know he feels it too.

This was never about us. It was always about *them*.

This is the feeling that we've been waiting for.

Madzikanda appears beside me in the crowd, clapping along with everyone else.

'*Huckleberry*,' I whisper, nudging her in the ribs.

Her eyes widen. 'It's *you*?'

'Me and Kellen.'

'Two of you?' she says. 'Well, whaddya know!'

'So you didn't figure it out?'

'I thought it was Josh! I've been saying "Huckleberry" to him all evening.'

I laugh. 'So he now thinks you've lost it.'

'Yeah, him and everyone else. Any fires this time?'

'Just one,' I say. 'Do you not think the prom committee should maybe ease up on the candles next year? You know, considering the tendency of this place to regularly go up in flames?'

'Don't get me started,' Madzikanda replies. 'Do you know how many times I've had that conversation? Every year I tell them, but the candles are "tradition" and none of them ever *remember* the school burning down, so to them it's as if it never happened! You see these grey hairs, Zach? This is exactly why I have them.'

'Well, I suppose they do set the scene,' I say, looking around the candlelit hall, moonlight breaking through the skylight.

'So this is it then? Your final day?'

'I think so,' I say, looking at my watch. 'Just a couple of minutes left . . .'

'What was it this time? A break-up? Enemies to lovers? Unresolved rivalry?'

'All of the above,' I say. 'But mostly a love story.' I nod to Josh and Owen. 'I thought it was about me and Kellen, but it was about them all along.'

'Well, maybe not *all* about them,' she says, just as the first fireworks go shooting up into the sky, raining down in soft pinks and blues. 'You've got a minute left, Zach. Do you really want to spend it here with me?'

I look down at my watch, the second hand ticking round towards midnight, and, when I look back up at Kellen, I realize he's looking at me too.

'Go on,' Madzikanda whispers. 'Make every second count.'

'Thanks, miss,' I say, walking across the hall to Kellen. He's walking towards me too, and it feels like the crowd parts just to let us through.

'So this is it?' he says, reaching me. 'We didn't fuck it up this time?'

'I think this is it,' I say. 'But, even if it's not, I'm not sure I care. As long as I'm stuck here with you.'

The fireworks come faster now, crackling above us.

'Well,' he says, 'whatever happens . . .' He offers me his hand. 'Kiss me.'

'You really think that's gonna make a difference?'

'Nah,' he says. 'I just want you to.'

'See you on the other side then?'

'Yeah.' He leans in. 'See you on the other side.'

8

'Prom night, baby!'

The video plays on an endless loop on Cameron's phone: Chase jubilantly popping a bottle of champagne for the camera as the cork goes flying and hits Mr Harrington squarely in the side of his head. That's what made the video go viral. That and the fact that it's nine seconds of pure chaos. There's just *so much* going on in the background.

Firstly, there's Josh and Owen – in their ridiculous outfits – running through the hall drenched in pig's blood. Then there's Bec dancing with Cameron. She spins him round so aggressively that he stumbles backwards into one of the candelabras. It no doubt would have sent the whole place up in a blaze if it wasn't for Madzikanda stepping in to catch it.

Then there's Rhys and Tiffany. If you look closely, you can see them arguing furiously up on the balcony. You can't hear what they're saying, but you can tell it's a *gloves-off* kind of argument. I don't know which of her heinous actions did it, but it seems that even Rhys – for all his flaws – had finally had enough of her. You can feel the venom through the screen.

And finally me and Kellen. Off to the side, barely even visible, sharing one single long, meaningful kiss. The fireworks explode above us all, setting the scene, like a modern-day *Feast of Dionysus*. Except instead of a painting it's a TikTok video that loops in perpetuity. I like to think that future generations will see this video playing somewhere in the Louvre.

'I can't believe it's hit three million views,' Bec says.

They've all come to Mum's house for my birthday.

'I think it's the look on Harrington's face that clinched the deal.'

'I'm just still shocked that you got away with corking the headteacher.' Cameron laughs. 'I'd have thought that would have got you expelled for sure!'

'God bless Madzikanda,' Chase says with a grin.

She stepped in and argued that the school hadn't done enough to protect him in the past. She said it would be a PR nightmare if they expelled him now. Mr Harrington didn't bend to that, so she threatened to walk out, and that's what finally did it.

'God bless Madzikanda' is right.

We stayed in touch after we left. Both me and Kellen got a blank email with the subject line *Huckleberry*. We knew immediately who it was from and replied straight away. Kellen had found this whole Reddit thread dedicated to a very specific subgroup of Oakbrook alumni. Amazingly, Madzikanda didn't even know it existed. The stories on there are absolutely wild – enough to make mine and Kellen's time at Oakbrook look *tame*.

Everyone uses fake names, of course – concealing their identities. I guess they don't want this somehow coming back to bite them. Nobody wants to google their husband-to-be to find that they're telling absolutely wild stories on the internet. And some of the stories really are *unbelievable*. To my dismay – and Kellen's absolute delight – there are, in fact, not one but *two* stories about encountering a bear.

I've sort of come to terms with the fact that nobody outside this exclusive club will ever really believe us. Madzikanda thinks I should write a '*fictional*' screenplay about our experience. I haven't committed anything to paper yet, but I like that idea a lot.

'Well, I think it's iconic,' Josh says, bringing my attention back to the video. 'What does your mum think, Chase? Has she seen it yet?'

'Of course she's seen it.' Chase laughs. 'That woman is obsessed with TikTok. She knew it went viral before I did. She's pretending to be mad with me, but I think she secretly finds it funny. I've heard her replaying it like a bazillion times. Half the views are her.'

'I still can't believe you're a viral superstar,' Owen says. 'Tiffany must be livid.'

'Oh, without a doubt,' he says with a mischievous grin. 'You should see the comments. My notifications are going nuts.'

The old guy is pisssedddddddddddd, one person has written.

Low-key the most chaotic thing I've ever seen, writes another.

Excuse me why wasn't my prom like this?! That one has twenty thousand likes.

'Oh my God,' Cameron says then, stopping dead as he scrolls through the comments. 'Gabi and Shanna have commented! They're famous TikTokers!'

I remember him telling me they were his biggest inspiration.

'Yeah!' Chase says. 'They messaged me! We're going to the same university!'

'You're not serious?' Cameron looks like he actually might burst.

'I'm serious!' Chase says. 'Gabi is trans too. They said they wanna hang out. I've never had a trans friend before! Not in real life anyway.'

'Not just any trans friend!' Cameron holds back a squeal. 'A FAMOUS trans friend!'

'You're really a big fan, huh?' Bec says, watching him light up.

'Do you want me to introduce you?' asks Chase. 'You could hang out with us?'

'YES!' He practically bursts. 'I mean, um, yeah, that would be so totally chill.'

'You're such a dork,' Bec says with a smile, kissing him on the cheek.

'Maybe they can help launch your solo Instagram career,' Josh says. 'Give you a few pointers? How many followers are you up to now?'

'I'm, like, three followers from a thousand!' He beams proudly.

That's actually really good going considering he only started it a few days ago. He already put up a post about the LGBT+ pay gap. He's finally doing exactly what he wanted.

'OK, celebrity,' Owen replies, 'don't forget about us little people when you make it to the top.'

'Oh, I've already blocked your number,' Cameron jokes.

'Well, I'm proud of you,' Bec says, squeezing his hand. 'Seriously.'

'I think we all are,' I say, looking round my small group of friends.

Owen, Josh, Bec, Cameron, Chase.

Everyone but Kellen. Where is he anyway? He should have been here an hour ago.

And that's when the lights suddenly go out.

'Shit, what happened?' I say.

The others pretend to act innocent, but the look on their faces in the gloom gives it away. I know what's happening now, and so I turn to see him standing in the doorway. Kellen.

He's smiling as he holds out the cake.

'*Happy birthday to you,*
Happy birthday to you,
Happy birthday, dear Zachary,
Happy birthday to you.'

'Make a wish!' Owen says.

'Fuck that, kiss him!' Josh shouts.

And so I do.

'Happy birthday, Zach,' Kellen says with a big grin. 'For real this time.'

'What do you mean *for real this time*?' Chase asks, confused.

'It's a long story,' I reply. 'How much time have you got?'

Acknowledgements

First and foremost, I think it's tremendously important to thank the trans community for the impact they have had on me during the course of writing this book. Many of my closest friends are trans, so it made sense that my protagonist would be supported by his trans best friend, too. What I didn't expect, however, was the extent to which the trans community would become targeted during the course of writing this book. It inevitably shaped the narrative. As much as I wish trans kids could live a life of unashamed queer joy – which had been my original hope for Chase – I know that oftentimes that just isn't the case. The sad reality is that there are villains like Tiffany out there in the real world, so I hope at the very least these pages are a safe place to see those villains get what they finally deserve.

I'd like to extend my particular thanks to Luxeria Celes, who acted as my sounding board for the trans storylines within the book, and to our brilliant sensitivity reader, The Mollusc Dimension, for their thoughtful feedback on how to make the diverse characters within the book as authentic as possible. I can never speak for the most marginalized members of our community, so thank you for helping me to show my support instead.

My next thanks go to my brilliant editor, Ben Horslen. For many reasons, this book was by far the most difficult to write (*if you don't like headaches, don't try to write about time loops*), but Ben was the constant calm within my storm. He contributed so much to this wonderful book – it was his idea to give Cameron an evil twin! – and I can't express my gratitude enough. Authors take far too much credit – the work is often an even split, and if it didn't mean I'd have to share the royalties, I'd probably insist his name be on the cover too.

Thank you also to the wider team at Penguin. It was always my dream to see the little penguin on the spine of one of my books, and the fact you've made that happen not once, but twice, is more than I could have ever hoped for. Jess Mackay, Josh Benn, Emily Smyth, Tanzim Kamali and Faith Young, thank you so very much.

Of course, my wonderful literary agent, Ella Kahn, played more than a small part in making that happen too. She's without a doubt my biggest champion. No idea is ever too extraordinary – if I'm passionate about it, she's passionate about it too.

And then to H.L. Gibby, for that stunning jacket. All I can say is that I really hope people *do* judge this book by its cover. Thank you for binding my words with your beautiful art.

And finally, to my friends, my cheerleading mum and dad, and my incredibly supportive online community – you're the reason I keep writing. Thank you.